THE BOYFRIEND

BOOKS BY KERRY WILKINSON

Standalone novels

Two Sisters

The Girl Who Came Back

Last Night

The Death and Life of Eleanor Parker

The Wife's Secret

A Face in the Crowd

Close to You

After the Accident

The Child Across the Street

What My Husband Did

The Blame

The Child in the Photo

The Perfect Daughter

The Party at Number 12

Ten Birthdays

Truly, Madly, Amy

The Jessica Daniel series

The Killer Inside (also published as *Locked In*)

Vigilante

The Woman in Black

Think of the Children

Playing With Fire

The Missing Dead (also published as *Thicker than Water*)

Behind Closed Doors

Crossing the Line

Scarred for Life

For Richer, For Poorer

Nothing But Trouble

Eye for an Eye

Silent Suspect

The Unlucky Ones

A Cry in the Night

THE ANDREW HUNTER SERIES

Something Wicked

Something Hidden

Something Buried

SILVER BLACKTHORN

Reckoning

Renegade

Resurgence

OTHER

Down Among the Dead Men

No Place Like Home

Watched

THE BOYFRIEND

KERRY WILKINSON

bookouture

Published by Bookouture in 2022

An imprint of Storyfire Ltd.
Carmelite House
50 Victoria Embankment
London EC4Y 0DZ

www.bookouture.com

ISBN: 978-1-80314-275-3
eBook ISBN: 978-1-80314-274-6

ONE

It was a few hours after her dad's funeral that Jodie stood on the pavement outside the house in which she'd grown up. She blinked into the spring sunshine that dappled through the thumbprint clouds and took in the bricks that were far more than simply bricks.

The upstairs bathroom window of the house was open a crack, as it always was. Her dad had been obsessed with potential damp and left tatty old dishcloths on every radiator, ready to clear windows of mist. The bathroom was the worst offender and that window remained open year-round. Jodie shivered at the memory of brushing her teeth while they chattered in the middle of December.

Dads could be weird. Hers in particular.

At the side of the house was the wheelie bin with the large '43' painted on the front, the same as it had been for years. The 'no free newspaper' sign was still taped to the inside of the front door, the words printed in her father's neat handwriting. As it had been for a decade.

All the same and yet... different.

There was a shuffling at Jodie's side and then, 'You don't

have to clear anything today,' Fiona said. 'Come back tomorrow, or the day after. It's not going anywhere.'

Jodie knew her friend was right, except the funeral itself had felt like a rallying call to get on with things. Since her father's death, there'd been endless amounts of paperwork. There were people to tell, phone calls to make, letters to send, forms to fill, text messages that needed a reply – and that was the day after he died. Then there was planning the funeral itself, the reading of the will, more forms, more phone calls, more letters, more texts.

Sorting out the admin around her father's death had turned into a part-time job.

The clearing of her dad's house was something Jodie had deliberately pushed back. It was as she'd stood in the church, listening to the vicar say her dad wouldn't hurt a fly, that she'd decided it was one job that needed to be done as soon as possible.

'I'd rather it was out of the way,' Jodie replied. Her throat was dry, and the words crackled their way out.

Fiona had been smoking a cigarette and she crouched before mashing it into the drain. She avoided Jodie's disapproving look.

'I can help if you want,' Fiona offered.

Jodie remained standing on the pavement, staring towards her childhood home. Words and thoughts were easier than action.

'I think I need to do it myself,' she said.

As she spoke, there was a flicker of movement from the neighbouring window. Curtain twitching was a sport in this area of town, although, on this occasion, the figure ducked out and back into view, then offered Jodie a solemn wave. Her dad's next-door neighbours had been at the funeral but weren't the sort to hang around for the wake. Neither was Jodie, for that matter. She'd been at the church hall but not for long. Given the sheer number of people, she doubted anyone would notice she wasn't there. Someone else could eat the cucumber sandwiches and fairy cakes.

Jodie felt Fiona shuffling at her side. 'They'll outlive all of us,' she said.

It took Jodie a moment to realise Fiona was talking about her dad's neighbours. Mr and Mrs Vickery were in their seventies and had lived in the same house for as long as Jodie had been around. *Longer*. Possibly since the dawn of time.

Jodie didn't reply, but the comment hung, possibly because of how 'outlive' sounded so insensitive considering what had happened to the Vickerys' son.

Fiona seemed to realise what she'd said when it was too late. She cleared her throat and shuffled some more.

'Is Mike going to help?' she asked, not bothering to be subtle about the change of subject.

'With what?' Jodie replied.

'Clearing the house. He is your brother.'

Jodie thought on it for a moment. Friend or not, there were some things Jodie didn't want in the open. 'I doubt it,' she said. 'I've not properly spoken to him since we found out what was in the will. Neither of us were up for it today.'

Fiona opened her mouth to say something, then closed it, then opened it again. 'What about your mum?'

'I don't think she's been in the house since she and Dad separated. Anyway, I think it's better if I do it.'

'Owen?'

That got a snort. It was enough effort for Jodie to get her teenage son to clean his own room, let alone an entire house.

Fiona rested a sympathetic hand on Jodie's arm. 'You sure you don't need a hand?'

A shake of the head. 'I'll catch up with you tomorrow.'

Fiona hovered for a moment. She'd been at Jodie's side all day and had seemingly made a promise to someone not to leave her alone. It was undoubtedly kind and yet Fiona now clearly wanted to get going.

'Text if you change your mind,' Fiona said as she took a step away. She waited on the edge of the pavement, as if half expecting Jodie to do precisely that.

'I will.' Jodie swallowed and then added a quick 'Thanks for today.'

Fiona muttered something that Jodie didn't catch. The sort of don't-mention-it that friends offer when thanks isn't necessary.

'When's the naming ceremony?' she asked.

'Saturday.'

Fiona nodded. 'Your dad deserves it after being mayor for so long, then all the other things around town. Naming the community centre after him is the least they can do.'

Jodie didn't disagree, though it would feel odd to walk through the centre of the town and see her dad's name on one of the buildings.

'Would've been nicer if they did it while he was alive,' she said.

It came out harsher than Jodie meant, and Fiona bit her lip before seemingly deciding not to reply. Jodie knew she should apologise but couldn't quite bring herself to do it. Lots of little things had been slipping out harder than was meant lately.

Fiona smiled with her lips pressed together, offered a quick 'see you' – and then turned, checked both ways, and crossed the road. She soon disappeared into one of the alleys that snaked through the estate without looking back.

When Jodie had been a girl, she would play in the street in front of the house. Now, cars were parked nose to tail along both sides of the road, leaving only a narrow gap in the middle. That sort of thing had crept up on her. One moment, she was living in this house – the next, nobody was.

Jodie shrugged the bag off her shoulder and flipped through

her keys until she found the same one she'd had since she was nine years old. Back then, her dad had presented it to her in a wrapped box, as if it was her birthday. He said having a front-door key was a sign of maturity and trust – and that she had to look after it. Over the years, that one key had joined those for the flats and houses where she'd lived, plus the cars she'd owned, and the offices she'd worked in. It had outlasted them all – and now it had outlasted her father.

Inside, Jodie stopped in the hallway to collect the last few days' mail. Despite what had happened, there would never be a time when it felt right to be opening something with MR MARTIN PARKER written on the front. She thought it was probably illegal to open someone else's mail – but did that still apply if that person wasn't around to open their own?

There was something from the building society – her dad didn't trust banks – plus a flyer about an upcoming change in bin days. She added them to the pile on the side table by the door. Each letter from a new place meant another phone call and endless passing around until Jodie had told the right person that there wasn't much point in sending mail to Mr Parker any longer.

Aside from the pile of post, the rest of the house was as it had been. The walls of the hallway were lined with memories that spanned her dad's thirty or so years of public service. The largest framed photo was of him as mayor, in his red gown with large ceremonial chain, while opening a garden centre. The strange mix of pomp and absurdity that Britain did so well.

Jodie took a moment to take everything in, as she did each time she entered the house. There were framed newspaper clippings about her father's various election wins before he'd become mayor. One of the things of which he was most proud was that he'd never lost a ballot at any level of government – not that he'd run for anything higher than district council. There were framed certificates, plus letters from people he'd helped.

Then there was the time he and some other local mayors had visited the House of Commons and had their photo taken with the Prime Minister. Jodie vaguely remembered talk that he might stand as an MP, except he'd decided that Westminster life wouldn't be for him. The town really was all he wanted. Sometimes, it was *too much* about the town.

It was a lifetime of public service spread across a hallway and, at some point in the near future, Jodie would have to decide what to do with it all. Would she throw it away, or would she put it in a box and keep it somewhere indefinitely? Would she display some of it at her own house? They all felt like decisions someone else should be making... except they were hers.

Jodie looked back and forth along the hallway, sighed, and decided she couldn't face this particular dilemma quite yet. She wanted easier choices, so headed up the dusty, creaking stairs onto the landing. There were no windows at the top of the stairs and the only light was the gloomy murk that shone from the floor below.

She opened the door to her dad's room, remembering the Christmas mornings when she'd be knocking on the same door, heart thumping with excitement. It would be barely 6 a.m. and her parents wanted to sleep but they would let her under the warm covers. Her father would give her the single gift he'd stored under the bed the night before, ready for her to wake them up.

As soon as she looked inside, Jodie knew she wasn't ready to clear her dad's bedroom. The bed was still made, all sharp corners and tucked sheets. That's the thing with heart attacks – they didn't give notice of when they were going to arrive. Her father got up one morning and made his bed, as he did every day, and fully expected to sleep in it again that night.

At some point, it would be Jodie who had to unmake it.

She returned to the landing, leaving open the door to her father's room and allowing light to pour through.

It was then that she noticed the hatch in the ceiling. Jodie had never been in the attic and it had firmly been the domain of her father when she was growing up. Whenever he needed something from inside, there would be something close to a small ceremony as he fetched the ladder from under the stairs and then clunked and huffed his way up to the landing before bellowing at Jodie's brother to hold it still for him. Presumably, holding a ladder was a job with which neither Jodie nor her mum could be trusted.

She could feel her father's ghost telling her not to as Jodie headed to the cupboard under the stairs and dragged out the famous ladder. She laughed to herself as the metal frame bumped and banged its way around the various banisters and posts that lined the staircase. No wonder her dad made so much noise and fuss doing the same. The ladder was heavy and didn't lend itself to bending around corners.

Jodie was huffing herself by the time she levered out the ladder's legs and shuffled it underneath the hatch to the attic. It was harder work than it had ever looked.

Each step creaked as she eased her way up and Jodie wondered if she needed someone to hold the ladder. Would it somehow slide sideways and bounce down the stairs, leaving her abandoned in the attic itself?

She figured she'd risk it – and gently pushed open the hatch, keeping one hand on the ladder as she balanced herself. On top of her grief, there was a growing kernel of excitement at doing something never done before. She couldn't say why she felt drawn to it, today of all days, other than there had always been the sense the attic was out of bounds. There was something unquestionably thrilling about doing the forbidden in the house where she grew up. The cleaning and clearing had to start somewhere.

Jodie levered up the hatch and then placed it on a wooden board at the side of the attic entrance before climbing a rung higher and poking her head into the greying haze. Everything above her smelled of dust and a sort of earthiness, as if picking up a crusty pair of wellies, where the mud had been left to dry.

She squinted into the gloom until she noticed a plug sitting next to the ledge. There was a socket next to it, so Jodie plugged it in – and almost fell backwards out of the attic as orange burst from a bulb that was hanging from the rafters. The dark was instantly a dim yellow, which sent lengthy shadows spiralling into the furthest corners of the attic. Jodie blinked some more, taking in the mounds of fluffy yellow insulation, some of which had been covered by a series of boards.

The beams screeched as Jodie heaved herself fully inside. The squeak scraped its way along the wood towards the darkest corners and Jodie had visions of the house crumbling around her as she clasped a wooden beam and had to explain to her brother that all she'd done was try to get into the loft.

Her dad would have been right after all.

There were a series of boxes scattered across the boards and Jodie sat with her legs dangling through the hatch as she reached for the nearest. It was long, with a picture of a fake Christmas tree on the side. She had barely touched the wilting cardboard when a thread of tinsel sprang from the side, which was quickly followed by a mound of shimmering silver stars and baubles.

The box of Christmas tat was one thing that Jodie would have no problem taking to the tip. Her dad had been a strict supporter of the fake tree, insisting it would be too much hassle to clean up after a real one. As soon as Jodie had moved into a flat big enough, she'd made sure to lug a proper tree home from B&Q. It had, of course, created an enormous mess – though she told her father she was happy to clean it up.

She was still picking needles from her socks in April. Another thing he'd been right about.

Jodie dropped the box of Christmas decorations through the

hatch and listened as it thudded on the floor below. It was one step closer to the bin and, if she did nothing else, she'd achieved one thing.

Back in the attic, there were rows of boxes carefully lined up on the wooden boards. The first Jodie tried was a box of boxes. There was one for an old phone and another for a DVD player. Keeping this sort of thing 'just in case' was very like her dad, so Jodie dropped that through the hatch to join the Christmas stuff.

Clearing any of the rooms below would have been depressing – but there was something cathartic about getting rid of this stuff.

The next box was smaller and almost pristine. It had a faded Heinz logo on the side: the sort of thing supermarkets would pile near the checkouts, so people didn't need a bag. Across the top, in faded black marker, 'KEEP' was written in her dad's handwriting. A scribble frozen in time that would never be repeated. There was a simplicity about her dad's handwriting when he was trying to be neat. He slipped into block capitals because his squiggled scrawl of joined-up type would make a doctor's look tidy.

Jodie slid the box across the boards towards her and spent a moment taking in the single word. She could picture her dad at the kitchen table, using the marker pen that always sat in the windowsill for some reason. She'd never thought to ask why.

With a sigh, Jodie levered apart the four flaps that had been interlocked in a crescent. She wasn't sure what to expect inside, perhaps more Christmas decorations, or other newspaper clippings that weren't quite good enough to be framed. Whatever it was had to be important enough to keep.

When she finally managed to wedge open the top, the first thing Jodie saw was something green. It would have once been bright, the colour of a field after a summer rainstorm. It might have been the light in the attic but it had that faded look of something that had been washed too many times.

Except, even with that, there was something familiar about the colour...

Jodie reached into the box and pulled out a T-shirt. It had been folded into a square, though it unfurled itself in her hands as she clasped onto the arms and let it dangle. The material was stiff and starchy, as if it had been left to dry in the sun. A darker, greener, shape was printed on the front. Green on green.

Jodie held the shirt with one hand and, with the other, ran her fingers across the raised print of a four-leaf clover.

It was something she hadn't seen in almost two decades.

Its wearer used to say he wore it for luck.

The shirt *couldn't* be in her dad's attic, let alone in her hands.

It was real.

It was impossible.

This was the shirt her boyfriend had been wearing the last time she'd seen him, nineteen years ago.

The last time *anyone* had seen him.

TWO

The T-shirt smelled faintly of fabric softener. She'd half been expecting the once-familiar scent of her old boyfriend, or at least a musty, attic kind of smell. But it had been washed at some point – and then folded into that box marked 'KEEP'.

Jodie held the top at arm's length and then pulled it closer to herself, taking in the cracked motif on the front. Even the fractured creases in the print seemed familiar.

Except it couldn't be true.

She stepped down onto the platform of the ladder and then carefully descended and stepped around the boxes she'd dropped. No matter whether it was the orangey light of the attic or the brighter daylight shining through her dad's bedroom window, the shirt was still green. It was in her hand.

Still unavoidably real.

Jodie moved along the landing and creaked open the door to the bedroom where she had spent more than half her life sleeping. She had moved out when she was nineteen and finally started to earn enough to afford the rent on a bedsit above the chippy on the high street. She'd lived in so many places since and yet there were times when it felt as if this room was the only place that would ever feel like her true home.

Perhaps not now.

It had been fifteen years and the room was obviously not as she'd left it when she moved out. The posters had gone long ago, so had the paperbacks she used to devour. Her dad had repainted her lilac walls an inoffensive magnolia, plus thrown out her old bedding and replaced it with a light brown set. He'd always said it was 'for guests', even though – as far as she knew – nobody ever stayed over.

Jodie put the green top on the bed and then knelt to look underneath. When she'd moved out, there had been far too many things for her to take. There were the photos and schoolbooks that she couldn't quite face getting rid of, plus magazines and gig tickets she thought she'd look through one day. She hadn't, of course – but she'd kept more than that and it had to be somewhere. Her dad wouldn't have chucked everything without asking.

She thought her boxes might be shoved to the wall underneath the guest bed – but the only thing there was a coating of dust on the carpet. Jodie took in the rest of the room, though there was none of the clutter from her day.

As Jodie pushed herself up, she picked up the shirt from the bed. Sniffed it again. Ran a finger across the motif. Wanted that rumbling, rising dread in her stomach to go away.

She left the room and closed the door, then stepped around the boxes and ladder on the landing and headed downstairs. If her things weren't under the bed in her old room, there was only one other place they could be. Well, two, if landfill was included.

Jodie left the shirt on the bottom step and then turned on the hallway light before digging back into the cupboard under the stairs. She'd dragged out the ladder but paid little attention to the other things inside. Old scraps of carpet squares lined the floor, though they were more dust than fabric, which left Jodie spluttering as she stretched and dragged a series of cardboard boxes and plastic stacking crates towards the door.

She knew instantly that these were what she was looking for. 'JP' was written on the side of the crates in Tipp-Ex, something that seemed a curious relic of its time. Did kids still even use Tipp-Ex, let alone write their names on things with it? It seemed unlikely.

There was dust on top of the crates, probably fifteen years' worth, given how thick and crusted it was. The madness of keeping any of the stuff inside was immediately apparent as Jodie unclipped a lid and pulled out a pile of cardboard wallets. They contained crusty lined papers, filled with lines of her own scrawl. Even her own handwriting seemed somewhat alien in the moment. She'd seemingly kept every essay she'd written – and, in a few pages, there were more words than she'd put to paper since leaving school. Jodie had forgotten the days when she had neat handwriting – and it was only as she was closing the cover of the first folder that it occurred to her how similar her writing was to her father's. Except that only reminded her of the box upstairs with 'KEEP' written on the side. Her dad's writing.

Jodie kept hunting through the boxes. There were many more essays and mock exams, plus class photos that had her stopping momentarily to take them in. She and Fiona were there in their modified skirts that were three centimetres shorter than the uniform guidelines allowed. They'd pushed their luck as teenagers, back before her boyfriend went missing and things didn't seem as funny any longer.

She kept pulling things from the boxes until she found another cardboard folder underneath her old school tie. The word 'Keep' had been written on the front of the folder but, this time, it was her own joined-up writing.

There was an uncomfortable itching up and down her back

as she opened the cover. The walls above her were surrounded by cuttings and photos from her father's life and there was certainly a degree of ego to it. Except the folder was full of family newspaper cuttings that Jodie had chosen to keep. The one on top was from where her year held their own vote on General Election day. She'd been in one of the photos, even though she was nothing to do with the actual election – and Jodie looked at her wide-eyed younger self wondering where that sense of mischief had gone. She didn't think she had it any longer, but the teenage Jodie oozed a misplaced confidence and cockiness. Another glance towards the shirt on the bottom step partly answered the question as to where that self-assuredness had gone.

Underneath that first clipping was one about Mike's band playing its first pub gig. Her older brother had somehow managed to get a photo in the paper, even though barely a dozen people had turned up. She eyed the image of him in his leather jacket, with the guitar that looked too big for him. His band had been woeful and the memory brought a hint of a grin until Jodie saw Ben at her brother's side. Ben with his bass that seemed an extension of himself. He actually *could* play and had been self-taught in the days before everything was on YouTube.

Jodie hadn't been to Mike's first gig because her brother was playing, she'd gone for the bassist.

The bassist who, even in a speckly, low-resolution photo, was clearly wearing a T-shirt with a four-leaf clover on the front.

THREE

Jodie stared at the photo. It had been taken before the smoking ban and there was a haze that cloaked the band, as if a dry-ice machine had gone wrong.

Her brother's leather jacket had been bought from a charity shop, with price a stronger concern than fit. He was swallowed by it, like someone layering up for a harsh winter's day.

The drummer's greasy hair was slicked across his face and the singer was shirtless as he wailed out what was sure to be a cover of some dad rock anthem. Jodie couldn't remember his name but she was fairly sure she'd seen him behind the bakery counter at Sainsbury's recently.

Then there was Ben. Ben from next door. Ben, her first proper boyfriend. Ben in his four-leaf clover T-shirt that she knew was green, even though the photo was monochrome. Unlike the other three, Ben was at home on the stage. The bass guitar hung low and he played it effortlessly, gazing into the distance and not needing to look at what he was doing. His black hair was messy, which suited his carefree, ruffled style.

Jodie looked at the clipping for a while longer before

returning everything to the boxes. This time, she put the folder at the top before reaching for the green shirt and putting that inside too. She reattached the lid onto the crate and then shoved everything into the cupboard.

Dust was clinging to her arms and clothes as Jodie pushed up from the floor. She moved through to the kitchen, *her dad's* kitchen, and set the taps running as she cleaned herself as best she could. Over on the counter, his mug with the Tottenham logo sat upside down, next to the kettle that was half-filled. She only realised she'd been staring at the mug and kettle when the water sputtered an air pocket and splashed in the sink.

Jodie dried her hands on the tea towel that was hanging from the handle of the oven, then quickly headed back through the house until she was outside. The air was cooler than before and stung her slightly wet hands.

Before she knew what she was doing, Jodie was at the front door of the neighbours' house. A door she'd knocked on many times before – though not recently. Perhaps not in the nineteen years since Ben had disappeared.

It was Elaine Vickery who answered. Ben's mother blinked at Jodie through tired, sagging eyes that seemed as if they'd not had a full night's sleep since Ben went missing. She leaned on the door frame and forced a gentle smile.

'You all right, love?'

Jodie suddenly realised she had no idea what to say. From deeper in the house, the vague, inoffensive nothing of something like Radio 2 or Smooth hummed. Jodie's mouth goldfished for a moment until she caught herself. 'Just wanted to say thanks for coming to the funeral,' she managed.

Elaine brightened a little. 'Of course we were going to be there. We've been living next to your dad for thirty-odd years. Couldn't have asked for a better neighbour.'

Jodie had to force herself not to shiver at the thought of their missing son's T-shirt. Had it really been sitting in a box in her father's attic for so many of those years? They might not have thought he was such a great neighbour if they knew.

Elaine paused as her husband joined her in the doorway. Jim Vickery wasn't much taller than his wife. He was hunched, his neck stooped, which Jodie assumed was down to his lifetime of being a lorry driver. He rested a hand on his wife's shoulder and offered a matching smile to hers.

'It was a lovely ceremony,' he said. 'The vicar did a really good job. It was great that so many came out.' A pause. 'Not surprising, of course. Everyone loved your dad.'

Jodie had wondered how old she would be when talk of birthday parties, anniversaries and births switched to that of funerals and goodbyes. Three times in the previous year or so, her dad had greeted her with statements like, 'You'll never guess who's died.'

And then, out of nothing, he was the one who'd died.

'I've been next door, doing some clearing,' Jodie replied.

It was impossible not to notice the way Elaine and Jim's faces fell in something close to unison. They both recovered almost instantaneously but the disappointment was already in the open.

'We were hoping you'd move in,' Jim said as his fingers tightened slightly on his wife's shoulder.

'Someone familiar,' Elaine added.

'If it's a stranger, you never know who you might get,' Jim said.

'You hear these stories on the news about nightmare neighbours and all that. The noise...' Elaine tailed off, though it was impossible for Jodie not to wilt slightly under the joint stares. It felt as if this was the topic they had been talking about daily ever since Jodie's dad had died.

Jodie glanced away, taking in the Van Gogh print on the wall of the hallway, unable to meet their accusatory stares.

'I don't think it would feel right,' she managed. 'I'm already living on the other side of town and...' She tailed off, not completing the sentence because she was yet to finish the thought. She didn't know what was going to happen to the house, other than that she wasn't going to move into it. 'I was hoping you could keep an eye on it,' she said quickly. 'While I figure out what I'm doing.'

Elaine replied almost instantly with 'Of course.'

Jodie found herself looking past the faded Van Gogh to the second photo on the wall of the hallway. She'd momentarily forgotten why she'd knocked on the door in the first place but the picture of Ben, that had been in the same place for as long as she could remember, was a forcible reminder. He was sitting in an armchair that engulfed him, an acoustic guitar on his lap. It was a moment frozen in time, with the sandy-haired boy focused on the instrument and the camera focused on him.

Aside from the fact he was her neighbour, Jodie hadn't really known Ben at the time. They hadn't been friends, or mixed in the same circles. She'd seen that photo hundreds of times since he went missing, though. Thousands. Tens of thousands. It had been a part of so many news articles – and it lived on the wall of the house in which he grew up.

Jodie had been looking at it for too long and both Jim and Elaine had followed her gaze.

'I know you were young,' Elaine said, 'but, when you started courting, I think we pictured you marrying and settling down. Like a movie. Next-door neighbours and all that.'

Jodie didn't look up. She'd heard similar sentiments from Elaine before. The word 'courting' had stuck because it was so old-fashioned – then there was the idea that two teenagers might have their entire lives mapped out. It felt so misplaced, especially now she was an adult herself – and yet there were people in the town who did precisely that. Jodie's brother had married his first girlfriend and Jodie had married her second boyfriend. Her own son, Owen, was only a year or so younger.

But it was that sort of place.

Elaine and Jim took a step backwards in unison and Jodie craned further into the hall, unable to help herself, taking in Ben's green T-shirt in the photo. The four-leaf clover was unmistakeable.

From there, she was back on the High Street, walking out of the cinema hand in hand with Ben. They'd just watched *Spider-Man*, the first one with Tobey Maguire, before it all got remade and then remade again. She had just turned sixteen, and it was a warm day at the end of May. Ben was wearing the same green top she'd held in her hands minutes before.

She wasn't thinking of her future back then, not at that age, it was all about that moment with Ben. That afternoon. She hadn't eaten popcorn at the cinema because she'd worried about it sticking in her teeth. She'd had a few sips of the Coke he'd ordered but not much because there were all those magazine articles about how fizzy pop was making people fat. She'd worried about the heat outside and her top sticking to her back. Whether Ben would notice, or care. Whether they'd run into any of her friends on their way home. So many little things, yet they had been embedded into Jodie's thoughts for all the years as she replayed every last second of the afternoon, searching for answers that weren't there.

Jodie and Ben had soon moved away from the high street, from the weekend shoppers, onto the side roads and the mazey cut-throughs around the estates they knew so well. They'd passed the church and Ben had asked if she believed in God. Jodie said she didn't and Ben said that he had as a child. He had grown out of it, in the way kids grew out of Santa Claus. It was the only time he'd ever mentioned religion to her. They'd carried on, talking about nothing and everything. Maybe school, maybe not. Maybe their friends, maybe not. Jodie could never remember.

She *did* remember the navy-blue van parked outside the

church, though – although she didn't realise how important it would end up being.

Ben had let go of her hand at some point and he'd tried a few car handles as they'd passed, checking to see if any were unlocked. Jodie had asked what he was doing and he'd said it was something to do. It was so odd at the time – and she'd always wondered whether it mattered. Would he really have stolen something from an unlocked car? Or simply taken the chance to peer inside? Was he doing it to impress her? She'd never know.

They'd got to the corner and the local chippy that soaked their bread in gravy for chip butties. They'd had tea there on some days but not that one. Ben had said he wanted to nip to the music shop, which was behind them. He'd asked if Jodie wanted to go with him – except she'd wanted to get home to change. She would never have told him why, but she was convinced there was sweat patches in the armpits of her top.

And that was it.

She had gone one way and he'd gone the other. It was the last time she'd seen him. The last time *anyone* had.

She couldn't remember whether she'd watched him go. If it had been a movie, there would have been that lingering shot of him disappearing into the alley while wearing that green T-shirt. Sometimes, that's how she pictured the afternoon – except she didn't think it was real. Or perhaps she *had* watched him head into the alley? In the years since, that afternoon had blurred into others and she wasn't sure what was real.

Except for the very real T-shirt he was wearing.

'Your dad was always so helpful...'

It was Elaine who brought Jodie back to the doorstep. Jodie blinked and looked away from the photo, back towards Ben's parents.

'Sorry...?' she said.

'When Ben went missing,' Elaine clarified. 'Your dad was always so helpful. He used his council connections to get onto the police. We'd have been left in the dark if it wasn't for him.'

'What do you mean?'

'It all went a bit quiet after a few days. Your dad kept on at the paper, making sure they didn't forget. Kevin-something was the journalist's name. Your dad got him to keep going back to the police.'

Jodie didn't know what to say about that. They had spoken about Ben in the frantic days after he went missing, and the years since, but Jodie couldn't remember her dad helping the Vickerys. Half an hour before, it wouldn't have mattered – would have even seemed normal, considering her dad's position at the heart of this town. Now, with Ben's top in her dad's attic, it was hard not to question everything.

'Keith,' Jim said, unprompted.

'Who's Keith?' his wife asked.

'The journalist. It's Keith, not Kevin. Keith Lincoln. He lives in that cottage out by the canal. That one with the chimney.'

Jodie switched off as they bickered gently, in the way couples do. He was definitely Kevin, but maybe Keith, then definitely Keith, who used to live in the flat above the old newspaper office. That office used to be something called 'Finnegan's', except it might have been 'Flannigan's', and perhaps he never lived there anyway.

By the time they'd agreed he was called Keith, and that he lived near the canal, Jodie had taken half a step away from the door.

'I know it's not the time,' Jim said, focusing in on Jodie. 'I meant to ask before but, with your dad and everything...'

'What?'

'People are saying he might be up for release...'

Jodie didn't need to ask who Jim was talking about. There could only be one person.

Ben had never been found, and neither had a body, but that hadn't stopped a local roofer being locked up for the murder. Traces of Ben had been found in a navy-blue van belonging to Paul McIntosh. It had been parked outside the church as Ben and Jodie walked past on that spring afternoon. Jodie was the person who'd mentioned it to the police as they asked what she remembered about the day. It was throwaway at the time. She'd mentioned the BT van at the end of her street and a broken-down Escort close to the alley. Little things that had stuck.

At the time, the court case and conviction had all felt right to Jodie. The police had got the man who did it and that was that. It was only as she got older that she realised how strange it all was. Someone had been found guilty of murdering her boyfriend, even though a body was never discovered. Even though nobody had actually seen McIntosh with Ben. Even though McIntosh said he didn't do it.

Jodie had zoned out once more, though Jim was still talking. '... don't know what to say,' he shrugged. 'You'd think the government would let you know if he was coming out, wouldn't you? Still, you never know with that lot.'

She blinked back towards him, lost between two timelines. 'I don't think he'd come back here,' Jodie said.

'I wouldn't put anything past that McIntosh,' Jim replied. 'After what he did. You know his wife died, don't you? About six months ago. There's been a 'for sale' sign up ever since, but who'd want to live there? After what her old man did?'

Jodie took another step away, unable to remember why she'd knocked in the first place. Everything had got lost in a jumble of memories.

'I've got to get home,' she said. 'I'll probably be back tomorrow.'

Elaine said something about looking after herself and that

the forecast said it was going to rain in the morning. The usual stuff. Kind and innocuous. It was only as Jodie was opening her car door that she realised the fact Jim knew that 'for sale' sign was up outside the McIntosh house meant he must be keeping a regular eye on it.

FOUR

Jodie sat in her car, on the other side of town from her dad's house, watching her own front door. She had no idea how long Ben's T-shirt had been in her father's attic. It could have been the entirety of the time Ben had been missing. She could have been sleeping in her childhood room with the shirt sitting above her.

In one way, nothing had changed.

Except... everything had.

She had to remind herself it had been her dad's funeral barely hours before. The day had turned into something she could never have imagined.

Should she tell someone about the shirt? If so, who? She and Fiona more or less told each other everything – but those conversations were mainly about what they were currently watching on TV. Or about the latest town drama that was playing out on Facebook. Or about Fiona's husband, or Jodie's ex. Things that were important in isolation but nothing compared to what Jodie had found.

If not Fiona, she could ask Mike. Her brother had been in the same teenage band as Ben and might have some simple explanation for why the T-shirt had been where it was. Perhaps Mike owned one that was the same as Ben's and it had somehow been left in the attic? Her brother was significantly bigger than Ben, so it seemed unlikely – though it was a better explanation than Jodie's dad having something to do with Ben going missing. Jodie couldn't think of a better explanation.

She *could* ask Mike... except he'd been a bit odd with her at the funeral. He had barely acknowledged her throughout the morning and, when she tried to speak to him before the service, had mumbled something about needing the toilet, then shuffled away to talk to someone else. Afterwards, he'd stuck rigidly to his wife's side before seriously hitting the bar at the wake.

If not Mike or Fiona, Jodie wasn't sure who else she could tell. If she'd gone into the attic a month before, she could have simply asked her father.

Despite that police visit to tell of her dad's death, despite his empty house, despite the reading of the will and the funeral itself, she wasn't sure it had quite sunk in that she'd never be able to ask him anything again. Someone had posted a news story on Facebook the week before about how councillors were considering a new bike lane in the town. Jodie's instant thought had been that her dad would be dealing with angry locals when he went for his daily walk. Then she realised he'd never be doing that again. That's what the last few weeks had been: thoughts of her dad, quickly erased by the knowledge that he was gone.

Jodie gulped away the lump in her throat and rubbed her eyes. She wouldn't tell either Fiona or Mike about the T-shirt. Not yet, anyway.

She climbed out of the car and headed along the path before letting herself into her house. The usual booming of Owen's Xbox echoed from above as he played some shooting game online with his friends.

After the funeral, he'd asked if he could head home and

Jodie hadn't seen any reason to drag him off to the wake, especially when she didn't want to be there herself.

Jodie considered leaving him to himself but headed up the stairs anyway and knocked on his door. She didn't think he'd hear over the explosions and machine-gun chatter from the other side – but a clear 'yeah' bled through as the sound lowered to something more acceptable.

Jodie nudged open his door and was met by the usual blend of feet, overflowing bins and Lynx Africa. She had tried talking to him about opening windows and the like, but fourteen-year-old boys had no interest in such things – and seemingly no sense of smell.

Owen was sitting on his bed, game controller in hand. His stare left the TV for a fraction of a second to take in his mum before returning to the screen. Since Jodie had last seen him, he'd changed out of his black school trousers, white shirt and too big suit jacket. He was now in oversize shorts, with a basketball vest that hung low on his chest, revealing the merest wisps of barely-there fluff. Much like his father, he was all skin and bone. Also like his father, he sat with his legs wide, in the way men do when they seemingly can't take up just the one seat on a train. Jodie had also mentioned that to Owen in the past – but it wasn't the time now.

'Are you OK?' Jodie asked.

Owen's gaze didn't leave the TV. 'Huh?'

'With your granddad's funeral and everything. I was making sure you're all right.'

'Yeah. Fine. Whatever.'

Owen had spent a lot of time in his room since his grandfather's death – though it was hard to tell whether it was his way of grieving, or if it was because he was fourteen.

Jodie stood and watched for a moment as Owen's thumbs fizzed across the controller.

'What's for tea?' he asked.

'What do you want?'

'Pizza...? Chips?' He sounded part hopeful, part demanding.

Jodie sometimes felt guilty at not having the sort of relationship with her son that led to them talking about their feelings. The only feeling he ever seemed to tell her about was those in his belly when he was hungry – which was most of the time.

'You had pizza last night,' Jodie replied.

'So?'

'I was going to do something with that leftover salad from Friday. Maybe mix it with some—'

'Yuck. I'll warm up a pizza in a bit.' He touched his ear, then added, 'Go round the back.'

'Back of where?'

He turned momentarily to Jodie before focusing back on the screen, which is when she realised he was talking to one of his friends via a headset. This was, presumably, the end of the conversation.

Jodie watched her son for a while longer, wondering if there was a time when he'd grow out of whatever phase he was in. She'd been much more sociable when she was his age, although a lot of teenaged stuff now seemed to happen via the internet.

'Owen.'

Jodie's son tapped his ear again and sighed theatrically, using his entire body and letting his shoulders slump. It was as if he'd been asked to do something heinous, like standing up, or go to bed before midnight. 'What?'

'Did your dad message you today?'

'About what?'

'I don't know. It was your granddad's funeral and I thought he might've been in touch.'

Owen didn't answer, not with words anyway. The way he focused unblinkingly on the screen as his thumbs flicked around the controller was an answer of sorts.

'Owen?'

'What?'

'Did he message you?'

'No.'

It was Jodie's turn to sigh, though it was less showy than her son's.

Even though she knew the answer, she figured she'd try one more time.

'Are you sure you're all right?' she asked.

'Yeah.' Owen touched his ear again and added with urgency, 'The other door.'

Jodie was about to turn and head out of the room when Owen started spamming a button. His thumb bash-bash-bashed the controller before he swore, with little regard for Jodie's house rules about such things. His language was something else she needed to speak to her son about, although she figured she might go through Owen's dad. Owen would sometimes listen if it was his father telling him something. 'Sometimes' was the key word.

For now, her immediate concern was the string of purply-black marks that ran along Owen's almost non-existent bicep.

'Are they bruises?' Jodie asked.

Owen ignored her, so she stepped across the room, deliberately walking in front of the TV, which got the expected tut.

Jodie craned in and then pointed to her son's arm. 'Why are there bruises on your arm?'

Owen glanced sideways – but only for a moment before his attention went back to the game. He tapped his ear. 'Dunno.'

'They must be from somewhere,' she said.

'I guess.'

'Where?'

'Dunno.' A pause and then, 'Probably PE.'

Jodie was ready to push for a better explanation, except she never got to ask because, as Owen tapped his ear once more, the sound of the doorbell echoed up the stairs.

She hovered for a moment, except there was only two of them who lived in the house – and Owen only ever answered the door if he was expecting one of his friends.

There was another tut as Jodie stepped across the screen, then she closed Owen's door and headed down the stairs. She half thought about trying to have a better conversation with her son after she'd dealt with whoever was at the door – but then remembered the green shirt she'd found in her dad's attic and, suddenly, Owen's moodiness didn't seem like such a big deal. If parents started worrying about teenagers being moody, there'd be no hours left in the day to think about anything else.

The doorbell had already sounded twice more by the time Jodie reached the front door. Each new ring sounded more impatient than the last, like a rogue church bell-ringer having a panic attack.

That annoyance was immediately reciprocated as Jodie answered the door.

'Can I come in?' the woman on the doorstep asked.

Jodie's instinctive 'no' almost popped out – although she could never actually say that. The visitor was family, after all.

Instead, and much against her better judgement, Jodie held the door wider for her sister-in-law. 'Sure,' she said, meaning 'no'. 'It's good to see you,' she added, meaning 'I wish I could slam this door in your face.'

Samantha smiled thinly as she stepped inside, her nose wrinkling with some sort of perceived grievance. She had the face of someone fishing an old egg sandwich out of a schoolbag.

'I figured it was time for a chat,' she said – which could only mean one thing.

Trouble.

FIVE

Samantha didn't wait for a reply, instead angling herself around Jodie and heading along the hall. By the time Jodie had closed the door and followed, her sister-in-law was already in the kitchen, crouching to squint at a coffee stain on the countertop.

As Jodie entered behind, Samantha straightened as if noticing her for the first time. 'I love your... uh, mugs,' she said airily, before wafting a hand towards the draining board, where there were three upturned mugs. They were chipped and mismatched. One with Mr Tickle on the front and the other two some sort of corporate freebies Jodie had stolen or been given at some point.

'Is something up with Mike?' Jodie asked.

Samantha went higher-pitched with surprise. 'Mike? No, why would there be?'

'I don't think you've ever come round on your own.'

Samantha took this in by pouting a lip and huffing slightly. Jodie wasn't actually sure they had ever been alone, without her brother to separate them. They didn't exactly feud – but there was no crossover in friendship groups. Strangers who knew one another.

Samantha moved on from this instantly. 'Oh, before I start, I left Jord in the car. Hang on.'

Jodie watched as Samantha marched out of the kitchen, along the hall to the front door, which she opened. She poked her head outside and bellowed her son's name. Moments later, Jordan appeared.

He was the same age as Owen, and Jodie had assumed he might be one of the people to whom Owen was talking to on his Xbox headset. The cousins often walked to school together, although it was rare Jordan came over.

Jordan slouched in the way teenage boys did, as if trying to walk backwards and forward at the same time. He mumbled something in Jodie's direction that might have been 'hi' before he headed to the stairs. She didn't think he was specifically trying to stomp but there was a series of solid thumps before Jodie heard Owen's door opening and closing.

Back in the kitchen, Samantha was perched on the edge of the dining table, ignoring the actual chairs. She glanced towards the kettle with sledgehammer subtleness and forced a smile that wasn't matched by her eyes.

'Do you want a tea?' Jodie asked, feeling obliged.

'That would be lovely. No milk or sugar. We're doing no-dairy at the moment.' She quickly and silently scanned Jodie and then added, 'It does wonders for your, er, skin.'

Jodie ignored the jibe and filled the kettle at the sink. She rolled her eyes when she was facing the window and her sister-in-law couldn't see. After flicking on the kettle, she turned to face Samantha.

'How can I help you?' she asked, forcing the politeness.

There was no hesitation in the reply. 'It's about the will.'

The two women stared at one another for a moment and there was an invisible fizz in the air. Jodie had suspected this would be coming – though not today.

'We've only just buried him,' she said.

'We didn't want to make a fuss before the funeral but—'

'So you gave it a few hours?'

Jodie had raised her voice without meaning to, though Samantha was apparently unfazed. Her features didn't shift as she continued to lean on the table, not quite sitting but not standing. She smoothed down a piece of hair that hadn't moved. It was as if she'd expected the reaction, perhaps even wanted it.

'We have to talk one day,' Samantha said. 'When's good for you? Tomorrow? The day after? How long do you want to leave it?'

Jodie could feel herself clenching her jaw at the direct challenge. A few moments passed as she ground her teeth into each other.

'What do you want?' she asked.

'You know what I want.'

'Dad left the house to me – that's what was in the will. You were there when they read it.'

'You know it's not—'

'That's what he wanted.'

Jodie had hoped for something of a reaction, but Samantha remained unmoved, despite being interrupted. She waited for Jodie to finish, took a breath, and then started again.

'It should be fifty-fifty,' she said. 'There are two kids – you and Mike. You know it isn't fair that you get everything and he gets nothing.' A pause and then, 'You're stealing from your own family.'

Jodie opened her mouth to reply but then closed it. The last line was meant to rile her. It sounded rehearsed, as if Samantha had stood in front of the mirror that morning, before the funeral, going over it.

'Does Mike know you're here?' Jodie asked.

It was the first thing that got a reaction. Samantha glanced past Jodie, to where the kettle had just plipped.

'I'll take that as a "no",' Jodie added.

She picked up the corporate mugs from the draining board, then dropped a teabag in each and filled them both with water. When she turned back to the table, Samantha was ready.

'Mike agrees with me,' she replied.

'Then where is he? He didn't seem that surprised when the will was read last week – and he's not brought it up since.'

'He was still in shock then. We both were. Imagine stealing from your own family.'

Jodie let that sit, determined not to rise to the obvious bait.

'I'm the one that visited Dad three or four times a week. I'm the one who did that hill walk with him last summer. It was me who cooked Christmas dinner last year and had him over. I drove him to the Ideal Homes exhibit the other year when no one else wanted to go. I never saw Mike doing any of that.'

Samantha's right eye twitched as she remained silent.

'Dad was on his own,' Jodie added. 'After he split with Mum, he only had Mike and me. If you're wondering why he left me the house, it's not too difficult to figure out.'

Jodie turned and grabbed a spoon from the draining board before going fishing for the teabags in the mugs. She dumped both in the sink – and then passed across Samantha's mug before getting the milk from the fridge to top up her own. Having wondrous skin could sod right off.

By the time she was back in place, leaning on the counter, Samantha had put her mug on the table and was standing with her arms crossed.

'You know you were always the favourite,' Samantha said. 'How do you think Mike felt? You were such a daddy's girl.'

Jodie didn't bother to turn away and roll her eyes this time. She did it to her sister-in-law's face. 'What's your point?'

'We're getting a lawyer to challenge the will – so don't even think about selling the house. We'll get an injunction to stop it if you try.'

Jodie hid her mouth behind the mug as she inhaled the

warm air. The truth was, despite everything about her spending time with her dad, she had been surprised that her brother had got nothing major in the will. She thought Mike might try to talk to her about it – though didn't think threats from his wife would be the first move. House prices in the town were ridiculously high, like everywhere, and that meant there was lots of money at stake. Money she needed...

Despite her previous coolness, the lack of Jodie's immediate reply seemingly sent Samantha over the edge. In a flash, she was wagging a finger in Jodie's direction.

'I don't know why you have to be such a *bitch* about it!'

She wasn't quite screaming but it wasn't far off.

Jodie put down her mug and nodded towards the table. 'Are you sure you don't want milk with your tea?'

Any pretence of calm was gone as Samantha trembled with sudden rage. She marched into the hall and paused momentarily at the bottom of the stairs to bellow 'Jordan!' before she stormed towards the front door. 'I'm not the sort of person to let things go,' she said, partly over her shoulder.

There was a thud from upstairs and the sound of Owen's door opening.

'Your natural hair colour seems to disagree with you.'

Samantha froze before tilting her head slightly to look at herself in the mirror that was pinned to the wall. She was trembling with rage, though neither of them had a chance to add anything else because Jordan half fell his way down the stairs before emerging into the hall. He nodded at Jodie and then slumped across to his mum, who'd opened the front door.

'You've not heard the last of this,' Samantha said, before holding it wider for Jordan to leave.

'What about your tea?' Jodie asked, forcing the politeness.

Samantha hovered for a moment in the door frame but then stepped through it and slammed it with thunderous, predictable and – to Jodie at least – somewhat satisfying fury.

SIX

Samantha's unexpected appearance had given Jodie something to stew about. She spent the evening going through imaginary arguments and conversations. She saw herself in court, arguing against some smart-mouthed, suited lawyer who was trying to say her dad didn't know what he was doing when he planned his will. She'd make sure the judge knew that *she* was the one who visited their father the most. *She* took him meals and kept him company when no one else wanted to go to the cinema with him. Or 'the pictures', as he called it.

She embraced her anger at Samantha, enjoyed it, grateful for something that didn't leave her thinking about that shirt in her father's attic.

She always returned to it, though. That image of Ben's green shirt niggled at the back of Jodie's mind. Not front and centre, not the main event, but since she'd found the top, there hadn't been a moment when it wasn't there. There were the questions that went with it. How did the shirt get into her dad's attic? Why was it there? Was it definitely Ben's?

Owen seemed oblivious to it all. Aside from making himself some toast in the evening, the next time he emerged from his room was the following morning. He was in his school uniform and put four slices in the toaster, buttered them all thickly with too much margarine and Marmite – and then headed for the front door with a grunt that was probably a 'goodbye'. They weren't the sort of family who sat at the dining table and told stories from their day. Jodie doubted that actually existed despite every movie pretending it did. There'd be perfectly set dining tables, with mounds of fresh fruit – plus bacon sizzling in the pan. Families would have conversations... but Jodie had never had that. Even when she'd been young, they'd sit with plates on their laps in the living room – or, as she became a teenager, she'd eat in her room.

After Owen had gone, she was back across town at her dad's house for the second day running.

She stood at the foot of the stairs, looking at the door that was built into the storage space underneath. The green shirt still rested in the crates where she'd left it. She unfolded it and ran her finger across the imprint, wanting to find something that might show it couldn't be Ben's. There was nothing attached to the inside. No label or tag to say it had been manufactured after he'd disappeared. The only marking was a faded black 'S' for small – a size into which neither her father nor brother could have fitted.

Jodie was trying to refold the shirt when there was a bang-bang-bang on the door. There was a doorbell but whoever was outside had seemingly decided mashing a fist onto the glass was the best way to get the attention of someone inside.

She had never been great at folding clothes, as her teenage floordrobe and the resulting parental arguments would attest. Jodie quickly tucked the arms underneath the main body of the shirt and slid it into the crate before shoving everything back under the stairs. As she did that, a man's voice was seeping through the front door. She couldn't make out every word but the end of each sentence was peppered with a sprinkling of 'mates' or 'pals'.

The man on the other side of the door was wearing jeans and a checked shirt and had a toolbox at his feet. A phone was pressed to his ear and he acknowledged Jodie with a nod as he told someone that he was 'snowed under' and that the roads were 'rammed to shite' because 'some tit in a van' had 'made a prat of himself' on the dual carriageway.

Jodie leaned on the door frame, waiting until the man finished his call. He slipped the phone into a back pocket and muttered an apology before turning to look at the door itself.

'Do you want front and back doing?' he asked.

Until she'd seen the toolbox, Jodie had forgotten she'd called a locksmith the night before. If nothing else, those hours pacing her living room while having imaginary arguments with her sister-in-law had given her one moment of clarity. If her brother was going to cause trouble regarding the will, then he had a key for their dad's house.

No, not *their dad's* house, *her* house.

The front door and the lock were the same as they had been when they'd each been given keys as children.

Back in the moment, Jodie told the locksmith that he could replace the locks at the front and back. His phone was already buzzing in his pocket but he ignored it as he started to unpack his tools on the ground.

'I can replace the whole door if you prefer,' he said. 'I'll have to measure it up and pick up the actual door – but that'd only take an hour and I'd be back.'

The old door was scuffed and familiar. Jodie couldn't quite face getting rid of the whole thing. It'd mean the house no longer felt like her dad's. It would be an end.

She told him to replace only the locks and then hung around awkwardly, not sure what to add. Her father was the sort who would find common ground with anyone and was seemingly as comfortable chatting to someone emptying the bins as he was glad-handing politicians. Jodie had never inherited any of that ability to make small talk. If anything, the opposite was true. Except for with people she knew, she lived from awkward silence to awkward silence.

She hovered for a moment, trying to think of something her dad might say – but all she could come up with was an offer to make tea. The locksmith was already fiddling with a drill bit as he told her he had 'loads of milk' and three sugars, so Jodie headed through to the kitchen, where she filled the kettle and flicked it on. She wondered what 'loads of milk' would do for someone's complexion, according to Samantha.

She listened as the locksmith whistled to himself before drowning it out with the bone-tingling buzz of his drill. She thought about whether the house would ever feel like anything other than her dad's. There were too many little things that stuck with Jodie. How her dad's car was full of petrol in the Sainsbury's car park because he'd just filled it up, moments before having his heart attack in the cereal aisle. How there was a full box of 500 teabags in his cupboard and six ready meals in the freezer. Her dad had done all those things, not knowing it was all unnecessary.

She was daydreaming again and Jodie blinked back to the kitchen as the drilling stopped momentarily. The kettle had finished boiling at some point, so she opened the cupboard and took out one of the generic off-white mugs of which everyone seemed to own six. She filled it with water and dropped in a teabag, then waited as more whirring filled the house.

The locksmith took less than an hour to replace the locks at the front and back of the house. He gave her three keys for each door and showed her they all worked before heading back to his van with his phone back at his ear.

Jodie watched him drive off, one hand on the wheel, the other clutching his phone, and then she closed the door. The house felt empty again and she had no idea what to do. She was supposed to be clearing it, ready for whatever she decided to do next. So far, the best she'd managed was to uncover something she'd have rather not known about.

It felt as if Ben's shirt was calling to her from under the stairs, whispering that she needed to discover its secrets. Jodie ignored it and instead headed up to her father's room, where she yanked the sheets off the bed, pulling hard so they untucked themselves from the mattress. She tugged the pillowcases off next and dumped everything in a pile before taking in what she'd done. Without the neatly made bed, the room felt less like her father's. He'd have never tolerated such mess – and the thought of that led Jodie towards the wardrobes that were built into the wall on the furthest side of the room.

Three suitcases were stacked on the top shelf and Jodie pushed herself onto tiptoes to drag them down before she opened them on the bed. Her father wasn't quite a hoarder – but he also wasn't the sort of man to replace something if it wasn't completely falling apart, or broken. His cases were the same ones he'd had when they used to visit the seaside for caravan holidays when she and Mike were children. They were made of brown, starchy leather. The sort of things that were so solid and heavy, they could survive a missile strike. At an airport, a weight limit would largely be taken up by the luggage itself.

As for the clothes, her dad had never been much of a fashion fan and he'd seemingly stopped buying clothes around twenty-five years before his death. There were chinos and buttoned shirts, jeans and jackets. Nothing expensive – although everything with a vague memory of when she'd seen her dad wearing it. There was the thin jacket he always wore at the cinema because he got cold – plus the polo shirt with horizontal stripes that he'd wear on his morning walks in the summer.

The only way to get anything done was without prejudice – so Jodie roughly crammed handfuls of clothes into the cases, trying not to think too much about what any of them meant.

It only took fifteen minutes until the cases were full and zipped closed. Jodie had cleared around two-thirds of her dad's wardrobe in a single, brutal swoop. She left the football shirts, wondering if her brother might want them, then dragged the cases down the stairs. She was unable to actually lift them. Jodie lugged them down the path and into her car's boot and back seat before locking up the house with the new keys.

Jodie was on autopilot as she drove into the town centre. The first time she realised where she was came as she drove past the community centre that was soon to be named after her dad. It was next to a set of traffic lights that had predictably turned red. Jodie found herself staring towards where a small girl was clambering up the slide in the small playground that sat to the side of the centre. Her shoes squeaked noisily on the metal as she heaved herself to the top and then slid down before starting again.

It was the beep of the car behind that made Jodie jump back to the road and the green light ahead. She surged across the junction, almost stalling the car as she tried to escape the thought that the world without her dad was never quite going to be without him if she remained in the town.

The ghost of Ben had hung over the area for a generation – and she didn't know if she could handle another spectre, even if it did belong to her father.

The next thing Jodie knew, she was pulling into an empty space on the road outside a charity shop. She heaved the first suitcase off the back seat onto the pavement and then dragged it across to the doorway of the shop. Hadn't someone invented wheels at some point? What was she doing?

Jodie was about to take it inside when she noticed the small card in the window that said they weren't accepting any more clothing donations. Her arms ached and Jodie's chest was tight as she realised she was sweating from the effort. She turned back to her car and considered leaving the case where it was, rather than attempting to carry it back.

She wouldn't, though. She knew that. She was the sort who returned shopping trolleys to the correct bays at the supermarket. Jodie realised it was the sort of thing that had been instilled into her by her dad.

Another 'sort of thing'.

'Is that what I think it is?'

Jodie looked up at the sound of the voice. A woman was standing in the shop doorway, holding open the door. Jodie vaguely recognised her, although she didn't know her name. The town wasn't big enough for anyone to be truly anonymous.

'My dad died and he, um...'

Jodie was stumbling but the woman wasn't listening. 'I've known your dad since we were at school,' she said. 'Terrible what happened to him. I couldn't believe it when I heard. Right there in Sainsbury's. Could've been any of us. He was such a lovely man.'

Because her dad was so well known in the town, Jodie had heard something similar on a daily basis since the heart attack. She didn't know if it was the same for Mike but people seemed drawn to Jodie, wanting to tell her how sorry they were for what had happened. There was no question her dad was loved – and surely someone that well liked would have a genuine reason for keeping a missing boy's shirt in his attic?

'I've been clearing his house,' Jodie managed. 'I don't know what to do with everything. I didn't want to take it to the tip.'

'We'll have it,' the woman replied, as she nodded towards the inside of the shop. 'I'm sure it's good stuff, seeing as it's your dad's.'

Jodie almost laughed at that. If second-hand clothes buyers had a preference for dated chinos, they were in luck.

With the woman's help, Jodie hefted the case into the shop before returning to her car for the other two. She left everything close to the counter and edged towards the door as the woman tried to continue the conversation. On another day, Jodie might have let her speak – but she couldn't face hearing all these good things about her dad when there was one enormous unanswered question hanging over him. Everything felt tainted.

Jodie muttered something about having to get back to the house and then returned to the street. She was so focused on returning to the car, away from conversations about her dad, that she almost didn't register the man saying her name. It was only when she started looking for the key in her bag that she realised her ex-husband was standing next to the driver's door.

SEVEN

Darren had the bemused expression of someone asked to do an algebraic equation on the spot. He squinted at Jodie and his brow wrinkled.

'Didn't you hear me?' he asked.

Jodie had been thinking about how it was impossible to escape a person's past in a town like this – and here it was in front of her. She ran into her ex-husband roughly once a week, not only because of Owen going from one house to the other but because they shopped in the same places, they walked the same streets and knew the same people. They weren't in one another's lives but they weren't out of them either.

'I was dropping off some of Dad's things...' Jodie half turned to the charity shop and then back to Darren. 'I've started clearing the house.'

He smiled kindly. 'Sorry I didn't make the wake. The funeral was so well done, but with Chandra being... y'know...' Darren glanced away, off towards nothing in particular.

'You can say "pregnant",' Jodie replied.

'I know...'

An awkwardness passed between them, as it often did

when they tried to talk about anything other than Owen. Some divorced couples would go around telling people they were still 'on good terms', 'still friends', as if to emphasise that neither of them were monsters. Jodie and Darren had never got to that stage, though they were never really at war either.

'Why didn't you message Owen yesterday?' Jodie asked. 'He just lost his granddad.'

Darren shuffled on the spot, still not quite looking at Jodie. The distance was apparently more interesting. 'I've been busy with Chandra and the... pregnancy. We've had classes and appointments. I never realised how much there all was.'

He clocked what he'd said a moment after it came out.

'I didn't mean with you and Owen,' he added quickly. 'Obviously, there was stuff to do back then.'

Jodie let him waffle his way into trouble and then attempt to waffle back out of it. She knew what he meant. When she'd been pregnant with Owen, there had of course been appointments at the clinic – but she'd never been offered the additional prenatal classes that were around now. Perhaps it was because she was younger, barely an adult herself. Perhaps she wasn't curious enough to ask. Perhaps, perhaps...

'I tried to talk to Owen at the funeral but he was with his cousin,' Darren added eventually, as he tried to steer the conversation back to their son. 'I don't think he wanted his dad around, so I left them to it. I did text him last week, Thursday or Friday. I asked if he was OK but never got a reply.'

'He's a teenager,' Jodie replied. 'Of course he's not going to reply to everything. He barely replies to me – and I live with him. You have to keep asking.'

Something about Jodie's tone must have been harder than she thought because, instead of arguing back, Darren nodded along. 'You're right,' he said. 'I'll try harder.'

He was looking at her properly now and sounded sorry enough. Jodie's dad had always told her to accept an apology at face value... except remembering that had her thinking of him once again. She never realised how much of her life he occupied.

'How's Chandra?' Jodie asked, wanting to change the subject.

Darren relaxed a little, back on a subject he was happy to talk about. 'Good,' he said. 'She's due in seven weeks, so we've been making route plans for the hospital, depending on what time she goes into labour. You've got to be careful around the dual carriageway, so I've been working on alternates.'

The enthusiasm was impossible to miss. On another day, at another time, Jodie would let it needle that her ex-husband was showing far more passion for an unborn child than he ever seemed to show for the son he already had. She didn't fancy an argument – especially not on the street.

She said something about that all being good and that parents-to-be had to be prepared. They talked in circles in the way people did around births, marriages and deaths. Other than 'congratulations' and 'sorry', nobody knew what to say, so they'd say nothing in as many words as possible.

Talk of the upcoming birth soon switched back to talk of the funeral – and then Darren was describing it to her, even though she'd been there. He talked about the people crowded at the back of the church because there were no seats left. How the vicar mispronounced 'peace' as 'pies' and got an unexpected laugh. How the weather couldn't have been better. And so on. Things Jodie already knew – but she let Darren speak because she was afraid she'd blab about what she'd found in her dad's attic if she didn't.

She only realised he'd asked a question when another silence settled between them. Darren looked at her expectedly before his features fell a little as he realised she hadn't been listening.

'You look like you want to say something...?' he added.

Jodie bit her lip, trying to stop herself, and then it came out anyway. It had been playing on her mind – and finding Ben's T-shirt had given it more significance. 'There was a bit where the vicar said Dad wouldn't hurt a fly and I suppose it sort of... stuck.'

'How do you mean?'

Jodie couldn't think of a way to put what she'd found in words. How to tell him about Ben's shirt without telling him – but her face must have given away some of it, although Darren instantly had the wrong idea. Clouds passed across him.

'You're not saying your dad used to hit you...?'

'No!' Jodie replied instantly, not quite sure why he had jumped to that conclusion. 'Nothing like that. Never...' She tailed off as someone walked past and slowed. Jodie might have imagined the change in speed but she waited until they were out of earshot. The conversation suddenly felt dangerous... but then Darren finished a thought.

'I didn't think you knew...?' he said.

They stared at one another, suddenly both confused as it dawned on Darren that Jodie had no idea what he was on about.

'Knew what?' Jodie asked.

Darren craned his head back a little, narrowed his eyes, glanced at that spot in the distance once more. He took a breath and it was as if time had stopped.

'I've gotta get home,' he said quickly, before taking a step to the side.

Jodie clutched his sleeve and pulled him back.

'You've got to tell me now.'

'I thought... It's just...' He sighed as his eyes darted sideways. 'There's no point in bringing things back up. Not now he's... died.'

Jodie felt chills along her back. 'What do you know?'

Darren pulled his arm away and glanced at his watch. 'That

thing you said about not hurting a fly. I thought that meant you knew what happened.'

'Knew what?'

Jodie had raised her voice and Darren looked both ways, checking there was nobody anywhere nearby.

'I shouldn't—' Darren started.

'I want to know.'

Another sigh. 'You free tomorrow lunchtime? Twelve-ish.'

'I can be but what's wrong with now?'

Darren took a small step away, angling towards the mini supermarket next to the charity shop. 'I have to get back. I'm on a Dairy Milk run for Chandra and we can't have this conversation on a pavement. Let's have coffee, or something. We'll talk then. I'll text you about a place.'

He ran a hand through his hair and muttered something Jodie didn't catch. He had the air of someone who wished they'd never spoken.

Jodie didn't get a chance to say anything because Darren was already turning towards the shop. 'Look after yourself,' he added – and then he hurried away, almost knocking over a woman who was on her way out the doors in his haste. He mumbled an apology to her, then stumbled up the steps and disappeared out of sight.

Jodie watched, wondering if he'd come back but suspecting he'd probably disappear out the back doors, rather than face her again. It seemed the secrets in her family weren't solely confined to her father.

EIGHT

Jodie started the car and drove along the high street before heading off into a side street close to the post office. She parked behind a red Royal Mail van and switched off the engine, then sat and watched a postal worker lug sacks from the vehicle into the back of the building. He was wearing shorts, even though it wasn't a particularly warm day – and there was a V-shaped sweat patch seeping through his shirt.

She needed a moment to herself, away from the High Street, where someone else might spot her.

It was hard for Jodie to figure out what had happened with Darren. She'd been talking about one thing and he'd come close to revealing something completely different, only stopping because he realised it was something she didn't know.

Something about her dad.

Jodie and Darren had endured a turbulent marriage, mainly because they were so young when they exchanged vows. Some of it was his fault, some of it hers. They'd not only married too young but they'd stayed together too long because of Owen. Their relationship was better now they were apart and grown up.

As she considered calling him, Jodie's phone buzzed with a message from Darren.

Sry. In a rush. Frys at 12 2moro?

Gonna Fry Now – or 'Frys' to the locals – was a greasy spoon on the edge of town. The name changed every few years – but the mix of cheap tea and heart-attack-baiting breakfasts had been on offer for as long as Jodie could remember. Her dad had loved it, obviously. It wasn't her type of place, which is perhaps why Darren had suggested it. He clearly wished he'd kept his mouth shut.

She replied with a quick 'cu there' and then pressed back into the driver's seat, wondering what to do next. If her ex-husband really did have something to say about her dad that could link to Ben, there didn't seem much point in telling anyone else about the shirt before she spoke to him properly.

Jodie thought about returning to her dad's house, to continue clearing, but it felt as if she was done with that for the day. She'd accomplished a partial clearing of his bedroom, which wasn't a bad effort.

She started the car again and pulled around the mail van, then continued along the street. The truth was, before she found that shirt, she had other worries – one of which could be addressed with a small detour.

Jodie hadn't travelled far when she stopped at a set of traffic lights. There was nobody behind her this time and, though she was away from the community centre, the tangled web of the town made it impossible for any spot to exist without the blanket of memories that went with it.

Off to the side was a slim alley that linked the centre of town to the newer housing estate that had been built at the back of an old factory. Beyond that, a good mile or so away, was Jodie's dad's house. The alley was the quickest way to get from there to town, or back again. At various times of the year, the berry bushes would burst from the mangle of thorns and start growing across the path. The council only seemed to cut everything once a year, which meant there would be weeks where anyone using the cut-through had to run the gauntlet of slicing their arms open.

Jodie stared towards the shortcut, to where the berry vines were starting to push across the top of the fence. People called it Bramble Alley when she was younger, though she hadn't heard that in a while.

Bramble Alley had been the last place she'd seen Ben. She had gone one way, towards her house, when he'd gone the other. Behind her, on the other side of the road, was the church where Paul McIntosh's navy-blue van had been parked. The same van where traces of Ben were later found, though not his clothes.

She hadn't planned to drive this way and yet here she was. Jodie took in all of that before realising that she'd missed an entire cycle of the traffic lights. Fortunately, the town was quiet enough that nobody was behind her.

The next time the light turned green, Jodie surged ahead. She manoeuvred her way through the town's endless series of junctions, traffic lights, one-way streets and chicanes until she pulled in at Bunnies Garden Centre. It was a fifteen-minute walk from her house and attracted old people in the same way the quiet carriages on trains attracted men in suits who refused to put their phones away.

She parked in one of the staff spaces and then headed into the main building. Although the sign read 'Garden Centre', the biggest attraction was arguably the café and bakery. Weekdays saw it packed with pensioners drinking their £1 teas and eating scones while talking about the weather. Jodie knew that because she worked in the office at the furthest end of the café – and the only way to get there was to navigate the tightly packed chairs and tables as if running an obstacle course.

As she headed through, the chatter was so loud it could make a plane taking off sound quiet. In her time away from work, Jodie had forgotten quite how deafening it was to host a group of people who'd rather shout than go for a hearing test.

She hurried as best she could, until bursting through the office door at the end and closing it behind her.

Her desk had been tidied since she'd last been in. The cordless mouse was nowhere to be seen and had presumably been tucked into a drawer, while her keyboard had been pushed under the monitor, out of the way. She felt a pang of annoyance that everything was seemingly running smoothly without her. She would never admit it but she liked nothing more than returning from a holiday or time away to find out something had gone badly wrong in her absence.

Her title was 'general manager', which involved everything from monitoring stock levels, being in charge of HR, placing job adverts, designing flyers – and more or less everything else that nobody else fancied doing.

It was stable work, which was about all Jodie had to say about it.

The desk next to hers, where her assistant would usually sit, was empty – which meant Anita was either on a break, or dealing with one of the regular catastrophes that needed hands-on attention. Someone would've spilled some compost, or knocked over a gnome. The usual stuff.

Jodie thought about going to look for her but didn't get a chance because a door clunked open at the other end of the office.

She heard the voice before she saw the man. Jodie might be the general manager – but the owner, Ian Bunnie, was very much the man in charge. He had the sort of voice that needed volume control. His idea of a whisper was one of the few things loud enough to be heard over the din from the café.

'What are you doing here?' he boomed. 'You're supposed to

be on leave.'

If Jodie didn't know Ian, his tone might have sounded harsh.

'I figured I'd see how everything was going,' Jodie replied.

'Don't you worry about this place. I told you to take the rest of the month off – and I meant it.'

Ian took a step forward, as if to start ushering Jodie back towards the door. When she didn't move, he stopped and perched on the edge of her desk.

'Was a good day yesterday,' he said. 'The funeral itself, I mean. Couldn't have asked for better weather – and everyone came out. You did your dad proud.'

Jodie smiled as best she could but she had already heard enough of the same thing. She'd never noticed how much people talked about weather until it came to small talk after her dad's death. Because people didn't know what to say, they'd always revert back to describing the sky.

'I heard they're naming the community centre after him,' Ian added.

'This weekend,' Jodie replied. 'There's going to be a ceremony and some sort of plaque. I'll send you the details.'

'Let's hope the rain stays away!'

It felt as if they were on the brink of another lengthy back and forth about sunshine and rain, so Jodie cut it off quickly.

'I needed to ask you something,' she said.

Ian frowned at this, which she took as genuine concern. He'd played golf with her dad every few weeks and they were members of the same club. Her dad had hosted charity auctions at the garden centre in the past and they had that sort of chummy Old Boys relationship that Jodie didn't think women really had. Someone had once said her dad was part of the 'funny handshake brigade' and Jodie had never forgotten it. She often wondered if Ian had offered her the job of manager because her dad had put in a word. She'd never dared ask – and she wasn't about to.

But there was one thing she had to ask.

'It's a bit awkward,' she added.

'What is?'

'It's just... when you told me to take the rest of the month off, you never said if it was paid leave. I can't afford to take it unpaid, so I need to ask whether—'

'Of course it's paid!' Ian looked down on her with a hint of bemusement, as if she should have somehow known. 'It's compassionate leave.'

Jodie took a breath and felt a small amount of weight lift. Ian must have seen it.

'You've not been worrying about it, have you? Not with everything else you've got going on...?'

'No, I mean... yes. I didn't know what you meant and didn't think I should ask...' She tailed off, fearing she was embarrassing herself.

Ian reached and squeezed her shoulder gently, offering a rueful smile, before removing his hand. He was the sort of old-school man who didn't seem sure of how to express feelings or concerns with words. He instead favoured that hand on the shoulder or arm. Too much like her dad.

'I know it's not my place,' he said, 'but are you OK for money...?'

It might have been the past week or so of concern over whether she was actually getting paid, or it might have been her dad's death, the funeral, and everything from the past twenty-four hours catching up to her. It might even have been the way Ian was showing genuine concern. Either way, Jodie did the one thing she absolutely did not want to do.

She cried.

It came in an instant. One moment, she was leaning against the filing cabinet behind her desk, the next her chest was heaving and she was struggling to breathe. The fact she was crying in front of her boss only made it harder to stop. The best she could hope for was for a freak tornado to rip through the area.

Failing that, Jodie turned her back and squeezed the bridge of her nose so hard that her nails dented the skin. She grabbed the box of tissues on her desk and wedged a ball of paper into her eyes before blowing her nose.

When Jodie turned back, Ian was frozen on the edge of her desk. There was something close to paralysed panic on his face, which also reminded Jodie of her dad. He never knew what to do with someone who cried in front of him either.

'Sorry about that,' Jodie managed, with a croak.

It was as if someone else had taken over in the moment. Now she had control of her body again, she couldn't remember what had set her off.

'It's fine,' Ian replied, although his voice wavered with the sort of nerves she would never usually associate with him.

'I never told Dad,' Jodie said. She didn't say that she hadn't told anyone, not even Fiona. 'I owe around eleven grand,' she added.

Jodie was looking directly at Ian, though her eyes felt puffy and sore. She hadn't come here for this but she was in too deep now.

For his part, Ian reached out and touched her shoulder a second time.

'I didn't know,' he said.

'It built up over time. No big thing. My car broke down twice and failed its MOT the other year. I had some loans when I first got married, then used credit cards to pay them off. Dad didn't leave any savings, so I shared the funeral costs with Mike. That went on my card too.'

She paused.

'I didn't realise how expensive funerals were.'

'You should've said. I could've had a word with Alan at the directors. He owes me one.'

Jodie didn't reply to that. The idea of haggling over funeral costs felt wrong. Having to think about the endless details after her dad's death had been bad enough.

She took a moment, not quite believing she'd said everything out loud. Nobody knew about her debt – and, of everyone, it was her boss in whom she'd confided.

'I'm on top of it,' she said quietly. 'But I can't afford to take unpaid leave. That's why I came in.'

Ian waved away the concern. 'Nothing's changed at this end. You'll be paid at the end of the month and you'll always have a job here.'

He took a half-step away and started scratching his head. Jodie suspected what might be about to come, so she cut him off before it could happen.

'Dad left me the house. It needs a bit of work but it'll probably be sold at some point and that will more than clear everything.'

Perhaps it wasn't what Ian was going to say – but she didn't want charity, or invented bonuses. They were her problems and she'd deal with them. It was also why she had no intention of caving to her sister-in-law's attempt at emotional blackmail.

'I suppose I'd not thought about what would happen to the house,' Ian replied. 'It'll be so strange driving past and knowing somebody else is inside.' He paused and then added quickly, 'Not that you shouldn't do with it whatever you think. It's yours, after all.'

He started to say something more but went silent as the outside door sounded and Anita blustered her way in, a jacket pulled tight across her.

She started speaking without looking up – 'You'll never guess what the binmen have done' – though she cut herself off when she noticed Jodie. 'I didn't know you were back,' she added.

'I'm not,' Jodie said. She rubbed her eyes self-consciously, wondering if it was obvious she'd been crying. 'I needed to check something with Ian.'

Anita looked between them, silently asking what was going on. When neither of them answered, she took off her jacket and slotted herself in at her desk. 'The funeral went well,' she said. 'Lovely weather for it.'

Jodie nodded along and the tears that had come so easily and unexpectedly felt so distant and stupid now. She wanted to get out of Ian's sight and away from work. She wasn't sure how she'd be able to face him again. At least she hadn't broken down in front of Anita.

'I should get off,' she said. 'There's still lots to do at Dad's house.'

She made a move towards the door and Ian stepped to the side. 'If you need anything, you let me know,' he said. 'I can move a few things around if you need and—'

'You don't need to do that.'

Jodie opened the door and offered a quick 'goodbye' before stepping through it and closing it behind her. The last thing she wanted was Ian mentioning money in front of Anita. The two women didn't have any particular problem with each other – but Anita and gossip went hand in hand. If she found out about Jodie's debts, then everyone at work would know. If that happened, the town was small enough that it wouldn't be long before it was common knowledge.

Jodie moved around the café tables again, heading back to her car. The din was as loud as ever but it was welcome this time. Anything that clouded those dark thoughts of her father's house being an asset. Being something to get her out of trouble, not the place she'd grown up, and where he'd lived his life.

That wasn't the darkest thought, though. What if it was the place where something had happened to Ben?

NINE

Jodie was thinking of Ben's parents as she drove away from the garden centre. They had spent almost two decades wondering about the fate of their son when, all the time, the answers could have been on the other side of a wall.

She didn't want to return to her dad's house – and Owen wasn't due home from school for hours. That left her with an afternoon and not much to do.

Except there had been one thing Ben's parents said to her the day before that might give a clue about Ben and his shirt. One thing that had been niggling.

Jodie drove to the far side of town, past Fry's, and out to the canal. On the weekend, the car parks were full of people pulling on walking boots before trekking up and down the edge of the waterways. It was one of the town's main tourist attractions, with a series of cafés and burger vans dotted along the towpath. Jodie's father had got into walking in later life, when his doctor told him he needed to be more active. Before that, his idea of exercise had been pottering around the garden and a walk to the shop to get a newspaper.

Even with that, Jodie had never seen the appeal of the

canal. To her, it was a bunch of people in fleece dragging their reluctant kids along a path for no real reason. As for those who did it in the howling wind or sideways rain, that's what sectioning laws were for.

There were only two cars parked when Jodie pulled in. She slotted in alongside a muddy Land Rover and got out. It was one of those days where the canal was seemingly in a different dimension to the rest of town. It had been cool but clear on the high street but, on the edge of the towpath, a wind was fizzing across the banks and there was dampness in the air. She had driven for fifteen minutes, yet seemingly passed a couple of international date lines.

Jodie's cheap trainers squelched through the mud on the steps as she made her way up to the towpath itself. The lock gates were closed and the canal water high as she trudged through the gale, past a series of signs and maps, until she reached a small brick cottage with a tall chimney poking from the top. She'd only walked for a couple of hundred metres but her face already stung and her fingers were numb.

Jodie headed down a second set of stairs towards a rickety white gate. The cottage beyond was the sort of place that didn't seem to exist outside of badly made Christmas movies. It was snug and secluded, with no road leading to it and only the canal for company. Jodie wondered what parcel drivers would do when faced with a delivery. Someone from Hermes would hoick stuff over the fence at the best of times, so walking along a canal seemed unlikely.

The latch was broken and Jodie had to lift up the entire gate to let herself onto the property. She half expected a furious dog to come charging but the only sound was the hum of the wind. The garden was a cluttered mess of at least two wheelbarrows without wheels. Just barrows, Jodie guessed. There were breeze blocks and bamboo canes, plus downed branches, even though there was no tree in the yard.

Jodie made her way to the front door and looked for a bell. Alongside her, the single-pane windows rattled in their wooden frames and the door was so flimsy she fancied her chances to kick through it, if that somehow became necessary.

With no sign of a bell, Jodie knocked on the soft wood and then took a small step back. She craned sideways, trying to peer through the glare into the front window but only managing to unbalance herself as the door opened.

A man stood in front of her wearing scruffy cords and a patchy cardigan. He had wild grey hair, wiry like a scouring brush, and eyebrows that were so overgrown they were almost waving to her.

He knew her right away. 'Jodie Parker,' he said as a statement of fact.

The greeting took her by surprise, which wasn't helped by Jodie trying to right herself after the failed attempt to look through the window.

'I didn't think you'd know who I was,' she replied.

The man smiled. 'Do you know, I first interviewed you when you were three years old.' A pause. 'Although I suppose "interview" is an exaggeration. I asked what you thought of your dad being mayor.'

'What did I say?'

'Something about wishing he was a dinosaur.'

Jodie laughed, to her own surprise. It felt like she hadn't done so since her dad died. She'd forgotten about her dinosaur phase as a child. She had a load of soft dinosaurs that she would have fight with plastic dinosaurs. She should probably pitch that to Disney.

Keith had been the local beat journalist when that was a thing. The office in the town centre where he used to be based had long since been knocked down and replaced by some flats. He'd retired about ten years before and there'd been a commemorative issue about it. The newspaper itself didn't even exist in a physical form any longer. Everything about him, from the clothes to the cottage to the job, felt like some sort of throwback. The sort of character that every town has.

'Do you want to come in?'

Keith held the door open wider and Jodie stepped inside. He hadn't asked why she was there – though that seemingly didn't matter.

The cottage was a warren of narrow halls and overflowing bookshelves. Every space that wasn't for walking was taken up by piles of books, yellowing newspapers, or stacked old computer keyboards, monitors and cases.

Keith led the way through and around the maze until they emerged in something that was probably a study. There was a desk and computer up against one wall – and more papers, books and old computers dotted around the cluttered space. It smelled vaguely of cigarettes and there were light brown stains dotting the ceiling.

Keith picked up a stack of hardback books from a chair and turned in a circle, looking for somewhere to put them before deciding on the floor. He then stepped back and settled himself in the chair by the computer, indicating that Jodie could have the newly cleared seat.

'I did wonder if you might come round,' Keith said.

Jodie thought of Ben's parents mentioning him the day before. How they'd told her Keith had kept Ben's case on the local police radar, wondering if they might have tipped him off for some reason.

Seemingly noticing her confusion, Keith continued the thought. 'Sometimes when a relative passes, someone from the family might drop round to ask if I have any cuttings.' He wafted a hand, indicating the rest of the room, perhaps the house, and the acres of newspaper. 'I've usually got something somewhere,' he added. 'I had a better archive than the paper itself – and that was before they closed the office.'

Jodie felt a twinge of connection in that he understood more or less why she was there. She wondered how many others had visited over the years, hoping to find long-lost photos of their loved ones. Out of nothing, there was a lump in her throat.

Keith probably recognised what was happening because he sat and looked past her, towards the chattering window, giving her a moment to settle.

'I've probably reported on your dad more than anyone,' he said after a while. 'Right back to when he ran for council before you were born. Then the various roles after that, throughout his mayorship and everything that came with it. The campaigns, the summer fetes, the fundraisers, the openings. I remember when he stuck the spade in the ground on the first day they started building the community centre. They'd been trying to raise the funds for years. Then he was the one who cut the ribbon to open it – and now it's going to be named after him. Quite the circle.'

Jodie didn't know how to reply to that. The life of the town was the life of her father.

She found herself looking to the side of Keith, next to the computer keyboard, where there was a smaller stack of newspapers. It was much more organised than anything else around the cottage seemed to be. It was a mix of browning, older papers and newer-looking grey ones.

Keith must have noticed her looking. 'There's no paper now, of course, but they asked me to write your dad's obituary for the website. I don't know if you saw it but they said I could write as much as I wanted. I went through a lot of old reports to make sure I had the timeline right.'

Jodie was only half listening. The newspaper on top of the stack had a headline that was etched into her memory. Six words she'd never forget.

GIRL PULLED FROM FIRE BY NEIGHBOUR

That was all it took and Jodie was fourteen again. Her dad was out for the evening, at some sort of function, and she and Mike were alone in the house. Her brother was seventeen and had recently started his carpentry apprenticeship. It was a couple of months after their mum had moved to a flat on the other side of town.

She couldn't remember exactly what was said that night but the sense of betrayal and fury was so close to the surface that Jodie could feel her breath shortening. She was so angry back then – at her mum especially, for not being there – but she was happy to lash out at anyone who looked at her the wrong way.

The precise words were forgotten but Mike had said something about the upcoming divorce not being entirely their mother's fault. That it took two people to break up. It wasn't what Jodie wanted to hear. Not as a fourteen-year-old with newly separated parents. She'd thrown a plate at him, kicked a chair, slammed a door. Fumed and seethed. She remembered him laughing, saying she should calm down – which only made that fury rage harder. She screamed and snarled and he laughed some more. They had always known how to push one another's buttons.

So she ran away. Not far. Jodie had slammed the back door on the way out. Kicked it. Reached down into the gravel and grabbed a handful that she flung against the back window. Then she'd stomped off to the shed at the bottom of the garden. Her dad wasn't the type for tools and mowers – and he hadn't minded that Jodie had taken over the space with some blankets and one of the deckchairs. She'd sit in the cold and gloom, writing in her diary and reading the same paperbacks over and over.

It was her space and she bubbled with rage in it that night. Overhead, the skies had responded with wondrous and manic reciprocity. There was barely any rain but thunder boomed and lightning poured through the cracks in the shed, illuminating the small wooden den. The storm raged and so did Jodie. She'd cried out to the heavens because there was no point in crying out to her mum.

She didn't remember it but, at some point, Jodie had fallen asleep in the deckchair. The next thing she knew, it was hot, so hot, and there were hands on her arm, pulling her. Grabbing. Her face had stung, her hair sizzled, her eyes streamed.

And then she was on the grass as the shed burned and flames surged high into the night. She'd cried out for lightning to strike – and it had, except it wasn't what she wanted, after all.

Her neighbour was there, Ben, to whom she'd barely spoken, despite living metres apart. He was more of a friend for her brother – boys together and all that – but he'd hauled her out of the fire.

He'd saved her.

And, back in Keith's cottage, there was the newspaper that reported it on the front page. She was the 'girl'. Ben was the 'neighbour'. A couple of years on, they'd been boyfriend and girlfriend.

Keith followed Jodie's gaze to the newspaper and then he plucked it from the pile and held it up. 'You can look through it if you want. I pulled all sorts to help with the obituary – although it's barely a fraction of everything I wrote about your dad over the years.'

Jodie's eyes stung with the smoke and the heat that she hadn't felt since she was fourteen. The memory could creep up on her from nowhere. Sometimes, it was the warmth of the sun prickling her arms, other times it was something as simple as a wooden shed. It never left.

She shook her head and Keith returned the paper to the pile. He sat forward and pressed his fingers into a triangle. It took Jodie a moment to realise he was waiting to hear why she was there.

'I've been clearing Dad's house,' she said, although the crack in her voice surprised her. Jodie cleared her throat and continued. 'It's had me thinking and I was wondering if you know anything about Dad that I wouldn't.'

Keith eyebrows fluttered like the greying embers of a dandelion. 'Lots, I would imagine. What sort of thing are you thinking?'

From somewhere deeper in the house, a landline started to ring. Keith didn't move for it and they sat, waiting for the call to ring off. Jodie was grateful for the moment.

'It's just... everyone thinks he's a great guy.'

Keith paused for a moment and seemed surprised. 'Are you saying he's not?'

'No... not that. It's just...' Jodie took a breath, knowing there wasn't a good way of putting it. 'I suppose I wondered if there was anything about him that never came out. Something that might make people think differently about him.'

Keith's wrinkles folded in on one another as he failed to hide his confusion. 'Why are you asking?'

'I'm not sure,' Jodie said. 'It's been a difficult couple of weeks.'

Keith rocked back in his seat and tugged at his hair before crossing his knees. She felt him eyeing her, asking silent questions.

'People usually come looking for happy moments,' he replied after a while. 'Births, christenings, fetes, that sort of thing. Nobody has ever come to me asking for dirt.'

'I wouldn't call it dirt...' Jodie tailed off and then added, 'I guess I want to know who Dad was. All of it. Obviously, there's a lot of good stuff. I suppose I'm at the point where I'm questioning whether it can all be true. People keep coming up to me, saying how much he did for the town.'

'Is that a problem?'

Jodie looked away, focusing on the pile of papers. 'No...'

She didn't know how else to put it, without telling Keith what she'd found – and she certainly didn't want to do that.

The silence between them was broken only by a clock in a far-off part of the house. Jodie hadn't noticed the sound before but, now she had, it was impossible to hear anything other than the rhythmic, numbing *tick-tick-tick*.

'I don't want to speak out of turn,' Keith said. There was a reluctance to his tone and the room felt colder than moments before. 'Are you sure you want to know?'

'I wouldn't have come otherwise.'

They sat across from each other, neither moving – and then, suddenly, Keith was on his feet. He started shuffling through the papers next to his keyboard and then turned to take in the rest of the room.

'There might be something,' he said cryptically, nodding towards the floor-to-ceiling stack of slim, unmarked hardbacks close to the window. 'I have to double-check some things. Triple-check. I've never thrown away a notebook.'

Jodie looked towards the window and what had to be at least five-hundred pads stacked on top of one another.

'I'll call you,' he said, nodding towards an open ringed pad on the other side of his computer keyboard. 'If you write your number down, I'll let you know when I've found the right notebook.'

Jodie did as requested, although it was hard to escape the thought that Keith was talking specifically about notebooks and not newspapers. Whatever he knew wasn't something that had ever been reported.

Keith showed her out of the room, into the corridor which somehow seemed more cluttered than it had before. The pendulum of a tall grandfather clock responsible for the ticking was busy clucking back and forth in a cubby next to another door. It was surrounded by more books and papers, plus another pair of old computer monitors with large domed backs.

Jodie edged her way around the mess, out to the front door. She stopped for him to open it and then he stood over her.

'I'm not comfortable with all this,' he said.

Jodie had no idea how to reply. She wasn't either. 'Thank you in advance,' she said – which was accepted with a gentle nod.

She headed along the path as Keith stood in the door frame and watched her pass through the gate.

As soon as she was on the towpath, Jodie checked her phone, wondering about how long she had until Owen finished school. Except for the immediate couple of days after her dad passed, Jodie didn't get much in the way of texts or calls. She and Fiona would send things back and forth, usually to organise where they were next going to meet. They were of the final generation used to doing things face to face.

She stopped, still in sight of the cottage when she noticed the missed call from Owen's school. Her phone was permanently on silent and she must have failed to notice the vibrations while she was in Keith's place.

Jodie pressed to ring back and waited as the call was answered by a secretary, who asked why she was calling. As soon as Jodie said her name, there was a knowing 'ah' – and then she was back on hold. A short while after, there was a click and then the same woman was talking again.

'We were hoping you could come in to the school tomorrow,' she said.

'Why?'

'It's not for me to say – and I don't actually know – but it's Owen's head of year who would like to see you. He said "as soon as possible", so if you do have some time tomorrow, that would be ideal.'

It took Jodie a moment to realise what had been said. 'Has something happened to Owen?'

'All Mr Timpson said was that Owen's fine – but that he

would like to talk to you.' A pause. 'How does ten o'clock sound?' The woman sounded annoyingly cheery, as if booking Jodie in for a spa day.

'Is he in trouble?' Jodie asked.

'I really don't know more than I've said. Mr Timpson is in the middle of a meeting, otherwise I'm sure he would have spoken to you.'

It was clear Jodie wasn't going to get anywhere over the phone, though an in-person visit sounded ominous. She wondered what might have happened.

'Are you sure Owen's OK?' she asked.

'Absolutely. Mr Timpson made it very clear that you shouldn't worry about that sort of thing.'

Another pause. 'I can do ten,' Jodie said.

The secretary said something about marking it in the diary and then listed the school's current security procedures for getting in. In her day, Jodie remembered various town residents strolling across the field as a shortcut home – but there was none of that in the present world. There were gates and buzzers, keypads and codewords. Jodie figured she'd never remember any of it but said everything was fine and then hung up.

She put the phone back in her bag, figuring Owen was due a grilling that night. He'd surely know why she had to visit his head of year.

It was as she was gathering herself that Jodie noticed Keith standing at his gate, looking up to her. He was barely a few steps away and she jumped at the proximity, wondering how he'd got so near without her hearing.

'Sorry,' he said. 'Didn't mean to scare you.' His eyebrows were swaying in the breeze. 'There's something else you should probably know.'

'About Dad?'

A shake of the head. 'Paul McIntosh was released from prison about two weeks ago and he's been in a halfway house. I was told he's determined to come home...' His words drifted into the wind as he gave a small, reluctant smile. 'Sorry to be the bearer of bad news.'

'Surely he wouldn't come back here...?'

A shrug. 'It was a good source. I suppose he could change his mind but I thought you should know either way. If I'd had a number for you, I'd have already called.' Keith drummed the top of the rotting gate with his fingers and then nodded back towards the house. 'Bit nippy out here.' He took a step away. 'I'll be in contact about the other thing. Only got a landline, so it'll be an oh-one number. I don't like leaving messages and I don't often answer the phone, so if you miss a call, you'll know who it is.' Another step away. 'I really *did* like your dad, you know. One of the good ones.'

Jodie didn't know what to say to that – but Keith wasn't listening anyway. He pulled his cardigan tighter and headed back towards the relative warmth of the cottage. She watched him leave, only realising her mouth was still open when the wind started to sting.

It had seemed unbelievable when Ben's dad had mentioned it – but if anyone knew, then Keith would. And he seemed convinced. The man sent to prison for abducting and killing Ben would be home any day.

TEN

There was still an hour and a half until Owen finished school – and Jodie felt on a roll of getting things done.

Her brother was the next on the list.

For someone who usually walked instead of drove, she was clocking up the miles. Jodie drove back across town, through the centre, and onto the outskirts of the trading estate. Large warehouses lined both sides of the road and there was an ever-present hum of machinery and lorries as Jodie turned into the car park of a small office block. The lot was empty, except for a scuffed green van that was parked across two spaces. Planks of wood were stacked against the fence at the back and a loud grinding seeped out from the office as Jodie got out of her car and crossed towards the van.

A lad with a wispy moustache was balancing a spirit level on a long piece of wood as Jodie approached. His overalls were a couple of sizes too big and he looked up, then frowned before pushing himself to his feet in an attempt to look taller.

'You after Mike?' he asked, poking a thumb towards the offices that were being worked on.

'Is he here?'

Wispy 'Tache was barely out of school. He was thin with youth and, as the power tools raged inside, Jodie almost laughed at the fact he was out in the car park with a spirit level. Mike had once been a carpentry apprentice and now, years later, here he was with his own business and his own apprentice.

'I can get him if you want...?'

Jodie said that would be good – and Wispy 'Tache edged towards the building before poking his head around the door. He shouted 'Mike', seemingly without reply because the howling whirl of a power saw continued as Mike's name was bellowed another ten or eleven times.

It took a while but the noise eventually silenced and then Mike emerged from the offices, his overalls coated with sawdust. He removed a set of goggles and said something to Wipsy 'Tache, who entered the now quiet building. Mike dusted his front and then crossed to Jodie.

'You look busy,' she said.

'Snowed under. *Sawdusted* under. There's five offices in there and we're fitting the lot. When that's done, I've got another ten on the other side of the estate.' He flapped a hand around his ears, scuffing away another dusting as he cracked a grin. 'Wanna help? There's plenty of sawing to be done.'

'I'm here about Sam.'

Mike's face fell. 'Oh. What has she done now?'

'Did you know she came over last night?'

A shake of the head. 'I told her not to! The day of Dad's funeral too. You know what she's like. I thought she'd gone to Tesco.'

If he actually *did* know his wife had gone to Jodie's, then he must have been on an acting course – because he was doing a great job of pretending he didn't.

'What did she want?' he added.

'I have a feeling you know.'

Mike rolled his eyes. 'I told her to let it go about Dad's house.'

'She's not letting it go.'

Those had almost been Samantha's exact words.

The siblings looked to each other with something close to a knowing acceptance. Mike was still shaking his head. 'She says we should have half.'

'You're married, aren't you? Don't you talk to each other?'

'Of course! I told her that if Dad wanted you to have the house, then it was up to him.'

'So what's the problem?'

There was a bang from the office behind and Mike frowned over his shoulder. He muttered something Jodie didn't catch and then spoke properly. 'When you were married to Darren, were you happy for him to speak for you, or did you have your own thoughts and ideas? I've told her what I think but she wants her own way. I tried talking her out of it but she won't listen.'

'She said she was getting a lawyer to stop the house being sold.'

Mike puffed out a long breath that sent a spiral of sawdust seeping from somewhere on his face. 'Are you going to sell it?'

'I've not decided. Probably. What about this lawyer?'

A shrug. 'I don't know. She said something but I didn't think she was serious. I'll talk to her later.'

There was a second bang from behind and Mike said he had to deal with it. He seemed grateful for the distraction as he strode into the office and closed the door.

Jodie waited next to his work van, knowing he had a point. She didn't want Darren speaking for her – and Samantha seemingly didn't want Mike acting on her behalf. It might be a lie but it felt as if trying to get half of the house might be Sam's obsession, not Mike's.

The relationship between Jodie and Samantha was complicated, not only because they were now related. The town had one secondary school, where all children over the age of eleven went. It meant everyone sort of knew everyone else – and, in some cases, it went further than that. Ben had been Jodie's first proper boyfriend – but she wasn't *his* first girlfriend. He'd gone out with Samantha and then, at some point around the time he pulled Jodie from that shed, they'd broken up. Jodie and Ben became an item and, years later, Samantha married Jodie's brother. It was an incestuous mess – and even though it was all teenage drama, there had always been something unspoken between Jodie and her sister-in-law. They had too much overlapping history to ever be friends.

A bang of the door brought Jodie back into the car park, as her brother strolled out of the office. 'I can't be long,' he said. 'I just wish you two would get along.'

'Tell your wife.'

It felt theatrical but Mike burst into a yawn, which he batted away with another flurry of sawdust.

'Do you want anything from Dad's house?' Jodie asked.

'Like what?'

'I don't know. I started clearing it and there's so much stuff. Dad had some old football shirts and I wondered if you wanted them?'

Mike shook his head. 'You know me, I'm not that fussed.' He took a half-step away and then bobbed on the balls of his feet. 'Actually, Dad has these old war medals. They were our granddad's and I used to polish them when I was a kid. If they're knocking around, I wouldn't mind them.'

'Do you know where they are?'

A shake of the head. 'Probably a drawer somewhere. I don't know. If you find them, put them to one side.'

He sounded emphatic, suddenly enthusiastic. Jodie couldn't help but wonder if he knew the medals were valuable and planned to sell them. She almost asked, except didn't fancy things descending into an argument. That's also why she didn't bring up how much he'd drunk the day before.

'Is something wrong?'

Mike's question took Jodie by surprise. They weren't the sort of brother and sister to check in on one another. They worked on nods and vague waves if they saw one another during the week. They'd plan to meet up at Christmas and maybe a summer barbecue – but that was about it. She only knew where he was working because he'd mentioned it at some point when they'd been talking after their father's death.

Jodie shook her head. 'No... I've just been thinking about Ben a bit. I saw his mum and dad yesterday and they mentioned it.'

Mike's nose wrinkled, his eyes narrowed. 'It was twenty years ago.'

'They were saying how Dad was really helpful after Ben went missing. I guess he's been in my head...'

She looked up and realised Mike had been watching her the whole time. It felt as if he might have something to say, except he changed his mind. He licked his lips and then nodded back over his shoulder. 'I really do have to get back,' he said. 'Let me know if you find those medals.'

ELEVEN

The usual thumping of virtual machine guns echoed down the stairs as Jodie entered her house. A part of her wondered how this was the norm. She wasn't the hysterical sort who fretted over violence in video games and yet she was never quite comfortable with walking into what sounded like a war zone when she got home.

Owen must have had half an ear listening for her because the volume decreased to something more acceptable as soon as she closed the front door. Instead of making the whole house rumble, there was now more of a gentle drumming.

Jodie waited at the bottom of the stairs, resting on the handrail, readying herself for what was ahead. It was hard these days to have a serious conversation with Owen without him seemingly believing she was out to get him. Asking him to put his clothes away after she'd washed them was her 'always having a go'. Asking him to move his shoes from the doormat, so she didn't trip over them when entering the house, got a huff of annoyance and mumblings too quiet for her to hear. Gentle enquiries about what he'd been up to at school, or where he was going, or who he was with, would be met by extravagant sighs and mini tantrums about how she was 'always checking up' on him.

It hadn't always been like that. He'd been something of a mummy's boy as a child. He'd want to go to the supermarket with her, or try to help out when she was cooking. He would pick up rounded stones from the ground and offer them to her as treasures.

And then... everything had changed.

Jodie hadn't been much different when she was a teenager. That's why she'd argued with her brother, why she'd stormed off to the shed, why Ben had ended up pulling her to safety. Her son had seemingly inherited the same persecution complex.

Jodie took a breath, then another, and went upstairs. She knocked on Owen's door, loud enough that it could be heard over the ongoing combat zone. There was no reply at first – but, as she knocked a second time, she got an annoyed-sounding 'What?'

It was no surprise to find Owen sitting on his bed, game controller in hand. He glanced momentarily towards her, scowling and not bothering to hide his irritation.

'How was school?' Jodie asked.

A shrug. 'Fine.'

'I need you to turn your game off.'

She waited as he ignored her, stare fixed on the screen, until she stepped sideways towards it, blocking his view.

'Owen...'

'Fine! God!'

He bashed the controller down onto the bed and then looked up with unconcealed annoyance.

'I got a call from the school today,' Jodie said. 'I have to see your head of year tomorrow.'

Jodie was expecting a reaction of sorts: perhaps surprise, or some sort of horror. Instead, there was the merest of shrugs.

'What's going on?' she asked.

'Dunno. Nothing.'

'It can't be nothing if the school called and asked me to go in.'

Owen glanced towards the screen, on which a man in all-black gear was paused mid-action: crouched, a machine gun in his hands.

'Owen.'

'What?'

'What's going on?'

'I told you – I don't know. Nothing.'

Jodie stared at her son, who was refusing to acknowledge her. There was clearly something, although she'd have had more response from the wall than she was getting from her son. This part of parenting felt like the hardest part. Owen had technically not done anything wrong that she knew of. If she got angry now, it would give her nowhere to go if she found out from his head of year that he actually *had* done something wrong. Besides, there was a chance she had to go into the school because Owen had done something good. He might be up for an award, or something. She knew her son well enough to know it was a *slim* chance...

'What's happening at Granddad's house?'

Owen's question took Jodie by surprise. He'd shown no interest in it since her father had died. She had told him that she'd been left it in the will but that had received the same sort of shrug as many of the other things she spoke to him about.

'How do you mean?' Jodie asked.

'Jordan reckons his mum is going to sue you.'

Jodie resisted the urge to roll her eyes. Of course Samantha had told her son about her plans. Jordan had then gleefully passed everything onto his cousin at school.

'You don't need to worry about that,' she replied.

'Why is she suing you?'

'She's not.'

'Jordan reckons it's because Granddad left the house to you.'

'Maybe you shouldn't believe everything Jordan says.'

Owen turned away from the screen and focused on his mum. Jodie was away from the TV now, perched on the edge of a table.

'Did Granddad leave anything for me?'

Owen's tone was softer now. The annoyance and borderline anger were gone.

'No. He probably would have done if he'd known what was going to happen. His will was written when you'd barely started school. That said, everything in the house is mine. I got rid of some of his clothes today but, if there's anything you want, just say. His TV's a bit bigger than yours, if you want that?'

Owen glanced between her and his own TV, mulling it over. 'What else is there?'

Jodie pictured Ben's shirt.

'You know your granddad. There's a lot of... tat. He didn't like to throw things out. I've got a lot of drawers and cupboards to go through. You can help if you want—'

Owen pulled a face at that.

'—Or I can put some things aside if you know what you might like. I asked your Uncle Mike earlier and he said something about some old war medals.'

'Medals...?'

'I thought he'd want Dad's football shirts but he says there are some medals somewhere that he wants. He says he used to polish them when we were kids. They belonged to your great-granddad and got passed down.'

Owen's fingers were twitching close to his game controller again, his interest clearly diminishing. 'I didn't know Granddad had things like that.'

'Neither did I. Anyway, if there's anything I think you'd

like, I'll put it to one side. Your uncle didn't want the football shirts, so you could have them? Or I can text you pictures of things and you can let me know what you think...?'

Owen nodded at this, which was as good an endorsement as she was ever going to get.

Jodie pushed herself away from the table, figuring that, as they were apparently on good terms, she'd try again. 'I'm not going to get any surprises with your head of year tomorrow, am I?'

Owen picked up the game controller. 'I told you, I don't know.'

She waited a moment, wondering if there might be more. When he unpaused his game, it was clear the moment had passed.

Jodie paused in his doorway for a few seconds, watching as the action raged on the screen. It wasn't that long ago that Owen would sit downstairs with her, playing Lego on the floor. Her dad had once told her that children grew up too quickly and she wished he'd been wrong.

She also wished she could stop linking everything back to her dad...

Jodie eventually closed the door and headed downstairs, to where a text from Fiona was waiting on her phone.

You OK?

They hadn't spoken since they'd been outside Jodie's dad's house the day before. Since Jodie had found Ben's shirt. If she was going to tell anyone about it, it would be Fiona... except she couldn't.

Jodie replied to say that Sam was arguing over the will – and threatening to get lawyers involved to stop her selling it. The response was instant.

REALLY?!!!!!!! Shall I come over?

Jodie almost replied to say that she could. A part of her fancied an opportunity to bitch about Samantha to someone who'd join in. She and Fiona hadn't had the chance to kick back, drink some wine, and gossip about someone else's Facebook drama in a few weeks. Family deaths tended to put paid to that sort of thing, considering Jodie herself was the drama.

Instead, she said she was going to get an early night. Finding Ben's shirt, then arguing with Sam meant Jodie had barely slept the night before. Rest had been patchy ever since she'd got that call about her dad.

The incoming message dots flashed as Fiona typed out a message at the other end, although it went on for so long that Jodie started to wonder whether her friend was ever going to finish it and send.

When it arrived, Jodie could have predicted the content. Robbie was being Robbie, apparently. The night before, Fiona's husband had got drunk – again – and had been thrown out of The Anchor – again. He'd spent the day sleeping off a hangover – again. Jodie said Fiona should come over if she wanted a break but Fiona messaged back quickly to say that she was trying to get an early night as well.

Jodie read the messages back and tried to think of how to reply. Ultimately, she sent a string of 'Zzzzzzz's – and then settled back on the sofa with some mindless game show on the TV to keep her company.

Her mind instantly wandered to Ben and that shirt, as she knew it would. Plus, the meeting with Owen's head of year and then her ex-husband. There was too much going on, too much to worry about – and before she even tried to close her eyes, she knew those hopes of a decent sleep were nothing more than misguided optimism.

TWELVE

Jodie took a couple of sleeping tablets that she'd been holding on to ever since her divorce from Darren. Her doctor had prescribed them and she'd only used a few, figuring there would be future nights when she'd need them more.

The future had become the present as Jodie slept dreamlessly until her alarm blared through the fuzz a few minutes before seven. It was only as she was dressing that she wondered if it had been dreamless, after all. She had vague memories of clunking sounds through the night – except there was nothing untoward around the house and, when she mentioned it to Owen, he shrugged and said he hadn't heard anything. As he ate his toast, she asked again if there was anything he wanted to tell her about what was going on at school. She got a mumbled 'no' in reply, which gave her the sense they'd be having a far more serious conversation in the near future.

Owen was about to leave the kitchen when he stopped in the doorway. 'He's got it in for me,' Owen said.

'Who?'

'Timpson. He's always hated me.'

'You've never brought it up before.'

'He's never called you in before.'

Jodie was sitting at the table, watching her son and wanting to believe him. It was hard to see this as anything other than a diversionary tactic to head off whatever it was Owen's head of year wanted.

'We'll talk later,' she said. 'Come straight home from school.'

'I've got—'

'Not tonight. I want you home.' A pause. 'I can give you a lift to school if you want. I've got to drive there anyway.'

Owen laughed, actually snorted, and then turned his back. He dragged up his schoolbag from the floor and hooked it over his shoulder. He muttered something that sounded like 'see ya' and then headed into the hall. The front door clunked open and banged shut – and then he was gone.

It was hard for Jodie not to question herself as she looked around the kitchen. Owen's crumb-riddled plate was on the table, there was a half-finished can of Coke on the counter next to the margarine, a buttery knife in the sink, the drawer from which it had come was half-open – and the toaster was on its side for some reason.

Owen had eaten two slices of toast and left a tornado's trail in his wake. He did it because he knew she would clean up after him – which she did. Again. Margarine and Coke can back in the fridge, plate and knife rinsed and left to dry, toaster shaken upside-down over the bin and then returned to the counter. She should say something... but if she did, there would be slammed doors and the silent treatment. She could face that if there was someone else to take away at least some of the load. Sometimes, she simply wanted to be around someone who'd tolerate her.

Jodie was stewing on that as she drove to the school. It felt as if she herself was in trouble. Owen went to the same one she had – although it had been updated since then. Half the school field had been sold off for houses and that money had been used to replace the cabins with a proper new wing. Jodie knew that because her dad had done some fundraising – and been part of the committee that posed with scissors and ribbon when it was opened.

There was always a ribbon.

There was also no escaping her father's legacy.

Jodie parked on the street and entered through the main school gates. There was a buzzer and someone read her a code through the intercom that she had to input to get inside. After that, it was up some stairs and through a large set of double doors before she was caught behind a plexiglass wall. A woman behind reception had to press a big red button to unlock a door – and then she was in.

Security had changed – but the long, gloomy corridor next to the office hadn't. There were doors on both sides, with plaques for various assistant heads and heads of years. The main headmaster had an office at the far end – but the receptionist stopped outside a door halfway along and said Jodie could wait on the seat outside.

As Jodie sat outside the head of year's door, it was hard not to picture herself all those years before. Until everything happened with Ben, she was one of those students who had been anonymous. Rarely in trouble and, even when she was, never for anything serious. Not the best grades but not the worse. Amazing at nothing but competent at most things. She existed her way through school. Then he had gone missing and, suddenly, everybody wanted to know her. Even the teachers looked at her differently.

She was brought back to the present as the door clicked open.

'Ms Alexander?'

Jodie stood and turned to face Owen's head of year. He was in black trousers and a white shirt, like the guy at the funeral parlour who'd boggled Jodie's mind with the cost of a casket.

Plain and normal: the sort of face she'd forget as soon as she left the room.

'It's Miss Parker,' she corrected.

Jodie had changed her name back after the divorce with Darren and it was only in that moment that she realised it was because her dad's name meant something in the town. Everyone knew the Parkers. Nobody knew the Alexanders, although it meant Owen had a different last name to her. She had asked if he'd wanted to change it, but he'd shrugged with indifference and she hadn't asked again.

Mr Timpson looked down to an iPad in his hand with momentary confusion. He glanced along the empty corridor and then pushed his door wider for her to enter.

'Sorry about that,' he said. 'I didn't realise your last name was, er... different.'

He made it sound as if Jodie had done something wrong and she instantly resented him for it. Perhaps Owen had a point when he said his head of year had it in for him?

Mr Timpson's office had a series of certificates around the walls, plus a chunky computer monitor on his desk. As offices went, he'd been given one of the boring ones, considering the view outside his window. It was the inside of some sort of quadrant and Jodie could see some stones and a wilting tree. Like a park that had been left to rot.

Jodie sat in the spare seat and Mr Timpson relaxed into his oversized office chair before typing something into the computer and then looking up.

'I may as well get to the point,' he said. 'I've asked you to come in because we're having some issues with Owen and bullying.'

He was sitting earnestly in his seat, pressed back with the tips of his fingers touching.

'Owen's being bullied...?'

'No...'

It took Jodie a moment to realise what was being said. She waited for some sort of punchline or reveal. Instead, Mr Timpson continued to watch her, looking for a reaction.

'Owen's the bully...?'

'I'm afraid so.'

Jodie was suddenly aware that her mouth was hanging open. She started a sentence. Stopped. Started another. Didn't know what to say.

When she went silent, Mr Timpson continued. 'We're not sure of the exact whos, whats, wheres and whys – but it appears Owen is part of a group of boys who have been picking on younger or smaller children.'

Jodie continued to stare and couldn't find the words. She'd assumed she'd been called in because Owen was behind in his classes or bunking off. She could have been given a hundred guesses and never figured he was a bully.

She started scratching her head, digging in her fingernail, waiting until a flake of skin crusted away.

'I'm having this same conversation with the parents of each of the older boys named,' he continued. 'I should stress, this isn't based on a single report and it's not a she said/he said scenario. We've had credible reports from numerous students about what's been going on.'

Jodie listened and couldn't think of anything to say. Multiple students were saying Owen was a bully.

Mr Timpson waited this time.

'I don't know what to say,' Jodie stumbled. 'Is he beating people up...?'

'We're not talking about physical evidence at this stage,' Mr Timpson replied. 'But enough people have come forward with similar stories that we have to take things seriously. We understand it's mainly threats at this stage – and we obviously don't want things to get any worse than that. The school has a very specific bullying policy about addressing issues when first reported.'

Jodie still wasn't clear about what had been going on. Owen had always been one of the bigger kids, to the point that there'd been a time at primary school when one of the mothers said he shouldn't be allowed to compete at sports day because his longer legs meant he was 'cheating'. He'd seemingly skipped from six years old to ten when it came to growing. She wasn't sure how that had progressed to him using his size to pick on the smaller kids.

'Who else is in this group?' Jodie asked.

'We're not revealing names to individual parents. We've got privacy rules and it means—'

'Is Owen the leader?'

'I don't know the answer to that. I don't know if there *is* a leader. In the end, I'm not sure it matters to the children being bullied. They just want it to stop – and so do we.'

Jodie sank into the seat. It felt as if her parenting was on trial, as if she was. If her son was a bully, then what did it say about her?

She'd always given Owen a long leash – and, probably because of his size, he'd always had a confidence around adults that she'd never had as a child. She never thought it could have led to something like this.

'Can you say anything about what he's been up to?' Jodie asked.

He hesitated for a second, perhaps mulling the question. 'A student's bag was thrown in the canal. Although we know the boys involved, we don't know who did it specifically. Our policy is that we get parents involved at the earliest possible stage, hoping things don't go any further.' A pause. 'I'd like to think this will be the end of it.'

Jodie allowed her head to loll back in the chair. There was a brown spot on the ceiling, as if someone had thrown a cup of tea.

'A bag...? The canal...?' She stumbled, not knowing how to continue. 'His granddad's just died,' she said, hating herself the moment the words came out. 'Sorry, I know that's an excuse. I'll talk to him, obviously. Find out what's been happening. Get him to stop. It's been a difficult few weeks.'

It was Jodie's turn to pause. She waited for a response that didn't came. Using her dad's death to explain Owen's apparent bullying was cheap – and she knew it.

'I'll support whatever you decide to do,' she said eventually.

'Hopefully, it won't involve any more than this.'

Mr Timpson stood and offered his hand, which Jodie found herself shaking. His fingers dwarfed hers, like octopus tentacles around a breadstick.

'Thanks for your cooperation,' he added.

Jodie nodded, still shocked by it all. The clock on his wall said she'd been in the office for less than five minutes but if it wasn't for that, she'd have guessed an hour. She was exhausted.

Jodie was at the door when a thought of worth finally popped into her head.

'Is Jordan Parker one of the other boys?' she asked.

'I can't—'

'He's Owen's cousin. They spend a lot of time together...'

'I really can't give you any other names.'

She waited for a moment, wondering if he'd say anything else.

He only spoke when she turned back towards the door. He stood and rounded his desk, then skipped ahead to open it for her. 'I'll come back to you if there are any further reports,' he said. 'I can't stress enough that we would much rather this was the end of things.'

Jodie muttered a 'thanks' and then Mr Timpson led her back along the corridor towards reception.

As she was leaving through the plexiglass door, another woman was on her way in. Jodie didn't recognise her, though she wondered if another parent was about to discover their child was a bully.

It felt unbelievable, as if Mr Timpson had been talking about someone else's child. Except, perhaps the signs had been there and she had been so invested in her own problems – her debt, her job, her dad – that she'd failed to see them. How could she have seen them when she let Owen spend all those hours in his bedroom, shouting at his friends via his headset?

Jodie made her way down the steps from the school as the braying howls of hundreds of children on their break raged behind her. She wondered what Owen was up to at that moment. Was he chucking some poor lad's bag around? When she'd been at school, she had been the sort that might look the other way if someone was being given a hard time. If it meant she escaped a bully's attention, that was preferable to anything else. It felt cowardly now she was older – but that was easy to think as a grown-up. She'd cried in her room when her friends had given her the silent treatment – and yet happily joined in as they did the same to others when it was their turn. It felt like part of being a teenager at the time. Now, she wasn't so sure.

She was back at the car, unsure who she was annoyed at most – herself or Owen – when she realised there was a missed text on her phone, from Ben's mother, Elaine.

Jim saw a window open at the back of your dad's house. Just checking if you want us to do anything. X

Jodie had to read the message twice before she realised what it was saying. It wasn't that a window was open at her father's house, it was that she knew for a fact she'd locked them all.

THIRTEEN

Elaine must have been watching from the front window because, as soon as Jodie pulled up, she was out the house and along the path to run interception. The car door was barely open before Elaine arrived at its side. She could seemingly move quickly when she wanted.

'Hope you don't mind me texting,' she said. 'Jim saw the window and said he was surprised you'd left it open. I said I didn't think you were the sort who'd leave a downstairs window open and he said that you'd had a lot on. I said I should probably let you know, just in case, and he said not to waste your time. Anyway, here you are.' A breathless pause. 'I hope everything's all right.'

Jodie was out the car, leaning on the door and trying to appear as if she wasn't picturing Ben's shirt. Wondering if someone had come for it, not knowing she'd already found it.

'Thanks for letting me know,' Jodie replied. 'I thought I closed it but I might have missed the latch. I'll check it now.'

She stepped around Elaine, who followed her to the end of the path, perhaps wondering if she should wait and make sure everything was all right.

Jodie stopped when they were a couple of paces apart. 'I need to tell you something,' she added.

The earnest tone stopped Elaine on the spot.

'You were right about Paul McIntosh. I've been told he's been released,' Jodie said.

Elaine was frozen, mouth half-open, one hand raised as if she was about to point to something. The only clue that time hadn't stopped was that her sleeve was flapping gently in the breeze.

'Who told you that?' she asked eventually.

'Keith, the journalist. I visited yesterday and he said a good source had told him that Paul's in a halfway house. He doesn't know where.' A pause. 'I thought you should know for sure.'

Elaine had turned white in the few seconds Jodie had been talking. If it was someone on a Facebook group, or someone gossiping at the market, rumours of the release could be swatted aside. If Keith had spoken, it was true. Her eyes darted sideways towards her house and then back to Jodie. 'He wouldn't come back here, would he? I know his house is still there...'

Paul McIntosh used to live in a farmhouse a little past the garden centre. Jodie vaguely remembered when the field at the side was full of chickens. There used to be a sign at the front advertising fresh eggs – but it hadn't been like that in a long while. Paul's wife had continued to live there after he'd been convicted, though rarely seemed to leave the house. As Ben's dad had pointed out, the 'for sale' sign had gone up outside around six months before, following her death.

Jodie hadn't spent a lot of time thinking of her over the years. There was an assumption – almost certainly unfair – that Paul's wife must have known what her husband was up to.

It wasn't only Ben. Paul McIntosh had a conviction for trying to abduct a girl when he'd been a teenager himself. Before he moved to the area, he'd tried to bundle some girl into the passenger seat of his car – but she'd managed to bite his hand and get away.

Nobody knew about that until it came out after he'd been arrested in connection with Ben's disappearance.

As well as that previous conviction, a couple of Ben's hairs were found in McIntosh's van that were never explained.

Looking back, it felt as if everybody assumed he was guilty as soon as the previous conviction was revealed. The police dug up his field, looking for Ben's body – which they never found.

Jodie certainly thought he was guilty, as that confused, frightened teenager. Frightened was the critical word. She'd avoid the cut-through, Bramble Alley, where she last saw Ben, even if it meant walking minutes out of her way. As for the McIntosh house, it was years after he'd been convicted that she allowed herself to walk past. With those chest-high overgrown plants and rickety gate, it seemed a lot less intimidating than she had convinced herself.

All that time avoiding the house – and Ben's shirt might well have been in her dad's possession. He might have known what had happened all along.

Jodie was back on the pavement with Elaine, who had aged in front of her.

'Keith said he thought McIntosh might come back here,' Jodie said.

Elaine breathed out with as her eyes widened. 'Surely not?' she said. 'Just imagine if he came back. Just *imagine*.'

The two women waited for a moment – but it didn't feel as if there was anything else to say. After a moment, Elaine offered a goodbye before they each headed along the paths into the respective houses. Jodie used the new key to let herself into her dad's – and instantly felt something wrong. Her dad's house was always warm, even in winter – but not in that moment. The hairs on her arm raised as she moved along the hall, into the kitchen, where the window wasn't simply open.

It had been *forced* open.

FOURTEEN

Cool air breezed into the house as Jodie edged forward to crane across the sink and get a better look. Her dad's marker pen was in the sink, instead of on the windowsill – and the window itself had somehow been levered open. It was hanging loosely on its hinges. Jodie pulled the window inwards but something was broken and it wafted open again.

She turned and hurried back into the hall, then crouched and opened the cupboard under the stairs. Someone knew about the shirt and had broken in, wanting to cover up whatever had happened. She never should have left it at the house.

Except...

The crates were still stacked as she left them and, inside, folded and untouched since she'd last been in the house, was Ben's green top.

Jodie felt a rushing that she first thought was because of the open window – but then realised was because her heart had thundered into overdrive.

She held Ben's shirt in her hands, gently rubbing the print, wondering who could have broken in. That's when she realised that, if someone had come in looking for the shirt, they wouldn't have been looking under the stairs.

Jodie returned the shirt to the crate and then pulled the ladder out and bumped her way upstairs. The ladder banged on the steps and the banisters until she emerged breathlessly at the top and placed it underneath the attic. She climbed and then pushed open the hatch, fiddling with the socket until light sprang from the bulb above.

If someone had looked in the loft the night before, they had returned everything to the places she'd left them. The box with 'keep' written on the side was a short stretch from the hatch, sitting on top of another unmarked box. She checked inside but it didn't seem as if anyone had disturbed it.

Jodie unplugged the light and lowered herself out of the attic before levering the hatch back into place. She descended the ladder and then went through the house, checking each room for a sign something had been taken. She almost hoped something *had* gone because it would give a reason for the forced window. The TV was still in place and so was her dad's stereo, which, admittedly, seemed a little outdated in the days of streaming.

Back in the kitchen, Jodie noticed the dishes on the draining board were still in place. If someone had come through the window, they'd done so carefully. It was possible – but it didn't seem like the sort of thing an opportunist burglar might do.

Jodie did another sweep of the house, moving slower second time around. The upstairs and downstairs televisions were untouched – and so were the pair of digital radios her dad owned. His photos remained on the wall and the kitchen appliances were in place.

If someone had broken in that carefully, then what were they looking for?

Her father had little of real value. He wasn't the sort of person to crave expensive things. He spent his money on meals and days out. He'd slip Owen money for his birthday and Christmas. He'd drop notes in the charity buckets, rather than coins. There wasn't much that could be stolen.

Jodie returned to the cupboard under the stairs and took Ben's shirt from the crate, placing it at the bottom of her bag as if it was padding. She wasn't going to take the chance of losing it. After that, she called the same locksmith from before and asked if he did windows. He laughed when she explained who she was, joking that he didn't do two-for-one offers, then said he'd be over as soon as he could.

With everything that had happened, Jodie had almost forgotten that she was supposed to be meeting her ex-husband, Darren. It was only a day on, but she could barely keep up. She texted him, saying she might be a little late, but that she still wanted to meet. Darren replied with a simple, and characteristic, 'OK'.

As she had to wait for the locksmith, Jodie spent the best part of an hour aimlessly sifting through her dad's things. Some of the obvious tat – a collection of old bottle tops, forty or fifty coasters and decades of old phone books – went in the bin. Other odd and ends were put to the side for either the charity shop, or to ask Mike if he wanted any of it.

She looked for the war medals her brother had mentioned. Her dad tended to keep things like that in the drawers of the bureau in the living room. That's where Jodie had found her dad's birth certificate, passport and paper driving licence when she'd needed them. Now, she also found a couple of old medals on red, white and blue ribbon. The metal was light and cheap, perhaps tin, and she didn't think they were what Mike had been talking about.

There was a gleaming fountain pen in a holder that she put to the side, figuring Owen might appreciate it, though knowing he wouldn't. Pens didn't seem like a twenty-first century gift, let alone for a teenager – especially one that needed ink to be added.

She was distracted by a bang on the door and, when Jodie opened it, the déjà vu made her shiver. The locksmith was standing in the same place he had been the last time he'd visited – though this time, he had an eyebrow raised and a half-grin.

'You should put me on retainer,' he said.

Jodie laughed, letting him have the moment. It was good to do something other than worry. She led him along the hall, into the kitchen, where the window remained on its hinges.

The locksmith let out a low whistle. 'Someone's done a number on that,' he said.

'Is it the sort of thing you can fix?'

He leaned in, peering at the hinges and then rocking the window back and forth. 'I'll check the van to make sure I have the parts.' He paused and then added, 'Looks like someone broke in.'

'That's what I thought – though I wasn't sure how.'

The man reached towards the window but then withdrew his fingers without touching it. 'These windows have a double lock. They're either fully closed – or you can leave them open a crack and half lock them. It must have been on the half lock. I guess someone worked something into the crack between the frame and window and yanked it open.' He puffed out a small breath. 'Gotta be strong to do that.'

Jodie looked between him and the window, trying to remember whether the windows had been on the half lock setting. They probably had. Her dad used to go on about air circulation a lot and it seemed like the sort of thing he'd do, while also being something she'd never notice.

The locksmith was eyeing her curiously. 'You should probably call the police before I do anything more. They can look for fingerprints, that sort of thing.'

'I've checked the whole house and nothing's been stolen.' Jodie nodded towards the living room. 'The TV's still there.'

That got a frown. 'Why would you break into a house and then let yourself out again?'

Jodie shook her head. 'That's what I've been wondering.'

They looked to each other for a moment and there seemed to be genuine concern in the locksmith's face. He eventually nodded towards the window. 'Are you sure you want me to have a go at this without the police getting a look? If there are fingerprints, they'll be gone.'

'I don't know what I'd tell the police. Besides, my neighbour had their car broken into the other Christmas and they only gave her a reference number.'

That got a shrug. 'Fair enough. Probably kids anyway.'

The man turned and lead-footed his way back through the house. Jodie moved out of his way, waiting in the living room as he clunked around his van, looking for the right part. She wasn't sure about it being 'just kids' – but he had made one good point.

Why *would* someone break into a house and then let themselves back out again?

FIFTEEN

In the end, Jodie was only fifteen minutes late arriving at Fry's. Darren was already in a booth close to the kitchen, tucking into a late breakfast. As well as a giant plate overflowing with beans, chips, toast, tomatoes, fried eggs, sausages, black pudding and bacon, he had a can of Coke and a huge mug of tea in front of him.

Jodie slotted in across from him as Darren looked up. 'I thought Chandra was the one eating for two,' she said.

Her ex-husband laughed, which rarely happened when the two of them were together. 'Get yourself one,' he said. 'Six quid the lot. I don't know how they make money, not that I'm complaining.'

A huge menu was on a board over the top of the counter. The prices seemed to match the décor, in being twenty years out of place. The booths were furnished with cracked leather that had foam spilling out – but a chip butty was eighty pence, so it evened itself out.

Jodie batted away the offer of food, though she got a fifty-pence tea from the counter and retook her seat.

'Before anything else, we need to talk about Owen,' she said.

Darren gulped, although it might have been the chunk of sausage he was trying to force down.

'What's he done now?'

Jodie titled her head, showing disapproval, even though Darren wasn't wrong. The assumption that he'd done something didn't help anyone.

'I got called into his school this morning,' she said. 'I had to see his head of year. They had me waiting in the corridor, as if I was the one in trouble.'

That got a hint of a smirk, though it didn't stop Darren diving in for a piece of black pudding that had previously been hidden. He dunked it in a mound of ketchup and then plonked it in his mouth.

'They say he's been bullying,' Jodie continued. 'Someone's bag got thrown in the canal.'

Darren momentarily stopped chewing before resuming and swallowing. He didn't seem surprised, which sent something boiling in Jodie's stomach. He should be shocked that his son – *their* son – was bullying other kids.

She gripped the underside of the table, trying to calm herself. 'The school said they call in parents to try to stop things before it gets too far,' Jodie added. 'I was wondering if you might talk to Owen? I will, obviously, but it'll be better coming from both of us.'

Darren was still chewing. Whatever it was seemed to be taking an age to go down, until she was sure he was doing it to annoy her.

'If it's just me, it'll seem like I'm always on at him,' Jodie continued. 'If it's both, we're more likely to get a reaction.'

Darren finally swallowed – and then reached for his tea. He swigged and swirled a mouthful, drawing things out. Surely doing it on purpose?

When he finally spoke, he did so through half a burp.

'I don't know why you think he'll listen to me.'

'Because you're his dad...?'

The dismissive shrug almost had Jodie picking up her ex-husband's plate and throwing it at him. Years before, she would have done. When they were younger, they'd have raged and screamed until burning themselves out.

'D'you want me to come over tonight?' Darren asked.

It was more than Jodie thought she'd get. He was dipping his toast into a runny yolk.

'I thought I'd talk to him tonight and then you could come over tomorrow?' Jodie replied. 'You know what he's like if we both try together.'

A nod. 'Fine.'

Jodie waited, watching Darren eat in a circle around his plate. Forkful of beans, then three chips squished into one another. Black pudding after that, then bacon, tomatoes, sausage. One at a time, around the plate until he was back with the beans. He gave the food far more attention than he ever gave their son.

'You sure you're not going to eat?' he asked.

Jodie reached for her tea and clung onto that. Around them, cutlery clanged and men mumbled to each other. In the kitchen beyond, food sizzled and pans banged. It was all a bit much and Jodie was starting to feel sick.

'What were you talking about yesterday?' she asked.

This finally brought Darren's frantic eating to a stop. He dabbed a bit of sausage in the bean juice but then put down his fork and winced. 'I wondered when we'd get to that.'

'It's why we're here.'

He looked past her, taking in the rest of the diner, perhaps wondering if anyone he knew was within earshot.

'You should forget it,' he said. 'No point in bringing up things from the past.'

'You basically told me there was something about Dad that you thought I knew. Something I didn't.'

She could see him wincing inwardly, wishing he had shut his mouth the day before. 'It's nothing... just that he lost his temper sometimes.'

'There's no way that Dad occasionally losing his temper is something you thought I might know. Everyone does. It's obviously more than that.'

Darren dug back into his food, shoving the sausage in his mouth and chewing until there couldn't be anything left of it. When he was done, he glanced across towards the toilets, then back to the rest of the room. Eventually, he leaned in and lowered his voice.

'I thought we were talking about the same thing yesterday. When you mentioned that bit where the vicar said he wouldn't hurt a fly. I thought you were telling me that specifically because you knew.'

Jodie couldn't keep the annoyance from her voice. 'Knew what?'

Darren banged his fork into the table with unexpected force. Tea bounced over the lip of his cup onto the surface, which left him dabbing it with a napkin as he desperately tried to avoid eye contact.

'That your dad made me leave you.'

Jodie stared at him for a second. Darren had walked out on her when Owen was barely two years old. She was struggling to cope anyway – and it had almost tipped her over the edge. She ended up moving in with her dad for a couple of months before settling into a different place. Meanwhile, she assumed Darren was around town, living up to his new-found single status. They barely spoke for the first six months of the break-up. She couldn't bring herself to see him, such was her anger at him walking out.

And now, Darren was saying he'd left her because of her dad.

She could see it was true. It was in the way Darren was

fidgeting, how he was obsessively cleaning the debris around the table – and straightening the salt, pepper and sauce bottles. Anything that meant he didn't have to look at her.

'Dad made you leave me?'

A nod.

'Why?' Jodie asked.

'You know why.'

Darren risked a glance up and nodded almost imperceptibly towards her face. That was all it took – and then Jodie knew.

There was a Friday when he'd been at work while she'd been home looking after Owen. When he got home, they'd argued about how much – or how little – Darren did around their flat. It was the only time in Jodie's life that someone had hit her. Actually put their hands on her. She could still feel it sometimes. That second of helplessness, at knowing he was bigger and stronger than she was. The moment of disbelief. Then that next second of seeing in his face that he was shocked by what he'd done. Then her absolute fury that he'd dare hit her.

There was blood and, later, a black eye. She told her dad she'd walked into a door. Was too busy holding Owen and wasn't looking where she was going. That's what she told everyone.

But her dad must have known. Perhaps everyone did? It wasn't as if the endless arguments were whispered.

'Sorry...' Darren said – and not for the first time.

He'd apologised at the time and had done so many times since.

Jodie realised she was rubbing the brow above the eye he'd once blackened. She didn't know how she felt about it now. He genuinely did seem sorry – and it didn't appear worth the effort of holding it over him so many years later. They were different people with different lives. But then she wondered if that was letting him off. If she should still be angry about it. If he deserved a lifetime of shame and remorse.

She didn't know – and, even if she did, he was still Owen's father.

'What did Dad say to you?' she asked.

The question seemed to take Darren by surprise. He'd been leaning in but pressed back into the squeaky leather. 'It wasn't what he said – it was that he had a hammer.'

Jodie looked up to where her former husband was now staring at her, his eyes wide. 'He what?'

'He had a hammer. I was outside our flat and he must have been waiting for me to get home. He was in the shadows and sort of jumped out. One minute he wasn't there, then he was. I almost didn't recognise him. He was in this big coat and had a beanie pulled down over his ears.'

The hat seemed almost more unbelievable than the hammer.

'Dad was wearing *a beanie*?'

'Yeah. I think I said his name, or something, then he pulled a hammer out of his pocket. Held it up to make sure I'd seen it. Said if I didn't get out of your life, then I wouldn't see him coming next time.'

Jodie stared at the father of her son. Looked for any hint he was making it up. It was fantasy. Surely?

'Dad said that?'

A nod and something close to a snort of disbelief. 'Word for word. You don't forget things like that. Next morning, I told you I was leaving and that was it.' A pause. 'Worked out in the end.' He gave a sad, sorry smile that said nothing, yet everything. It *had* worked out in the end – but if it wasn't for Owen, the destination would never have been worth the journey.

Now, Jodie was discovering the journey wasn't even what she thought it was. It wasn't solely that Darren had hit her, it was everything that led to it. Their total unhappiness in the life they'd created, the fact they had nothing in common and couldn't even agree on simple things such as what they wanted to eat. Darren showed little interest in helping to raise Owen and seemed to think Jodie's place was very much in the home, while he went out to work. Everything about them was incompatible. They had only married because she was pregnant. They were so young.

When Darren told her he was leaving, it was a relief – even though it made her life harder in the short term. She worried that Owen's life would be worse because she was a single mother, even though she didn't think having warring parents would make it any better.

And now it turned out that her father had taken the decision out of her hands.

She'd never known her dad to be violent – and he'd certainly never hit her. As far as she knew, he hadn't touched Mike or their mother either.

This was... new. A side of him she never knew existed.

Darren was seemingly not hungry any longer. He shuffled the food around his plate with the fork, though made no attempt to eat anything. He didn't look up when he next spoke.

'I don't want to make you think badly about your dad. Mess up his memory, or whatever. I'd never have told you – but, yesterday, it sounded like you knew...'

Jodie didn't reply. She could see how he might have thought that. She had been wondering if her father was somehow capable of harming Ben – and in asking that without asking, Darren had thought she was talking about the time her dad came for him. It was hard not to feel a sense of unease at hearing about this different side to someone Jodie thought she knew.

She wanted to talk to her dad. To ask why he'd turned up with a hammer. Whether he knew she hadn't walked into a door and that Darren had hit her. She wanted to thank him for making her life better because if she and Darren had remained together, something awful would have happened to one or both of them.

She wanted to ask about Ben.

Now he was gone, she suddenly had a list of questions that left only an emptiness.

'I'd do the same now,' Darren added quietly.

'What do you mean?'

'If someone was hurting Chandra, or our baby, I'd have no problem turning up with a hammer.'

Jodie didn't reply to that either. She wasn't jealous of Chandra, or the child she was carrying – but something certainly stuck that Darren was so emphatic in his love and support for them, when he hadn't been for her. It said something that he was unequivocal in saying he'd protect them, while Jodie had needed protecting from him.

She almost reminded her former husband that he had another child to think about – Owen – but there didn't seem much point in getting into an argument.

And so, as she did so often, she let it go.

Darren had finally given up on his food, nudging the plate off to the side and picking up his tea. 'I have to get back to work,' he said.

'Sorry for being late.'

Darren shrugged. He'd never asked why she wasn't on time. 'I'll come round tomorrow night and talk to Owen,' he added.

Jodie pushed herself up and reached for her bag. It was only as she picked it up that she realised the top wasn't zipped and that it had been sitting on the seat next to her, hanging open the entire time.

And there, sitting on top for anyone to see, was Ben's green T-shirt.

SIXTEEN

Jodie pulled out of Fry's car park, intending to drive home and wait for Owen to get back from school. She would have to psych herself up to talk to him about the bullying. It was one of the things people never spoke about when it came to being a single parent. If you fell out with your only child – even if it was over something as justified as addressing bad behaviour – then there was no respite from it. If Owen didn't talk to her, she could go an entire day or longer without speaking to anyone. Every moment at home would feel as if she was on a precipice. There was none of the emotional support of having a partner in whom to confide. She had Fiona, except her friend was having her own issues with a marriage going off the rails.

As she drove, Jodie found herself passing her house and continuing past it. She had no specific plan, except perhaps she did. She headed through the town, out towards the garden centre and then further out towards the town's boundary.

Jodie pulled in on the opposite side of the road to the house she actively avoided at other times. She got out of the car and leaned against the bonnet as she took in the sight across the road.

The field at the side of Paul McIntosh's house that once contained chickens was riddled with grass and weeds that were higher than the fence which ringed it. The fence was almost more holes than wood – and an entire section facing the road had collapsed into a mangled heap. The house itself was a faded, peeling yellow with a rail of guttering hanging down on one side. There were boards across the downstairs windows, on which someone had graffitied a giant cock and balls with an amount of detail that indicated an impressive level of talent.

From the outside, the house didn't look liveable. There were holes in the roof and as least one of the upstairs windows didn't have glass in it. Despite what Keith the journalist had said, it was hard to imagine anyone living here. After all those years in prison, could Paul McIntosh *really* want to return to a place so grim?

Jodie was about to leave when she realised the thing she wasn't seeing. Ben's dad said a 'for sale' board had gone up outside the dilapidated farmhouse – but there was no sign of that as Jodie stared across towards the ramshackle building. She crossed the road, feeling a pull towards the house that she couldn't explain.

Now she was closer, she could see the stack of old appliances at the side of a wheelless car that was on bricks. There were at least two microwaves, a rusty old oven and a couple of old-fashioned televisions with domed backs. A bent 'for sale' sign had also been dumped upside-down next to a battered metal bin.

Jodie shivered.

Her evidence had been part of the case that had sent Paul McIntosh to prison, even though it now felt so weak. She'd seen his navy-blue van outside the church, which was the only reason the police had questioned him. If she had been looking in the opposite direction as she and Ben had walked past, everything would have been different. If she hadn't paid attention, life would have been different for both of them. She might have pointed a finger in one direction as, in the other, her dad perhaps knew what had *really* gone on.

The weight of Ben's shirt sat heavy in Jodie's bag.

She didn't know how long she'd been staring, although it was definitely a couple of minutes. A chill whipped along the street, gathering a gritty cloud of dust and fizzing it into the distance. A car horn honked somewhere out of sight.

Jodie shivered again.

She was about to turn and leave when a clunk had her turning back to the house. In the moment she'd looked away, the front door had opened – and a man was standing in the frame staring at her. He had long, wiry grey hair and an unkempt, white beard. His black trousers and check shirt were hanging loose, like someone wearing their older brother's hand-me-downs.

They stared at one another for a moment and then the man dropped the bin bag he'd been carrying and walked slowly along the path towards her, never once turning away from Jodie.

She felt stuck on the spot, unable to move or look away until he was a couple of metres ahead.

He was so different, so much older than the last time she'd seen him, except those brown eyes were the same. They were so dark it was as if he had no pupils – and they were staring into her.

'Jodie,' he said croakily. 'Jodie Parker.'

They'd not seen one another in twenty years and yet they each knew who the other was. Jodie stared into Paul McIntosh's eyes and had no idea what to say. She'd been fourteen when Ben had pulled her from the shed, sixteen when he went missing and when she'd given evidence against Paul McIntosh from behind a screen. They did it so she didn't have to look at him, but she'd seen him around town before that. There were those photos in the papers too – and now he was in front of her.

'Hello...'

She wasn't sure why she said it, wasn't sure why she spoke at all – but Jodie's voice was as croaky as his.

McIntosh took a half-step backwards, holding his hands out palms up, as if trying to tell her he was no threat. 'Petrol station's gone,' he said.

Jodie blinked at him. 'Huh?'

He nodded towards the end of the road. 'Used to walk and get a paper every morning. There are flats there now.'

Jodie followed his gaze towards the junction in the distance, where a modern-looking set of apartments had been built. She'd forgotten a petrol station used to be there but could picture it now. It was one of the old independents with a car wash around the back.

When she looked back to McIntosh, he'd taken another small step away – although he was now staring at her again.

'I've got to go,' Jodie said, suddenly aware of who he was and how close they were.

Without waiting for a reply, she turned and hurried across the street. She'd had her car keys in her hand the entire time, though she fumbled with the fob, trying to unlock the vehicle with the wrong button and accidentally opening the boot.

By the time she'd closed that, dropped her keys, picked them up, bundled herself into the car and got the engine started, her heart was thundering. She turned to the side before pulling away – and there, still standing at the gate of his house, still watching her, was the man convicted of killing her boyfriend.

SEVENTEEN

Jodie set off towards her house, though her mind wasn't on the road or the route. The residents of the town wouldn't know yet – but they soon would.

Paul McIntosh was back.

She had no idea what would happen when word went around but she couldn't imagine it would be good.

Jodie was still thinking of that when she let herself into the house. She'd expected the usual buzzing din from upstairs – but everything was quiet. She checked the time on the microwave and then double-checked it with her phone. If Owen had finished school on time, and walked directly home, as she had told him, he should be back by now.

Her phone was buried in her bag, underneath Ben's shirt, and she took it out before typing out a message asking her son where he was. She sent it and then plucked out the shirt and put it on the counter.

It felt wrong to have it in this house, in the place she shared with her son. A child was supposed to feel safe at home and, despite everything that had been said about Owen at the school that morning, he was still a child. Ben's shirt represented the opposite of safety. It might have been washed and neatly folded but it was mystery and murder. She'd spent years thinking that was because of Paul McIntosh but now... she didn't want to think too much about what it might mean.

Jodie was in the kitchen and found her eyes drawn to the lighter wand that sat next to the cooker. She used it to light the gas rings because the built-in trigger hadn't worked in a long time. A frying pan was sitting on the stove, unused from the night before, and Jodie placed the shirt in it, watched it, then flicked the switch that sent a flame springing from the lighter. She felt the prickle of heat dancing across her thumb. She could burn the shirt, forget she ever saw it. Nobody would know.

The flame flickered and extinguished itself, so Jodie clicked the switch a second time, then a third. The fire appeared at the end of the wand again and again – and she tilted it towards the shirt in the pan...

She could end it all in a moment. Watch the shirt wilt and flake to nothing.

She should do it...

The scratching of a key in a lock echoed along the hall. There was a bump and bang – and then the sound of Owen falling inside. He could never simply enter the house, he had to barge his way through the door, shoulder first, and then trip over the step as he bundled his way inside. It was the same when he went up a set of stairs. Going one at a time was seemingly an impossibility as he bounded two or three at once.

He'd usually head for the stairs but Owen entered the kitchen and dropped his bag onto the table with a whump. He looked between Jodie and the empty pan on the stove, nose wrinkling with confusion.

'Did you burn something?' he asked.

'Some toast – but don't worry about that. Where've you been? I told you to come straight home.'

Owen sighed elaborately and slumped into one of the

dining chairs. He reached into his bag and pulled out his phone. 'I was walking.'

'It doesn't take an hour and a quarter to walk a mile.'

He shrugged and started fiddling with his phone, probably knowing what was coming.

'I talked to your head of year today,' Jodie added.

'OK.'

'He told me you've been bullying other kids.'

Owen didn't reply at first. He continued tapping on his phone until Jodie stepped across and snatched it from him.

'Hey!' he said, reaching for it. 'That's mine.'

'I paid for it.' Jodie stretched across and put the phone on the counter, next to the ignition wand. 'I didn't bring you up to be a bully,' she added.

'You didn't bring me up.'

Jodie stared at her son, replaying what he'd said and wondering if she'd misheard. 'What?'

'You were always arguing with Dad. Then I was with you in the week but him at weekends. You'd *bitch* about him; he'd bitch about you...'

'Don't use that word.'

Owen huffed something halfway between ridicule and annoyance. He turned away and stared into the distance, muttering under his breath. The venom of his reply felt as if he'd hit her. She wondered how long he'd felt like this.

'I always tried my best for you.' Her voice cracked as she said it.

'Did you?' Owen's reply was something closer to a snarl and, before Jodie could say anything, he pushed himself to his feet and grabbed his bag from the floor. He moved quickly, snatching his phone from the counter and stomping away.

Jodie wanted to call him back but the words wouldn't come. There was a series of elephant-style thumps and then his bedroom door slammed with a *whump* that made it feel as if the entire house was quaking.

The house wasn't the only thing. Jodie held up her hand and it was trembling. She was supposed to be grilling him about his bullying and, instead, *she* felt attacked.

Worse, she couldn't escape the awful feeling that he might have a point. He *had* been shunted between her and his dad. He had listened to them argue at those drop-offs more than any child should. Silly things about being a few minutes late or getting home with muddy shoes. It felt so inconsequential years on.

Did he *really* think that she hadn't raised him properly...?

Jodie considered going upstairs to ask him what he meant but, in the few seconds she spent think about it, the steady *doof-doof* of his game started to seep through the ceiling.

He'd be downstairs when he was hungry, though whether he'd want to engage with her was another issue.

Somehow, despite being called in by her son's school to discuss his bullying, she was the baddie. And none of this helped those at his school, who had suffered at Owen's hands.

Jodie reached for her own phone and typed out a quick message. She really needed some company.

Fiona pressed back into the lounger as Jodie sat on the sofa across from her. They'd been friends when they were younger than Owen. Fiona had been Jodie's only bridesmaid back in the days when it felt like people only had one or two. That was before the endless cast of extended family and friends began to occupy Facebook photos. Hashtag blessed, and all that.

Jodie told Fiona about the meeting with Owen's head of year, how Darren was coming round the next night to talk to their son – and that she felt incapable of having a tough conversation with him in between times.

Fiona sipped her tea and listened, which was more or less the only thing Jodie wanted.

'I feel like I'm failing,' Jodie said. 'Other parents, other mums, would have got to the bottom of things already.'

'You've had a lot to deal with this last month,' Fiona replied. 'If Darren's going to talk to him tomorrow, then maybe that's all it'll need. It's about time he did his share.'

It felt good to hear that. Darren's lack on input into his son's life had been a growing problem, even before Chandra's pregnancy.

'Speaking of separations...' Fiona was hiding behind her mug, eyes peering over the top towards Jodie.

'You and Robbie?'

Fiona took another sip of her tea and then put down the mug before nodding gently. 'It's been coming. I'm waiting for the right moment to talk to him. I don't know how he'll take it.'

For a second, Jodie was back in the old flat, face stinging as Darren apologised for slapping her. She now knew that, days later, her dad had threatened him with a hammer.

'Do you need me to be there?' she asked.

There was a moment in which it felt as if Fiona was going to say yes. As far as Jodie knew, Robbie had never been violent with Fiona, even though his drinking seemed to be a constant and increasing problem. Then again, Darren had never been violent until he was.

It was slow but Fiona eventually shook her head. 'I want to do it myself,' she said. 'It'll be for the best. All we ever do is argue. I can't believe he's happy. I know I'm not.' She paused for a moment and then added, 'Look at how things worked out for you. You're so much better off without Darren. I should have taken your lead and left Robbie years ago.'

Jodie thought of the eleven thousand or so that she owed across various cards and loans that Fiona didn't know about. If Jodie had the choice, she still would have split with Darren. It had been for the best – but Fiona made it sound as if it had been easy – which was far from true. It still wasn't.

She didn't say any of that. It'd be hard to explain without making it sound like she was saying her friend should stay with Robbie.

'There's always a room here if you need somewhere,' Jodie said instead. 'And I'm only down the road if you need me.' She paused. 'If you change your mind about having someone there when you tell him, let me know.'

Fiona nodded along and they sat quietly for a moment. One of the best things about their friendship was that they each understood when to say nothing. Sometimes, it meant more than words.

Jodie gulped the remains of her own tea, which had long since gone cold. She thought about telling Fiona of the shirt she'd found in her dad's attic – except there'd be no going back. Even for a best friend, it was too big a secret. As she'd discovered, knowledge could be a burden – and Fiona had her own issues, without needing to add Jodie's.

'Look at the state of us...'

Fiona was smiling sadly from her spot in the lounger and Jodie matched it. 'You look tired,' Fiona added.

'I am.'

'I should go—'

'I didn't mean—'

Fiona stepped across the room and perched on the sofa before leaning in to put an arm around Jodie. 'You've been through a lot,' she said.

'You too.'

Jodie pressed her head into Fiona's shoulder and they stayed there for a few moments until her friend stood. 'I need a smoke anyway,' Fiona said. 'Get some sleep.'

'I'll try.'

. . .

Jodie's alarm went off at the same time it always did. She had it set for quarter to seven, which gave her time to have a shower and make sure Owen went through the motions of pretending to do the same. He wasn't quite at the age where impressing girls was a priority – and she didn't know if that change would make things better or worse around the house. It might make his room smell a little more pleasant, which would be a start.

'We'll talk tonight,' she told him as he was eating his breakfast.

It didn't quite get an agreement but there was some sort of grunt as he stuffed toast into his mouth.

She watched as he sat at the table, eating and then stopping to fiddle with his laces. Jodie's dad had taught Owen to tie them in his living room, telling Owen to make 'elephant ears' with the laces. It was almost yesterday and yet it must've been a decade before.

'Is that your phone?'

Jodie was leaning on the counter, daydreaming when she realised Owen was talking to her. It was the first thing he'd said since their argument that wasn't in response to a question.

He was looking towards the other side of the counter, where her phone was buzzing across the surface.

Jodie picked it up, taking in Elaine's name on the screen.

'Hello...?'

There was a nervy, hesitant voice on the other end. 'Is that Jodie?'

'Yes.'

'It's your dad's house. There's a strange man standing outside.'

EIGHTEEN

Jodie told Owen not to be late for school and then drove the few miles across town to her dad's house. She assumed the stranger described by Elaine would have disappeared by the time she arrived. Instead, as she parked on the road, he paid her no attention.

The man was in black trousers and a shirt, standing near the end of the path and technically trespassing by a metre or so. He was facing her dad's house while talking into his phone and flapping his free hand around like a market trader offering two pairs of flip-flops for a tenner.

Jodie got out of her car and approached the man from behind, not that he noticed her. He was speaking so quickly that the words rolled into one another. She heard snatches of 'tell her to do it herself then', 'don't ask me' and 'what are the solicitors saying?' before she gently tapped the man on the shoulder.

He spun, his free arm still flailing as he yelped as if electrocuted. He then jumped back, further onto the property. 'What—?'

'This is my house.'

The man was around Jodie's age, with a fake tangerine tan

line along his hairline. He seemed vaguely familiar, although she couldn't place him. The man muttered 'Call you back' into his phone and then slipped it into his pocket.

'Jodie, is it...?'

She stared at him, momentarily confused. 'Do I know you?'

He held out a hand. 'Luke O'Reilly.'

Jodie looked at his hand, though made no attempt to shake it. 'Am I supposed to know who you are?'

Luke's face fell momentarily, although his toothy façade returned almost instantly. He pulled his hand back towards his body and scratched his thigh, as if that was what he meant to do in the first place. 'O'Reilly's Property And Letting. You might've seen our boards around town...?'

Jodie *had* seen the advertising boards – as had anyone who lived in the area. There was a huge one in the centre of town that had a picture of Luke's orange face next to the slogan 'let me let for you' – or some such nonsense. There were at least two more boards on the main road in and out of the town.

Not that Jodie was going to give him the satisfaction. 'I don't think I've seen them,' she said, shaking her head.

'Oh...' Luke seemed confused by this, but only for a second, before he was back into his spiel. 'I was trying to figure out who's responsible for the house,' he said.

'Why?'

He slid a card from a gleaming holder and offered it to her. Jodie could see his face beaming on the front of the card, plus his name and a string of contact details. He really did like his own face.

'If you're the owner of the house, I'm sure we could work together.' He waved a hand in the vague direction of the opposite end of the street. 'It's a seller's market at the moment – or, if you want to rent it out, we have some incredible offers for people who want to let with us.' He paused momentarily to flash another white-toothed grin. 'Let me let for you!'

Jodie didn't take the card, which had no effect on Luke as he slipped it seamlessly back into the holder, which then disappeared into a pocket.

'My dad's funeral was three days ago,' Jodie said.

'Sure, sure. I realise that. I was simply going to put a card through the door. Everything's at your pace.'

'You've been here at least twenty minutes. That's a long time to put a card through the door.'

Luke's stoic front wilted for a couple of seconds this time. He looked both ways along the street, wondering how she knew. Jodie didn't give him the chance to add anything else.

'I think you should leave,' she said.

For a moment, she thought he was going to reach for his business cards again. Instead, he gave a *suit yourself* shrug that would've impressed Owen. He then turned and strolled off towards a shiny red convertible that was parked a few doors down. The engine growled and roared – and then he disappeared around the corner in a guff of exhaust fumes.

Jodie wondered how her dad would have handled it. He'd have probably been amused by the idea of someone trying to sell his house when he was barely out of it. That was his sort of humour. He'd joke about death and age; about his creaky knees and aching back. Nothing was ever taken too seriously.

But then Jodie wondered whether that was actually who he was at all. Someone like that didn't turn up with a hammer to threaten his daughter's husband. Someone like that didn't have a shirt belonging to a missing teenager folded neatly in his attic.

She was brought back to the moment as the neighbours' door clicked open. Ben's father, Jim, was standing in the frame; Elaine a step behind and peering around her husband's shoulder.

'I see he's gone then,' Jim called across.

Jodie stepped over the low fence and crunched across the gravel until she was on the neighbouring path.

'It was an estate agent,' Jodie replied.

Jim turned to his wife. 'That's what I said, wasn't it?'

'You said it was a burglar.'

'That was before! Then he started taking photos and I said it was an estate agent.'

'I don't remember that.'

'Course you do. I said it right after you said you were going to call the police.'

'I never mentioned the police. That was you.'

It felt as if the couple could bicker back and forth for the rest of the day. They'd been married so long that endless, meaningless squabbling was their language of choice.

'Thanks for letting me know,' Jodie said, talking across them.

In an instant, their arguing was over.

'You're welcome, love,' Elaine said.

'We're here if you need us,' Jim added.

Jodie angled towards her dad's house and said she was going to check inside. She stepped back over the divider and then searched through her bag for the keys. All three of the new ones sat on the same ring and she let herself inside and headed through to the kitchen.

She'd checked the window was fully locked before leaving the day before – and it remained clamped in place. Whoever had broken in before hadn't returned, which left Jodie wondering whether they'd found what they were looking for. If that was the case, it meant they weren't after Ben's shirt. It didn't feel like something opportunistic, given the window had been forced open – although enough people in the town would have known the house was empty.

Jodie leaned across the sink and checked the window to be certain – which is when a bright beam of sunlight reflected into her eyes. She stepped to the side, shielding herself from the glare, as she noticed that the light was bouncing off something attached to the house over the back fence.

She was too far away to know what it was, so Jodie unlocked the back door and went into the yard. It was after she and Mike had left home that her dad had replaced the turf with paving slabs. When they were children, they'd play in the garden – but, once he was living alone, her dad didn't want to mow the grass and he certainly didn't want to pay someone to do it for him.

Weeds were starting to poke through the gaps between the blocks and there was a mossy green coating across the top of the concrete.

When the grass had been replaced, it meant the scorched patch on which the shed used to sit had gone. That didn't stop Jodie looking across to the corner of the garden where it once sat. When Ben had pulled her clear, he'd gone out the back of his own house, into the alley and then leapfrogged their gate to get to her. She didn't remember ever spending time in the garden after that. She'd see the blackened, ashy earth from her bedroom window but that was as close as she'd get.

It was after the patio had been put down that her father decided he wanted people to come over for barbecues. She'd bring Owen and they'd sit in fold-down chairs as her dad burned burgers and made terrible jokes – but she never felt safe in the space.

That was perhaps the biggest reason why she didn't think she could ever live in the house now her father was gone. It wasn't only full of *his* ghosts, it was riddled with hers.

Jodie was staring towards the paved corner when she remembered what she was doing. She edged towards the fence, squinting towards the house over the back.

When she was growing up, it seemed normal that the view outside her bedroom window was not only their back garden – but the one belonging to the house behind. She'd sometimes see children younger than her playing in a paddling pool or hear the vague chatter of adults around a barbecue. She didn't realise until she was older that most houses weren't built to give a direct view into someone else's garden.

She hadn't thought about that since she'd moved out – but, as she got closer to the back, she realised the reflection she'd seen from the kitchen window had come from something metal and cylindrical attached to the opposite house.

From... a security camera.

The camera was pointing towards the alley that separated the rear of her dad's house from the house on the opposite side. The angle meant it probably had a view of the back yard – and the window that had been forced.

Jodie unlatched the back gate and stepped onto the alley. A wind bristled along the narrow lane, skittering between the mismatch of different fence types and assorted wheelie bins. Jodie stepped around them and followed the path until it reached the main road. She followed the route in a loop until she was on the street that ran parallel to the one on which her dad's house sat.

She counted the houses as she passed – but everything looked so similar: two-storey red-bricks with tidy, boxy front gardens. With no clear view towards the back, she wasn't sure which house backed onto her dad's and the best she could manage was narrowing it down to a pair of semi-detacheds.

Jodie was trying to think of the best way to figure out which was the right house when she spotted a white, cylindrical camera bolted to the wall above one of the front doors.

Jodie felt its watchful stare as she strode along the drive, eyes on the floor, until she reached the front door. She pressed the bell and waited, trying to force a confidence she didn't feel.

She only had a moment to consider it before the door swung open, revealing a woman cradling a baby with one arm. She looked past Jodie towards the street, as if expecting someone else.

'I'm not selling anything,' Jodie said quickly, which did little other than to draw a frown.

'Only people who are selling something say they're not selling something.'

'I'm really not.' Jodie pointed past the woman, towards the back. 'I'm Jodie. My dad owns the house behind you. Well, *owned*, I guess.'

The woman hoisted the child higher onto her shoulder. Jodie couldn't tell if it was a boy or girl, though the enormous googly eyes felt as if they were drawing her in.

'Martin's house?'

'I'm his daughter.'

The woman nodded slowly, lip pouted, apparently not convinced. 'I saw on Facebook that he'd died.' She chewed the inside of her mouth for a moment and then added, 'Rest in peace and all that.'

Jodie almost laughed. She liked the sentiment of 'all that'. It was the opposite of all the careful commemorations everyone had been offering. 'I noticed you've got a camera at the back,' Jodie added. 'Someone tried to break into Dad's place on Monday night and I wondered if you might have footage?'

The child was gaping at Jodie, his or her eyes seemingly growing wider and more bulbous by the moment. Jodie was doing her best to avoid the staring contest but she was feeling an increasing urge to say something about how cute the child was. That's what it felt like people did.

'Not my thing,' the woman said. Jodie also sagged with momentary disappointment, although she kept talking. 'My son knows all about the cameras. He's at college today but he's off tomorrow. He'll sleep 'til twelve but I can get him to have a look then. If you drop round after that, I'll let you know if he has anything.'

Jodie was about to suggest leaving her number – but the child had other ideas. It started with a belch, was quickly followed by a 'shite' from the mother, and ended half-a-second later with a flood of yellow-browny goo across the front of her top.

The woman angled down and eyed her top with a grimace. 'I've gotta go,' she said.

Jodie was halfway through a 'thanks' when the door banged into place. The 'I only washed this yesterday' was clear enough, even through the double glazing.

She turned, quietly laughing to herself as she walked away. She'd been there. It was always grim when it happened to you – but there wasn't much else funnier than when it happened to someone else.

Jodie followed the street around to the alley and then into the back yard of her dad's house. She stopped at the kitchen window, turning and eyeing the camera now she knew what it was. If it kept recordings and worked at night, it would surely have a clear view of whoever levered open the frame.

She was thinking of that when her phone started to ring. Jodie almost pressed to ignore the call from the oh-one number. If it was important, they'd call back – except then she remembered she was waiting on a call from Keith.

The journalist didn't bother with introductions. 'I've got what you were after,' he said.

NINETEEN

Keith's house had been a cluttered mess the first time Jodie visited – and her second visit was like visiting the path of a tornado in the hours after it landed. The stacks of books and papers had apparently been breeding, spawning new piles that quivered dangerously as she slipped around them. Despite the chaos, and his size, Keith navigated his hallway with the ease of a ballerina. He glided around the jumble while talking over his shoulder and not looking where he was going.

'I know more or less where everything is,' he said, asking a question Jodie hadn't asked.

It was as she followed him into the study that she started to feel nerves. Since his death, Jodie had found out things about her dad she didn't know before. It wasn't only the mystery of Ben's shirt, there was the hammer threat to her ex-husband. She'd had an image of her father and now, not only was he gone, that impression was in danger of disappearing too.

A nearly full ashtray was in the windowsill – and the room smelled more distinctly of cigarettes for Jodie's second visit. Two chairs were clear, so Jodie sat in one as Keith slotted himself in at his computer. A pile of *Private Eye* magazines, a bottle of gin, and a photo of a brown and white bulldog had all appeared since she'd last been in the study.

'I had to go through my old shorthand,' Keith said. He picked up a battered spiral notebook that was resting on the radiator. The paper had yellowed and the front was torn. None of that seemed to faze Keith, who flipped pages until he was almost at the back. 'I take it you haven't changed your mind,' he asked.

'I wouldn't have come if I had.'

That got a short nod. 'It's not entirely about your father – although it obviously includes him. It's also about Mike.'

Jodie stared for a second, wondering if she'd misheard her brother's name. She found herself repeating 'Mike...?' as if she didn't know who it was.

Keith continued anyway. 'It could be a quirk of timing. A coincidence. I know people say coincidences don't happen – but, when you've done this job as long as I have, they appear with alarming regularity.' He wafted a hand. 'I'm waffling. Anyway, I took these notes about a year after your fire.'

He pointed to a series of squiggles on the pad, which Jodie couldn't make out, even if she had known shorthand.

'I checked everything against the other stories I wrote,' he added. 'I wanted to be sure.'

'About what?'

From somewhere deep in the house, the landline started to ring. Keith's gaze flickered with something close to annoyance. Jodie's dad had never been much of a phone person either. He waited for it to ring off and then continued.

'You know the council offices? They were renovated and there was this area at the back where they were piling everything being ripped out. Wood and brick, that sort of thing.'

As he spoke of it, Jodie vaguely remembered a time when

her dad said he'd had to move offices because of the construction. It was one of those things that she'd considered for half a second at the time – and forgotten about ever since. It had no effect on her life, then or in the present.

Keith flipped a page on his pad. 'One of the builders had accidentally left some tools on-site and went back that night to get them. He heard something and went around the back – where he found Mike trying to start a fire next to that rubbish pile.'

Jodie stared at the journalist. She'd had no idea what to expect when he'd called her back. After hearing from Darren about the hammer threat, she wondered if Keith might relay the same story to her. If not that, then something similar.

But, no. This was something unrelated and unexpected.

Jodie floundered for words that didn't come.

Her whole life had changed because of a fire blamed on a lightning strike... and now Keith was talking to her about a different blaze.

'He was using a lighter and some paper,' Keith continued, 'but he was caught before any real damage was done.'

Jodie could barely get the words out. 'What happened after?'

'The contractor called the police. Back in those days, a local bobby would come out – and the sergeant who turned up was someone who went to school with your dad. Rather than arresting your brother, he called your dad.'

Jodie stared, still unsure how best to reply. It felt impossible and yet she knew instinctively that it had happened. She was fairly sure the sergeant had been at a few fetes and functions where her dad had been opening things. She couldn't remember his name, though she did remember a moustache. Her dad seemed to know everyone back then.

'What did Dad do?' Jodie asked.

'Kept it quiet. I'm not saying he was wrong. I only found out because I know that sergeant too. *Knew*. He told me after a couple of pints one night.'

Jodie took a few seconds, remembered the heat on her arms from her own fire. 'Did you ask Dad about it?'

Keith pressed back into his chair and scratched at his hair. For the first time, he seemed a little off-guard. 'Once.'

'What did he say?'

Keith took a breath and started scratching his palm. 'This happened around a year after you were pulled from that shed – and sometime around when Ben Vickery went missing. I know what you must be thinking about your fire and this fire. About your brother. I'm not saying any of it was linked, although the thought obviously occurred.'

'But what did Dad say?'

'He asked me to sit on it. If it got out that his son had tried to start a fire, people would obviously link that back to the fire from which you'd been pulled.'

He was right – because Jodie was making those exact links herself. It was impossible not to.

'Is that why you never reported it?' Jodie asked.

When the nod came, it was slow and considered. 'I suppose. There was other news going on at the time – this was not long after Ben had gone missing – and I guess I figured I knew your dad well enough to trust his judgement.'

'That feels like a big call.'

That got a nod. 'I'm not sure I would've sat on it with anyone else.' He scratched his head a second time and then closed his notebook and put it on top of an old computer monitor that was sitting on the floor near his feet.

Jodie thought for a few seconds. 'They said the shed fire was a lightning strike.'

Keith shook his head. 'I read the reports back. They said it was an *assumed* lightning strike – and it probably was. There were three other strikes across town that same night. A tree near the school was brought down and a farmhouse was hit about a mile from there. One of your neighbours reported a loud bang, so there was no reason to assume anything different.' He paused for a second. 'Again, I'm not saying you should read anything into this. I'm only telling you what was reported to me. You wanted to know about your dad – and this is what I have. He did all he could to protect your brother.'

Jodie wondered if he'd done all he could to protect her. If the fire from which she'd been pulled was really unconnected to the one her brother had tried to set a year on. If he was a potential arsonist at one point in his life, could it really be true he'd never tried before? Or since? Keith's line about coincidences now felt less throwaway. He knew what she'd think because he'd thought it as well.

From nowhere, she was back in the hospital room that had become a temporary home in the week or so after Ben pulled her from the shed. None of her burns were serious but doctors kept her in because she was having difficulties breathing. Every time she inhaled, a clawing, wheezing itch would tickle her insides.

The first time she paid Ben any real attention was when he visited with her brother. She didn't know it at the time but he'd already been named on the front of the local paper as the 'hero' who pulled his neighbour from a fire. In a town the size of theirs, it was enough to make anyone a celebrity. Her brother had been the bold one that day, crouching at the side of her bed and joking that she'd do anything for attention. Ben hovered a little behind him, not wanting the credit, even when she thanked him for pulling her clear.

He shrugged and mumbled that anyone would have done the same. That was when he couldn't quite bring himself to look at her. She thought it was modesty at the time, and it probably was, but he was shy as well. Then he'd become her first boyfriend – and that discomfort disappeared.

When she got home from the hospital, Ben was part of the greeting party, along with his parents and her family. He asked if she wanted to go to the cinema – and then it had become part of their weekly routine.

It had all seemed so natural at the time – but, like so many things, it felt different now she was an adult. She thought it was love, and perhaps it was, but she'd idolised Ben as well. She was obsessed about being his girlfriend to what she now knew was an unhealthy degree. His low-level fame suddenly meant people wanted to see his band, which inevitably meant girls wanted to talk to him. He was already at home on the stage – but the arrival of *actual* fans into his life only gave him more confidence.

Every time a girl spoke to him, Jodie would send herself into a spiralling panic that he liked them more than he liked her. She couldn't imagine not having him in her life – which wasn't a good thing for anyone, let alone a girl who was just turning fifteen.

And then, just over a year after he'd saved her, he was gone. The intensity of her feelings for him evaporated into a deep hole, from which she only emerged because she decided Darren was actually the boy for her.

That had, of course, gone as badly as it was always going to.

'Do you want to copy any of the papers?'

Jodie blinked back into Keith's study, where he was motioning towards a stack of papers near the window.

'You can photocopy whatever you want. There's one at the library, or—'

'It's fine,' Jodie replied. 'Thank you for going through everything.'

They stood and waited apart from each other for a moment – and then Keith sagged slightly, his shoulders drooping. 'I'm not sure I should've told you this. I knew your dad fairly well over many years. I knew lots of politicians. Some were in it for themselves, some wanted it as a stepping stone to higher office, or well-paid board positions. Your dad was different. He actually cared about this town and the people. I could tell you about the woman who lost her benefits because of a technical glitch – and it was your dad who stepped in and dealt with it. He sorted out wheelchair ramps on the high street when nobody else thought it was an issue. He pressured BT to get a broadband line fitted at a residential home. I could list a dozen more things without thinking about it.' He paused for breath. 'These aren't things he told me, or anything bragged about in a press release. These are things I was told by the people involved. Almost none of it got into the paper because it's not really news – but that's who your dad was. That's why the church was packed for his funeral. That's why there'll be a big crowd when they do the naming ceremony at the community centre on Saturday.'

Out of nothing, there was a lump in Jodie's throat. She had to turn half around and face the wall as she blinked away the inevitable.

How could everything be reconciled? This calm, compassionate man who did so much for so many. He'd once found a bird with a broken wing in the garden. With some advice and help from the local vet, he nursed it back to life and then asked Jodie to stand with him when he'd released it.

He cried over that bird.

And yet...

And yet he had that shirt in his attic. Jodie wished she'd never found it. She could have carried on with her life and continued seeing him in the way she always had. She didn't want to hear about him threatening Darren with a hammer or protecting her brother from attempted arson charges. Except, without those tales, would she ever get to the bottom of why her dad had that shirt?

When she finally turned back, Keith was sitting in his chair, pretending to read something in one of his notebooks and silently doing his best not to make her feel self-conscious.

'I should go,' Jodie said softly.

'You're welcome to come back any time. My archives aren't going anywhere and if you change your mind, I can always get you a copy of something.'

Jodie nodded meekly, not quite trusting herself to speak in case she broke again. And then, just as she thought she was going to walk away, she couldn't stop herself. 'Do you think good people do bad things?'

Keith blinked and puffed out a long breath. He was a stranger and yet it felt like he was the closest chance she'd get to asking the same question of her dad.

'Unquestionably,' he replied.

'What if it was something *really* bad?' Jodie asked. 'What if that one bad thing undid all the good stuff?'

His eyes narrowed slightly – and it would have been impossible for him to miss that she was talking about her dad.

'I'm not sure I can answer that,' he said.

Jodie was so close to telling him about what she'd found in her dad's attic. Asking if he had any idea what it all meant.

She felt her dad's presence looming over her, looming over the town. Over everything. He had a legacy and even asking the question could be enough to destroy it.

'I should go,' Jodie said for the second time.

'As you wish.'

Neither of them moved for a few seconds – and then Jodie's legs finally started to work. She wobbled slightly, and then clasped the corner of the desk to right herself. She edged through the hall, accidentally clipping a stack of books on her way through. Jodie crouched, picking them up and trying to re-stack them, even as Keith said he'd deal with it.

When she finally got outside, the crisp air grabbed and slapped her back into the moment. She couldn't believe how close she'd come to telling a stranger – a journalist, of all people – about her father's secret.

About his *secrets*.

Because if Mike, her own brother, had started one fire, who was to say he hadn't started another at the bottom of his own garden?

TWENTY

The roads were quiet as Jodie drove away from the canal and Keith's cottage. Every time she scratched the surface of something, she came away more confused than when she started. It wasn't only her father about whom she had doubts and questions, it was now her brother as well.

Autopilot was working again as Jodie headed in the vague direction of home. She turned onto a quiet residential street that had cars parked along both sides and barely room for one vehicle to fit through the middle. Jodie would often take the longer route around town to avoid this area.

She was a third of the way along the street when a car raced around the bend at the other end. With the lack of space, the second driver to enter the street would usually pull in to let the other pass. Jodie only realised this wasn't happening as the other car roared past a gap in the parked cars and continued towards her.

It was a game of chicken – and Jodie was in half a mind to carry on driving and block the road. She was in no particular rush and if the other person wanted a lengthy stand-off, that was fine by her.

Except it wasn't.

It would be a man, because it always was, and she couldn't be bothered having some guy beep his horn and call her a bitch, all while someone filmed it all from their bedroom window. Before she knew it, she'd be on the internet – and then she'd somehow seem like the crazy one.

The car continued driving at her, passing a second pull-in spot and, if anything, speeding up.

Jodie slowed, indicated, and swerved into the gap on her left. She seethed as the other vehicle continued accelerating, though it was only as it got nearer that something didn't seem quite right. It wasn't some boy racer with a chuntering exhaust that was haring towards her. It was a stoic and sensible green Skoda – and that wasn't the strangest thing. Jodie had no interest in cars and knew very little about models and makes – except she knew the one coming towards her.

They were in a 20 mph zone – but the approaching car ripped past at what had to be twice that, or more. It was all a blur, but Jodie not only recognised the car, she recognised the driver.

For some reason, Ben's dad was thrashing through a residential zone in the way she couldn't imagine her father's neighbour doing.

Unless...

And then Jodie knew exactly why he was driving like such a maniac.

TWENTY-ONE

Jodie did a three-point turn in the road, which wasn't easy with the tight space. By the time she was retracing her steps, Jim's Skoda was already in the distance. Jodie accelerated more than she should.

As she got to the traffic lights, Jim was out of sight – except Jodie knew where he was going. There was no traffic coming, so she edged through on red and accelerated past a pub, out towards the ring road.

They'd never make it that far because Jim wasn't leaving town.

She saw him on the next straight. There was another set of red traffic lights and, with cars flowing across, there was no gap for Jim to head through safely.

They were in a thirty zone now and Jodie eased down to a little over forty as a car pulled out of a side street, separating her and Jim.

When the cross-traffic stopped, Jim didn't wait for the green light. He surged through on red and floored it, sending a rubbery squeal into the air as the car between him and Jodie slowed for the light.

Even though she knew where he was heading, Jodie didn't want Jim to have too much of a head start in getting there. She had a horrible sense of what might be about to happen.

The car between them turned at the lights and Jodie drove wide around them before accelerating off in pursuit of the Skoda. It was open road now, only intermittent houses, a couple of pubs, and the garden centre.

By the time Jodie reached Paul McIntosh's farmhouse, Jim's car was already parked at an angle outside. She pulled in behind and managed to turn off the engine and get out almost in the same movement.

Ben's father was already along the path, hammering on the door of the farmhouse.

'I know you're in there!'

He was shouting in a way Jodie had never heard before. He'd always been the friendly neighbour next door. The man who offered her sweets when she was a kid and waved from his front window whenever he spotted her. There had been grief, of course. It had been quiet and calm when Ben disappeared – but she'd never seen the fury.

'Come on, McIntosh! I know you're there!'

Jim stepped away and then kicked the door before moving to the side and thundering on the window with his fist.

'Come out, you coward!'

Jodie edged along the path, nervous at the fury in front of her. Despite the story of her dad with the hammer, despite her arguments with her ex-husband and that one time, violence had never been a part of her life. She'd not been one of those kids at school who bounced from aggro to aggro. She didn't have enemies, or, at least, she didn't think she did.

'Jim...'

She spoke softly, in between his shouts. She saw his shoulders tense and he must have heard her – except he didn't turn.

Instead, he walloped his fist on the flimsy-looking glass once more.

'I know you're there.'

Jodie continued on, until she was a couple of paces away from Jim. 'Mr Vickery...? It's Jodie, from next door.'

His shoulders tensed again and his head twitched. This time, he did turn, though not entirely.

'What are you doing here?' he said. He wasn't quite yelling but his voice was gruff and hard.

'This isn't going to help,' Jodie said, ignoring the question.

'But he—'

'I know.'

Jodie closed the distance between them and put a hand on Jim's shoulder. He loosened at her touch, slouching and taking a huge breath as he turned. When he faced her, the anger had been replaced by the look of a man who was broken. His bottom lip bobbed and his entire body had shrunk in front of her.

'He killed my boy.'

There was a sob in the middle of the sentence and Jodie pulled the older man towards her. He rested momentarily on her shoulder, chest heaving until he stepped away and launched another furious round of door hammering.

Jodie stood and watched. Waited.

He was trying to be angry now, desperately wanting the furious thunder to remain... except Jodie could see it fading.

'Let's go home,' she said quietly. 'I'll drive behind you.'

Jim's head drooped. 'It's not right,' he said. 'How can he come back? How can they let him out?'

Jodie didn't have the answers but she angled herself sideways and Jim took the hint. He moved past her one small step at a time, hands trembling, as Jodie slotted in a step behind. They moved back along the path towards the pavement and their cars – which is when the door behind them clicked open.

Jim and Jodie turned together to see the windswept man in

the doorway. Paul McIntosh was wearing the same oversized black trousers and check shirt Jodie had seen him in before. His hair was wild and untamed, his beard matted and messy.

The air between them bubbled dangerously. The moment in between dropping something and the smash. When nature is in charge and the outcome is inevitable.

Jim moved first. It should have been Jodie but she was a frozen bystander. It all felt preordained.

Jim stepped around Jodie and returned along the path, slowly at first and then at a stumbling run. McIntosh didn't move from his doorway. He had his arms out, palms up, welcoming what was to come. He wasn't scared. He didn't mind.

Which is when Jim reached into the pocket of his jacket and pulled out a knife.

TWENTY-TWO

It was a long triangular blade, thick near the handle, pointy at the end. The sort of thing sold in every supermarket.

Jodie watched, still unable to move, as Jim held the blade in front of him, making sure McIntosh could see it. There was no reaction from the other man. Still no fear. If anything, he moved his arms wide, welcoming Jim and his knife.

'Please...'

It was McIntosh who spoke, although his voice was no louder than if he was calmly talking to someone next to him. It was a single word and yet impenetrable. He could have been begging Jim not to do it – or it could have been a plea to end everything.

The men were a pace apart: Jim heaving breathlessly, McIntosh still and calm.

Jim's voice was a sob again. 'Why him?' he asked. 'Why not me? Why not anyone else?'

McIntosh's only reply was a long sigh before he turned towards his house.

'Don't turn your back on me!'

Jim was trembling, the knife raised to shoulder height, still a pace away from its apparent target.

'What do you want me to say?'

McIntosh's voice was gravelly, as if it had been a long time since he'd last spoken.

'Just say why you did it?'

McIntosh was watching Jim over his shoulder and Jodie felt the hairs rise on the back of her neck. She could move again and she took a couple of steps along the path.

'I said twenty years ago,' McIntosh replied.

'What did you say?'

A pause. 'I didn't kill your boy.'

Jodie took another step towards the men. Her body was tingling as she saw Jim's fingers tighten around the knife handle.

'Why can't you admit it?' Jim said with a growl. 'Be man enough after all this time.'

McIntosh altered his stance momentarily, glancing towards the knife, and then back to Jim. Time stopped and then, slowly, deliberately, McIntosh stepped into his house.

Jodie only realised she'd been holding her breath when she let out a long, low gasp as, finally, the door closed with a solid click.

TWENTY-THREE

Elaine was waiting at the front door as her husband parked on the road in front of their house. Jodie pulled in behind him and was out of the car first. She hurried to the other driver's door and helped Jim out of his car. She'd worried about letting him drive home but there was little she could do to stop a grown man from doing precisely that. The journey itself had been mercifully uneventful. Jim had stopped at all the traffic lights and kept to the speed limits.

'He just took off,' Elaine said, as Jodie helped her husband towards the front of the house. Any fight that had been in him was long gone as he leaned on Jodie's shoulder for support. He suddenly felt very old and vulnerable.

Jim limped past his wife into the house without another word, leaving the two women on the doorstep.

Elaine seemed close to tears. 'One of our friends called. They said they'd seen McIntosh at his old house – and Jim set off. He didn't even hang up. What happened?'

Jodie said she'd seen Jim driving near McIntosh's house, glossing over the speedy chase that went before. She then reached into her bag and handed across the kitchen knife she'd taken from Jim. Elaine's eyes widened as she took it. She looked over her shoulder towards the kitchen, as if checking it was theirs.

'He didn't use it,' Jodie said.

Elaine was holding the knife pinched between two fingers, her gaze blank and unfocused. 'I didn't know he took it.'

'All they did was talk for a bit,' Jodie said.

'Talk...?'

'Sort of. Jim asked him why he did it and McIntosh said it wasn't him.'

There was no reply other than the wide-eyed, bleary stare into the distance. 'I should check on him,' Elaine said. 'Thanks for... y'know.'

Jodie turned and headed back along the path as the door closed behind her. She was back in her car when it finally dawned on her how badly things could have gone. The irony wasn't lost that an apparently kind and considerate man could turn in an instant and become something else.

She switched on the engine and sat, looking towards her childhood home... *her* house now – and only then did she know it was time to do the thing she'd been putting off ever since she found Ben's shirt.

It was time to visit her mum.

Jodie's mother had always been a housewife. In her lifetime, that had gone from being the norm to the exception. She'd been ever-present in the house as Jodie grew up: the person who walked her to primary school and the one who made tea when Jodie got home. It was all she wanted to do and, after the separation and divorce from Jodie's father, she'd married another man who was more than happy for her to spend her days cleaning and cooking.

Her house was a few miles outside the town in which Jodie had grown up: a tidy little cottage that had a row of 'Britain in Bloom' nomination signs planted equidistantly from one another on the front verge. There were no broken gates or assorted junk on the lawn on this side of town. The grass was in perfect symmetrical lines; and cutesy, rainbow flowerbeds lined all sides.

Jodie unclipped the pristine gate and let herself in before closing it. There was no point in starting an argument about nothing if her mum heard the gate bang closed or, worse still, if it was left open.

She first headed along the path but then spotted her mother off to the side, kneeling on a thick foam pad and wearing gloves as she picked and plucked at one of her flowerbeds. She'd not heard or seen Jodie and was busy humming tunelessly to herself as her daughter approached.

'Mum...?'

The older woman rocked backwards, almost toppling over as she jumped and tried to turn at the same time. She clutched a hand to her chest, putting a soil stain on her light green top.

'Jodie! How many times have I told you about sneaking up on people? You'll be the death of me.'

It almost made Jodie laugh. She couldn't ever remember her mum telling her about sneaking up on people, let alone at any point in the past twenty years or so.

Jodie's mum stood and cricked her back before holding her arms out. Jodie hugged her momentarily – chest in, arse out – and then they stepped away from each other. It was less than a second but summed up everything.

Jodie's parents had divorced in the year between Ben pulling Jodie from the burning shed and him disappearing. At the time, it felt as if she was walking away when Jodie needed her the most – and she'd never quite forgiven her for it, even though it wasn't really the truth. In reality, Jodie's parents had been out of love and coasting for years. They had remained together for their children but it wasn't a healthy long-term thing. Jodie had sided with her dad, even though no side needed to be taken. She had always been a daddy's girl – and her mother probably knew that long before the divorce.

The older woman shielded her eyes from the sun. 'Is everything all right?'

'Yeah.'

'Owen...?'

'He's fine too.'

'Oh...'

There was confusion because Jodie never visited her mother unannounced unless she needed something – while her mum never visited at all. A few miles apart geographically and yet continents between them where it mattered.

'Is this about the will?' her mother asked. 'Because I told Mike I wasn't getting involved. You need to sort it out between yourselves.'

'It's not that, Mum.' Jodie paused and then added, 'I spoke to Darren after the funeral. Did you know Dad once threatened him with a hammer?'

Jodie wasn't sure what she expected. That confrontation had happened after her parents were divorced, though they still spoke afterwards. She thought there'd be a reaction from her mum – perhaps surprise at the violent connotation – but, instead, there was a blank look.

'It was for the best, wasn't it?'

'That's not the point, Mum. You can't just threaten people with hammers.'

'Didn't Darren hit you?'

Jodie had started to reply before she realised what had been said. She stopped and started again. 'How do you know that?'

'I think your father told me. I warned him about going too far.'

'How did *he* know?'

'Everyone knew! You spent all your time arguing – and then had a massive black eye. Did you really think anyone was going to buy the whole walking-into-a-door, or whatever it was?'

Jodie took a moment, trying to remember if that's what it was truly like. Did everyone *really* know Darren had hit her? Nobody had said. They hadn't been such close friends at the time but Fiona hadn't mentioned it.

Her mum angled back towards the flowerbed, not bothering to disguise the hint. 'Why'd Darren tell you that now?' she asked.

'No reason. We were just talking.'

That got a narrow-eyed squint which made it very clear Jodie's mum didn't believe her. She'd always been a ridiculously good lie detector.

'Did you tell him he should spend more time with the son he has, rather than the child who's not been born yet?'

'Something like that.'

That got a roll of the eyes. The upbringing of Owen was a constant thorn between the two women – and, given the bullying reports, Jodie really didn't want to get into all that again. Then she remembered the line she'd skipped over.

'What did you mean about Dad going too far?'

Her mum had returned to the flowerbeds and casually turned to peer over her shoulder. 'Huh?'

'You said you warned Dad about going too far when he found out about Darren...'

Jodie couldn't quite finish with 'hitting me'.

Her mother was in full breezy mode, eager to get back to her work. 'I could see how angry he was, so I told him not to do anything stupid.'

'But why would you need to say something? I don't remember Dad as the type of person who'd do stupid things.'

They looked to one another, a pace and a mile between

them. Jodie's mother wanted no part of the conversation because she'd rather be working.

'Why are you asking about this now?' she said. Her tone was strict and probing, as if asking who'd drawn on the wall.

'It's just...' Jodie took a breath, puffed out her lips, stared towards the corner of the garden where a pristine wheelbarrow stood, ready to be filled. Who cleaned wheelbarrows?

She barely had conversations with her mother, let alone confided in her. They didn't have that sort of mother-daughter relationship... which is why she might be perfect.

'I found something,' Jodie said, turning back around. Her mother hadn't moved.

'Where? What?'

'I was trying to clear Dad's house and started in the attic. I figured I'd work my way down but there was a box up there, with "KEEP" written on the side. I opened it and...' She tailed off, picturing the shirt.

'And what?'

'And I found Ben's T-shirt in there. The green one he was wearing when he went missing.'

Jodie couldn't quite look at her mother. The silence hung between them. Nothing was said but everything was. Her mother was no longer facing the flowerbeds. She momentarily crossed her arms, almost hugging herself, and then released it.

'Burn it.'

The breeziness of her mother's tone had been replaced by something firm and final. A declaration, not a suggestion. Jodie felt drawn to the piercing stare that was now boring into her.

'Burn it,' her mother repeated. 'And never tell anyone you found it.'

From nowhere, the silence between them felt dangerous.

'Did you know it was there?' Jodie asked.

The reply snapped back almost before Jodie had finished speaking. 'Of course not.'

A lump was in Jodie's throat and she couldn't face her mother any longer. Her world was changing and she couldn't stop it.

'Do you think he... killed Ben?'

The question was out there now. That thought which had been niggling Jodie for four days was finally more than simply a devil on her shoulder.

Her mum waited, waited... *waited* – and then, finally Jodie looked back to her once more. 'Why would you say that?' her mother replied.

'Why would he have the shirt?'

'Any number of reasons. It might not even be the right shirt. It's not as if there's one green shirt in the world.'

She sounded dismissive and annoyed.

'It has the same four-leaf clover on the front, Mum.'

'Lots of things have clovers on the front.'

'It's Ben's shirt, Mum. I know it is.'

That got a huff of annoyance. 'Where is it now?'

The hairs on Jodie's neck raised again. This time the danger wasn't from two men and a knife – it was her own mother. She felt as if she'd missed a large part of the conversation. That she was supposed to know something she didn't.

She'd put the shirt in that pan the night before and held a lighter to it – but she hadn't managed to burn it. She couldn't.

Despite that natural lie detector her mother seemed to have, Jodie couldn't stop herself. She knew she couldn't tell the truth.

'Dad's house,' she said.

'Where in Dad's house? Still in the attic?'

'Why do you want to know?'

Jodie's mum crossed her arms again, which is what she did when she wanted to get her own way. She'd be having a conversation with Jodie's dad about where they should go on a sunny Sunday. Her dad would suggest the coast but her Mum would fold her arms and say it would be too cold.

With no answer coming, other than those folded arms, Jodie took a step away. 'I'm going,' she said. 'I thought you might...' A pause. 'I don't know what I thought.'

TWENTY-FOUR

Jodie stewed at the kitchen table, running through the events of the day. It had unquestionably been a mistake to confide in her mum. She had spent twenty-odd years *not* sharing secrets with her, only to blab about the important one. She wasn't sure what had come over her, other than temporary madness.

It had been that sort of day.

Owen's war game chattered down the stairs and, after the day she'd had, Jodie didn't feel ready to confront him again over what had been said at the school. For once, his dad could do the talking – if he remembered to come over.

Her father's death could have been something to bring together the family but, instead, they were further apart than ever. She'd learned her brother had apparently tried to start a fire, which her dad had covered up. Her mum showed no surprise that the T-shirt belonging to a missing teenager was in her ex-husband's attic. Her son was apparently a bully – and then there was Jodie herself, with her five figures of debt and a series of questions that seemed destined not to be answered.

It occurred that the connecting part in everything was her.

Jodie was in her kitchen, nursing a mug of tea, lost in those dark thoughts, when the doorbell sounded three times in quick succession. She didn't need to answer it to know her ex-husband would be on the other side. He'd always had that annoying habit of pressing buttons three times in rapid sequence. He did it at pelican crossings, or in lifts. A rat-a-tat-tat reflex that he likely didn't know he did but which had always driven Jodie crazy. He did a lot of things like that.

She pushed herself up from the table and headed along the hall. When she opened the door, Darren was thumbing his phone and seemed almost surprised to be interrupted.

'Is he in?' Darren asked.

'Nice to see you too,' Jodie replied.

Darren shrugged his way into the house, not making eye contact as he pocketed his phone. He dealt with things he didn't want to do by trying to avoid them – and then sulking if there was no alternative.

He paused at the bottom of the stairs as Jodie closed the door. 'Do you want to come up with me? We can double-team him.'

'That's exactly what I was trying to avoid.'

Darren sighed and started tapping his foot, trying to come up with another reason to get out of talking to their son by himself. It was the same when Jodie asked him to talk to Owen about shaving when the first wisps of stubble appeared on their son's face. The same when Owen needed to be fitted for his school uniform and she asked Darren to go with him. The same with dozens of things before. Hundreds.

'Shall I call him down, or…?'

'Just go up.'

Darren put a foot on the lowest step, paused, half turned. Jodie could sense the cogs whirring as he continued to look for a way out. She'd ducked out of the same chat for a day – but there was a part of her who always had to be the bad cop to Darren's indifferent cop. For once, she wasn't going to let him wheedle out of it.

Darren took a second step, wavered, then took the third. Jodie was almost enjoying it. Actually, she *was* enjoying it.

Darren stopped on the fourth step, one hand on the banister as he turned back. 'Maybe I should let him finish his game...?'

'If you do that, you'll be here all night – and I don't think either of us want that...'

Darren sighed once again and then took another step. He was out of excuses and stomped the rest of the way up to the landing.

It was easy to see from where Owen got his moodiness.

Jodie waited at the bottom of the stairs as she heard the knock on Owen's door before the sound of it opening. The blather of the game was silenced and then there was Darren's chummy 'all right, mate'. That's how he spoke to anyone male – his son or a randomer at a bus stop.

The door closed, so Jodie headed through to the kitchen and set the kettle boiling again.

She waited. And waited. If she'd been the one to address Owen's bullying, there'd have been two raised voices within seconds, then a full-on shouting match, then a day or two of Owen pretending she didn't exist. Ostracised in her own house by her own son.

There was none of that from above. Instead, three-quarters of an hour later, there were footsteps on the stairs – and then Darren appeared in the kitchen by himself.

'I'm going to get off,' he said.

'How did it go?'

'Fine. We played a bit of Xbox. I showed him that I know how to use a joypad.'

Jodie could feel an all too familiar sinking feeling. 'Did you even ask about the bullying?'

Darren took his car keys from his pocket, dropping the hint with the subtlety of an imploding building. 'A bit.'

'What does that mean?'

Darren and Owen had the exact same shrug – except it was more annoying when the grown man did it. 'I didn't want it to seem like we were ganging up on him, so I tried to be a bit softly-softly.'

Jodie clenched her fist tightly, digging her nails into her palm. 'How is it ganging up when it was just you in the room? *You* were supposed to do the talking.'

'It didn't feel right.'

'So what *did* you do...?'

'I said he should be careful about who he's hanging around with.'

'Is that it?'

Darren passed his car keys from one hand to the other and nodded towards the front door. 'I really do need to get off.'

'You just spent forty-five minutes playing Xbox.'

'I don't know what you want me to say. You wanted me to talk to him, so I talked to him.'

Darren took a couple of steps into the hall.

'You talked about the new baby, didn't you?' Jodie asked.

'So what? It'll be his half-brother or sister.'

Jodie was on her feet now. 'Just go. I knew I should've done this myself. All you had to do was find out what's been going on with the bullying. Try to make sure it ends now. Instead, you had to remind our son – again – that there's going to be a new child along any day who'll get way more attention than you've ever given him.'

If Darren had denied it instantly, Jodie might have even been tempted to believe him. He didn't, of course. He knew she was right. In the end, this was the argument to which they always returned.

'I need to go,' Darren said. 'Text if you need something else.'

Jodie followed her ex-husband along the hall and just about stopped herself from slamming the door behind him. Darren was the bloke who got asked to wash up, so did it badly enough that he'd never be asked again. Except he used that method for parenting.

She waited at the bottom of the stairs, wondering if she should follow up with Owen and try to talk about the bullying again. The problem was that, as Darren had apparently mentioned it in passing, it really *would* seem like them ganging up on him if Jodie went upstairs to ask about it. Plus, Darren knew what he was doing. He'd gone soft on their son, so if Jodie had to add anything else, she'd be the bad cop.

Feeling useless, she headed through to the living room and switched on the television. She flitted between channels, not taking in any of it. She exchanged some texts with Fiona, who was yet to have her own conversation about leaving her husband, and then kicked off her slippers and lay on the sofa.

She blinked and the drama on the screen had turned into the news. Another blink and it was some after-midnight talk show where everyone argued with everyone else. The room was dark, with flickering bluey light dancing in the corners.

Another blink and the news was on again.

Another blink and it was dark.

One more, and...

A knocking echoed through her dreams, bringing her back to her living room. Darren was there again with his stupid triple knock that drove her mad.

Knock-knock. Knock-knock.

She wanted him to go away... except it wasn't a triple knock. There were two gentle thumps – and then two more.

Jodie rolled over and almost slipped onto the floor from the seat of the sofa. Her neck and back ached as she oohed and aahed her way to her feet.

Knock-knock. Knock-knock.

The clock underneath the TV read 04:51 and Jodie dragged herself through the house into the hallway. The street light on the front pavement was illuminating the silhouette of someone standing at the front door. She edged past the stairs, closer to the front. Whatever it was, this couldn't be good news.

'Who is it?' Jodie's voice echoed hauntingly around the empty hall.

The man's voice crept eerily through the door. 'It's the police, Ms Parker.'

TWENTY-FIVE

'I can pass my ID through the letterbox if you want to check...?'

Until the man said that, the thought hadn't occurred to Jodie that she shouldn't open the door.

The letterbox clanged and a leather two-fold wallet plopped onto the mat. Inside, there was some sort of police seal, next to a card that had 'police officer' in capital letters, alongside a man's photo and warrant number. Jodie checked it over – but there was no way she'd know a genuine police ID card from a fake.

'Has something happened?' she asked.

The same man's voice seeped through the door, haunting and solemn. 'There's been a fire.'

It jolted Jodie into action. She unlatched the door and pulled it inwards. A man in a police uniform was standing on the doorstep, with a second officer sitting in a car on the road beyond.

The officer was immediately all business. 'I believe the house belongs to your father,' he added. 'Or perhaps *belonged*.'

There was a noise from behind her and Jodie turned to see a

sleepy-looking Owen standing on the bottom step. He was wearing boxer shorts and a raggedy T-shirt.

'Mum...?'

'Everyone's fine,' she told him. 'There's been a fire at Granddad's house.'

'A fire...?'

His confusion echoed Jodie's own as she turned back to the officer. 'Are Mr and Mrs Vickery safe? Jim and Elaine? They live next door.'

'As far as I'm aware, everyone is fine. You know better than me but I believe the house was empty – and nobody else was affected.'

Jodie felt a surge of relief. 'What do you want me to do?'

'That's up to you – but if you want to follow us over, we're heading there now.'

Jodie turned back to Owen, who was still on the stairs. 'Go back to bed,' she said. 'If I'm not home in time, make sure you're not late for school.'

There was no arguing as he fought away a yawn. 'Whatever.'

Police cars were blocking either end of the street when Jodie arrived in convoy behind the patrol car. The marked vehicle slowed next to the one doing the blocking and the officers exchanged words through the wound-down windows, until Jodie was waved through.

Two fire engines were outside Jodie's dad's house, with floods of water pooling on the road outside, dribbling towards the drains. There was no obvious fire but the air smelled of burnt toast – and every other house either had someone standing outside or watching from the windows.

Jodie had half expected her father's house to be a smouldering ruin – but the slanted shape of the roof glimmered in the orangey glow of the street light and everything appeared intact. The only sign of things not being right was the lack of a front door and the charcoal stains on the surrounding brickwork.

As she neared the house, a thickset man wearing a fluorescent tabard over the top of a heavy dark coat approached. He asked if she owned the house and after stumbling over saying it was her dad's, before remembering she *did* own it, the man explained he was the fire investigation officer. Jodie nervously joked about him starting work early, though neither of them laughed.

'You're really lucky,' he said, nodding towards Elaine and Jim's house, where lights were on downstairs. 'If the person who tried to start the fire knew what they were doing, both houses could've gone up.'

Jodie was no expert but, even to her own eyes, the charred brickwork around the front door made it seem obvious someone had tried to burn down the house, starting at the front.

'Did someone do this deliberately?' she asked.

'Looks like someone poured something through the letterbox and then tried to set it on fire. It didn't catch for whatever reason, though it made a lot of smoke – and you'll need a new door.' He paused a beat. 'Your welcome mat is a goner.'

Jodie pictured the locksmith who'd already visited twice. She had to stop herself from laughing at the prospect of bringing him back a third time. She should ask for a bulk discount. Either that or get him on retainer, as he'd suggested. It was laugh or despair.

'At least nobody was hurt,' Jodie found herself saying. The same sort of weak, meaningless platitudes people had been saying to her ever since her father died. *Nice day for it,* and all that. When something bad happened, all the cliches came out.

'It's a bit early to knock on doors,' the fire officer said, 'but enough people are up and out of their houses anyway. We've been asking if anyone saw anything – but it's all very premature at the moment.' He nodded at Elaine and Jim's place again. 'Your neighbours called 999 because they smelled smoke but they didn't see anyone.' He stopped to cough and then added, 'Good job your neighbour has a weak bladder.'

'Huh?'

'He said he only got up for a wee – which is when he smelled smoke through the bathroom window. There's a chance him turning on the light is what disturbed whoever tried to set the fire. That weak bladder might've saved his life.'

Jodie thought on that for a second – picturing the scene if the semi-detached property really *had* burned down, with Jim and Elaine asleep on their side. The horror...

She blinked it away. 'Someone forced the back window a few days ago,' Jodie said.

This got the officer's attention. He had been looking in the vague direction of the house but spun to face her. 'You had a break-in?'

'Maybe. I don't think anything was taken.'

'Did you report it?'

Jodie squirmed under his gaze. 'I didn't see the point in wasting the police's time. Nothing was missing and I got the window fixed.'

She felt as if he might scold her for this but, instead, he turned back towards the house. 'It might not be connected. Sounds like lots of people knew the house was empty...'

He didn't phrase it like a question but, when he glanced sideways to Jodie, she found herself answering him.

'It was Dad's funeral at the weekend. Loads of people were there and it was in the paper and on the internet. If people knew where he lived, they could've guessed it was empty.'

The officer considered that for a few seconds. He had the unflappable look of a man who has the same expression in any number of official photographs. Birth, death, or marriage, he'd be there, face-front, without a flicker of emotion.

'The official verdict won't be in for a while,' he said.

'Is someone more likely to burn down an empty house than an occupied one...?'

Jodie didn't get an answer. 'We'll knock on some doors when the sun comes up,' he replied. 'It'll be easier to see a few things around here once it's light.'

'Can I go inside?'

A shake of the head. 'Not yet. You might be better going to get a coffee and coming back – or going home to get some sleep. We'll let you know when it's safe.' He batted away a yawn and then reached into one of his inner pockets before passing across a card. 'My number's on that. I'll take yours and let you know when we can allow you in.' Another pause and then, 'Unless there's something else you want to say...?'

Jodie hovered for a moment, thinking of Keith in his cottage, saying that her brother was a failed arsonist – and that her father had covered it up. But if she mentioned that, she'd be starting something that couldn't be stopped. There was only Keith's notes to say Mike had tried to set a fire – and, if the investigators looked into him about this new failed arson – and he had a perfectly good alibi – he'd know Jodie had given them his name. She couldn't see any way their brother-sister relationship could survive that.

Plus, did she *really* believe it was him? Not really.

Fire was defining her life.

'No,' she said. 'I'll wait for your call and see you later.'

TWENTY-SIX

Jodie thought about returning home to sit in her kitchen and wait for the call. The only reason she didn't was that she was as certain as could be that Owen had gone back to bed. Waking him up for no reason didn't seem particularly fair – and he was more than capable of getting himself up and walking to school. When the garden centre was busy around Christmas, she worked early mornings and he'd done it then.

Instead, Jodie drove to Fry's and sat in a booth by herself. The 'big breakfast' was somehow the smallest on offer, with meals increasing through 'bigger', 'biggest', 'gigantic' and 'colossal'. Jodie ordered the 'big' and then poked around her plate, feeling guilty about the calories. Around her, truckers and drivers chatted to each other, or sat and read the papers as they inhaled their food. Jodie was halfway through her meal when she realised she was the only female customer.

She poked at her egg with the tip of her toast and dragged it around the plate, making more of a mess. Her stomach gurgled from the mass of fat and because she wasn't used to being up at this time of the morning, let alone eating.

She wanted to sleep. She could feel her thoughts

chuntering sluggishly into each other. She'd struggled to rest since finding that shirt in her father's attic. Perhaps even since his death itself. She had technically slept well last night – but it had been on the uncomfortable sofa and then she'd been awoken by the police officer at the door. Her neck ached and so did her back. It had been one thing after another for weeks.

'I think that's your phone...'

Jodie blinked up to the lad who was cleaning the tables. She must have dozed off momentarily because her fork was in her lap, yellowy-white egg yolk was drizzled across the table – and, as he was pointing out, her bag was buzzing.

She thanked him and retrieved her phone from her bag, managing to answer the unknown number moments before it rang off.

It was, unsurprisingly, the fire officer – who said they were ready for her back at the house. She picked up the fork from her lap and put it back on the table. She'd eaten barely half of the food and her stomach was gurgling its disapproval.

'I'll be right there,' she said.

Her dad's house somehow looked both better and worse in the crisp morning daylight. From the pavement at the end of the path, it could easily be the case that the front door was open. It was only from closer that it became clearer that there was no front door – and that the black marks around the frame had been licked by flames.

The other clue was that the twisted, partially melted, remains of the door were leaning against the fence at the side.

The fire officer explained that the house was 'structurally sound' and that officers had left the top windows open to help clear the smell. He said Jodie might need a dehumidifier to clear the water from the hall but that everything else should be safe enough. He also pointed out the obvious in that she'd need a new front door.

With that, he said he'd be in touch – and then left her to it.

Jodie's shoes squelched as she entered the unguarded front of the house. The carpet would definitely need replacing – as would the wallpaper in the immediate area around the door.

She took off her shoes and left them at the front – and, within a few steps, everything was more or less as it was. Her father's photos and pictures still hung on the wall untouched and the only real difference was the lingering smell of something being left in the oven for too long.

Jodie moved into the kitchen, where the newly replaced window was open and a stinging breeze was filtering through.

She felt so tired. So unable to process the way one incomprehensible thing had happened after the other for what felt like weeks.

She'd changed the locks, meaning family members could no longer let themselves into the house. And then, hours after telling her mum about Ben's shirt being inside, someone had clumsily attempted to burn the house down. All that happened a short time after someone actually *had* tried – and possibly succeeded – in getting through the back window.

That was all something for the future. In the moment, Jodie took out her phone and scrolled through her recent calls. She was in danger of becoming a stalker...

The locksmith slid open the door to his van and wrestled a new door from the back. He lowered it onto the pavement and then nodded towards the house. 'Is this all right?' he asked. 'I can get you something different if you prefer? You said anything normal and white on the phone.'

The door chosen by the locksmith was standard uPVC, with rippled glass across the upper half. Jodie had no particular preference because a door was a door. This was closest to the one that had been damaged overnight.

'It's fine,' she said.

He looked towards her curiously. 'Are you sure everything's all right? I'm not complaining – but I've never had so much repeat business from one person.'

She laughed gently. 'I think it's because the house is empty. Things keep happening.'

That got a snort. 'You can say that again.' His phone started ringing from his back pocket but he ignored it. 'I'll do the door at cost and only charge you labour. You're basically keeping me in business by yourself.'

Jodie thanked him and said she'd make him some tea while he worked. By the time the kettle had boiled, he was already sanding part of the old frame, ready to fit the new one.

Jodie used some towels to soak up much of the water from the hall and, though it was still damp, it no longer squelched underfoot. After that, she left the locksmith to work, while she pottered around the house, vaguely piling up a few things that could probably go in bin bags.

Her heart wasn't in any of it. It was hard to consider whether it was worth keeping her father's old branded beer glasses when someone had tried to set fire to the house barely hours before. Possibly, or perhaps *probably*, someone she knew.

Time passed, bin bags were filled, and then the locksmith called her through to the front of the house.

'See you on Monday?' he said, dusting down his front with a hint of a laugh.

'More like Saturday,' Jodie replied.

He picked up his bag of tools and beckoned her to follow before he showed her that the door opened and closed. That done, he passed across yet more keys. She was building a collection.

Jodie thanked him again. 'Don't take this the wrong way,' she said. 'But I really hope I never see you again.'

That got a much bigger laugh than she expected, though the moment was quickly lost as his phone started to ring once more. It rarely seemed to stop.

He ignored it and was packing his tools back into his vehicle as a green van pulled up in front. Jodie was still on the path and stopped to watch as her brother got out of his work van and headed across to her.

'I just heard,' he said, nodding towards the house. 'Why didn't you call?'

'How did you hear?' Jodie replied.

'Someone on Facebook. Sam saw it and called me at work.'

Something must have twitched in Jodie's expression, probably an involuntary eye roll.

'She was concerned!'

'Concerned that she wouldn't be able to cheat her way to grabbing half the house.'

Mike let out a low breath. 'I've told her to leave you alone.'

'Fat chance of that. She said she's going to sue me.'

'I'm trying to stop all that. You'll have to leave it with me.'

Jodie purposefully rolled her eyes this time – though anything she was going to say was drowned out by a solid toot-toot from the locksmith's van as he beeped his horn and waved his way off down the street.

Mike watched him go and then offered Jodie a curious look. 'Who's that?' he asked.

'He's basically turning into one of my best friends.'

Jodie didn't bother following that up as Mike gazed past her towards the house. The new door shone bright and white, though it was offset against the blackened brickwork.

'What happened?' he asked.

'Someone tried to set the place on fire.'

He continued staring and sounded slightly disbelieving. 'Why?'

'How would I know?'

That didn't get a reply. 'What did the police say?'

'The fire guy said more or less what I just did. Someone tried to set the house on fire – but they didn't succeed.' She turned to him. 'Good job whoever it was is a total failure.'

She wondered if there'd be a reaction – except Mike was watching the house, not her, and his expression didn't change. She couldn't stop thinking about what Keith had told her about Mike starting a fire at the council offices.

'Why *this* house?' Mike asked.

'Because people know it's empty? I don't know. The police were going door to door and the fire investigators took a load of photos. I suppose I'll hear back at some point.' Jodie motioned towards the house. 'I've got to go,' she fibbed. 'Thanks for checking in.'

Mike apparently wasn't ready to go himself. 'What happens now?' he asked.

'I told you. They're investigating and I'll hear back.'

'Is there insurance?'

Jodie hadn't thought of that. Her father would have had some sort of buildings and contents policy – but, as far as she knew, it hadn't transferred into her name. She'd certainly not set up anything herself. It was one more thing to look into.

'I sorted the door and there's no real extra cost for now. Everything smells a bit but it could've been worse. I might have to replace the carpets in the hall.'

Mike opened his mouth to say something – and then seemingly decided against it. They stood together as brother and sister, looking at the house in which they had grown up. They'd fought in the way brothers and sisters did – but there had been good times too. More good than bad, especially when they were really young. They'd played *Buckaroo* and *Operation* with each other, then, when they were a little older, there were those original PlayStation games. That was when the idea of playing online against someone else seemed like some sort of magic. They'd even shared Lego back in the day.

It seemed incomprehensible that Mike could have set fire to the shed, knowing she was inside. Incomprehensible and yet, after that chat with Keith, suddenly not impossible.

'I didn't find your medals,' Jodie said, trying to keep things friendly. 'I looked earlier, when I was clearing some of the kitchen and living room – but there was no sign.'

Mike took a moment to reply, almost as if he'd forgotten about the war medals he'd asked for days before. 'I think they used to be in Dad's bureau,' he said.

The front door was still open and Jodie poked a thumb towards it. 'That's the first place I checked but they weren't there. We can look together, if you want?'

'I thought you had to go?'

'I've got five minutes.'

They headed into the house together for what was probably the first time since they were teenagers and they'd accidentally get home from school at the same time. Jodie closed the new door and followed her brother through to the living room, where the bureau had sat in the back corner for as long as Jodie had known. It was heavy and old-fashioned, from before the days when everything was flat-packed.

Mike opened the drawers and began to sort through the same pens and pads Jodie had when she'd looked. Their father's birth certificate, passport and paper driving licence sat in the same pile she'd made – but there was little else of interest, except for the cheap tin medals on the red, white and blue ribbons, which Mike didn't bother to pick up.

'They'll be somewhere,' he said. 'No rush. It's not as if Dad's stuff is going anywhere.'

Jodie took a moment, wondering if it was a dig. Some of his

stuff clearly *was* going to either the tip or the charity shop. It didn't feel as if there was an edge to the remark and, when Mike didn't follow up, she figured he was simply saying he would wait.

They turned to leave together, Mike a step ahead as they moved through the house towards the front. It had been a strange few minutes. There had been a lot Jodie had stopped herself from saying – and she had the sense it had been the same for Mike.

It was when she was locking up that she realised he was hovering a step too close. 'I guess they had to change the locks,' he said.

'That's what happens when you get a new door.'

Jodie didn't mention that it was the *second* recent change. She wondered if he already knew.

'Are you going to give me a key?' He held out a hand, half expectantly, as Jodie finally managed to lock it. She had three new keys attached to the same ring – and it was obvious her brother had seen.

'Why do you want one?' she asked.

That got a curious mix of frown and confusion. 'Because I've always had one.'

'It's not Dad's house any more.'

Jodie had meant to sound firm and decisive – and she had – but it still was shocking to hear the words from her own mouth. An acceptance that their father was gone and not coming back, that his house was hers. That she could do what she wanted.

They stood a pace apart – and yet it was so much further.

Mike slowly withdrew his hand and scratched his arse, as if that's what he'd been meaning to do all along.

'Fair point,' he said.

It was only two words and yet the hurt was unmistakeable. In the instant afterwards, Jodie felt so bad, she almost handed across a key.

She didn't, though.

'I should get off,' Mike said.

'Me too.'

'See y'around, I guess.'

Jodie nodded and waited for him to step away. He was blocking the path, after all. When he finally moved, there was a reluctance about his step. Something unsaid, or perhaps unseen. Jodie wondered whether he really *had* heard about the fire from Facebook, or if he already knew. Whether he'd turned up to check out the aftermath of his failed attempt to burn down the house. She couldn't think of an obvious motive. Even if he knew, or *thought* he knew, Ben's shirt was inside, it seemed extreme.

Jodie made a point of dropping all three keys into her bag. Making sure he saw. 'See y'around,' she said.

TWENTY-SEVEN

Jodie sat in her car and waited for Mike to roar off in his van. Once he'd gone, she got back out and walked the same route around the street as she had the day before. When she reached the house that had the camera pointing at the front door, she rang the bell.

An irritated 'hang on' echoed from the inside and then there was a series of bumps and bangs until the door was wrenched open. The same woman as from Jodie's previous visit stood in the frame and, though she wasn't cradling a child second time around, there was a greeny-brown stain on her top.

'Oh,' she said, blinking towards Jodie. 'I forgot you were coming back today.'

Jodie needed a moment to remember that she'd first been to the house the day before. It felt as if days had passed.

'Is everything all right over there?' the woman added, poking a thumb backwards. 'I saw some spinning lights and someone said there was a fire. I didn't see anything...'

'Nothing major,' Jodie replied, not wanting to get into details. 'But I was wondering if your son managed to look at the camera footage...?'

'He did. It was a bit annoying, actually. I've been telling him it's all overkill, that nothing ever happens here – and then you come over and ask for his footage. He couldn't believe his luck when I asked if he'd got anything.'

She stepped back into the house and said something over her shoulder that Jodie didn't catch. There was a small unit of drawers inside the hall and she opened the top drawer, then fished around for a few moments. When she turned back, she handed Jodie a white envelope.

'He left this for you,' she said.

The front of the envelope had a lengthy Google Drive web address written on the front in neat capital letters.

'I made him print it tidily,' she added. 'There's no way you'd have been able to read his regular handwriting. The college are always going on about how bad it is. He said it would be easier to email you – but I didn't know how to get in contact. Anyway, hopefully it's what you want.'

Jodie asked the woman to thank her son and it was only once the door was closed that she realised she didn't know either of their names. She was at the end of their road, turning back towards her dad's house and her car, when curiosity got the better of her. She sat on a low wall and typed the web address carefully into her phone's browser. It took a few seconds for the page to load and, when it did, it revealed a gallery of stills from the camera. Each was date- and time-stamped, spread across around twenty minutes from the night the window was broken. The night vision of the camera displayed everything in a greeny grey – but the quality was as if a professional had been filming from metres away.

Jodie clicked from photo to photo as everything was documented.

It *had* been a break-in – and there was only one perpetrator. It had happened as the locksmith had said. Someone had come armed with something that was probably a crowbar, which had been jammed into the small gap where the window was only half locked. By the next photo in the sequence, the window was hanging open. One more picture and an arse was on display as the person headed into the house. They were inside for seventeen minutes until they came out the same way they'd gone in.

The penultimate picture had a perfect freeze frame of the person who'd broken into her dad's house – and Jodie knew precisely who it was.

TWENTY-EIGHT

Jodie was sitting on her sofa, scrolling through the Google Drive photos in an endless loop. Each time she hit the final two shots – each with a view of the intruder perfect enough to take to the police – she'd go back to the beginning and start again.

Seventeen minutes. She wondered what had happened inside the house during that time.

The list of awkward conversations she needed to have was growing, though she was in half a mind to take the photos to the police and let them deal with it. She went through lengthy scenarios in her mind of how it would be better in the end – even though she knew she wouldn't do it.

Couldn't.

It wasn't only that talking to the police would start a chain of events she wouldn't be able to control, it was that her past experience with them had left her wary.

The older she'd got, the more she'd understood how odd the investigation into Ben's disappearance had been. There was a big part of her that wished she'd never mentioned Paul McIntosh's van because, as soon as she had, that's all they seemed to focus on. They went over and over that view she'd had of the van in the church car park. They made her draw the route she and Ben had taken on a map. They'd asked questions as to whether she or Ben had even been in contact with McIntosh. Whether they knew him. They'd asked if she'd actually seen him on the afternoon Ben had gone missing and, when she said they hadn't, they'd asked her to think and think – as if that would help. She had insisted she *hadn't* seen McIntosh that day – and only vaguely knew who he was. As far as she knew, she'd never spoken a word to him – and neither had Ben.

Then traces of Ben had inexplicably turned up in McIntosh's van and that was the end of it. The police dug up the fields around his farm but found nothing. Later, there had been a campaign for McIntosh to tell everyone where Ben's body was buried – except he always denied it was him, even after conviction.

When Jodie was a teenager, it felt simple and straightforward. Of course it was McIntosh. Now, well into her thirties, it felt a bit... simplistic. A bit obvious. It had been tickling the edges of her thoughts long before she knew McIntosh had been released and certainly ahead of her seeing him. It had niggled away before she had found that shirt in her father's attic.

She wondered if anyone else had the same doubts.

And then she was back in her living room, those Google Drive pictures in front of her, still worrying about the police twenty years on.

A knock on the door distracted her. She put down her phone on the arm of the sofa and headed through to the front door. Fiona was there, a duffel bag in each hand.

'I was hoping you were home,' she said.

'What's happened?'

'I've left Robbie. I was hoping I could stay a few nights...'

TWENTY-NINE

Jodie took a bag and led Fiona into the house. They almost immediately headed back outside for Fiona to have a smoke. She fiddled with her lighter, swore because the ignition fuel was used up, and then borrowed the wand lighter next to Jodie's cooker to set it going. They stood together, Fiona smoking, Jodie not, as they had so many times over the years. Jodie had been so engulfed in her own issues, she found herself anticipating hearing about someone else's.

'What happened?' Jodie asked.

Fiona sucked on the cigarette and let a long plume out into the air. It felt as if she'd been anticipating the moment as well. It was likely Jodie was the first person she was telling.

'We had a big argument,' she said. 'Robbie got in at half-one last night and sat up smoking weed in the kitchen. It stank so bad it woke me up. I came down and told him to pack it in. He slept on the sofa but then woke up at about ten in a foul mood. The kitchen still stank and I suppose that was the final straw.'

Jodie laughed gently. 'I thought last week was the final straw, when he went to the pub and left the front door open.'

'I'd almost forgotten that.' Fiona slumped a little. 'I finally told him that we're done and he has a month to find somewhere else to live.'

'How did he take that?'

Fiona took two puffs before replying. It felt as if she was fighting away a yawn, even though there was a degree of relief as well.

'He stomped off and said he was going to the pub. That was about an hour ago and I doubt he'll be back 'til later. I packed a few things because I can't bear to share the same space with him. That's why I'm here. I was hoping I can stop for a few nights. Maybe a week at most. I told him a month but I'm hoping he'll end up with one of his mates sooner than that. If he's still there next month, I'll go back and start doing his packing for him. I'll dump it out front if need be.'

Jodie doubted it would come to that. She'd known Fiona a long time and, though they weren't friends as such, she'd known Robbie for almost as long. They were another couple who'd met at school and ended up together years later. The town was full of the same. Internet dating had nothing on sitting behind someone in maths class. Robbie had been one of those boys who always seemed to be in the middle of trouble. Never the leader, never the worst – and yet, if anything bad happened, he was somehow connected. Even though they'd been friends a long time, Jodie had never been quite sure what Fiona had seen in Robbie – although it was also true that Fiona probably didn't know what Jodie had seen in Darren.

Fiona finished the cigarette and nodded towards the house. After making them both tea, Jodie sat with her friend in the living room and listened to the list of grievances she'd heard before. She ummed and aahed. She said things like 'I don't blame you' and 'That's ridiculous' in all the right places, even though her own problems continued to dominate her thoughts.

Fiona and Robbie had been on holiday the month before which – for Fiona at least – had been 'make or break'. It had ended up as 'break' after Robbie made a fuss at the airport when they wanted to charge him for his bag being over the limit. There were arguments with the woman checking them in and more again with a stewardess on the plane.

On the holiday itself, they'd argued over where to eat, how much he drank, how late they stayed out, and an apparently limitless amount of other things.

The holiday story was interrupted by the front door opening and closing with its usual force and bluster when Owen was involved. Jodie was on her feet and in the hall before he reached the stairs, much to her son's surprise. He'd been looking at his phone and almost bumped into Jodie as she appeared in front of him.

'What happened with the fire?' he asked.

Jodie had forgotten that she'd left him to take himself to school that morning. The last time he'd seen her was with the police officer at the front door.

'The investigators are still looking into it,' Jodie replied. 'I had to get a new front door fitted, but everything else is fine.'

He looked to her somewhat blankly for a moment before glancing towards the stairs.

'We need to talk,' Jodie said.

'What about?'

'Things. I'll be up later.' She motioned towards the living room. 'Fiona's going to be staying with us for a few nights. She'll be in the spare room.'

He frowned slightly. 'Why?'

'She and Robbie are having a few problems.'

The eye roll wasn't entirely unexpected. Fiona had stopped over for odd nights in the past and it usually followed arguments with Robbie.

'He's got the new Warzone,' Owen said.

'The new what?'

'Robbie's got the new Warzone.'

'Is that a game?'

Owen smirked, though not necessarily unkindly, and Jodie suddenly felt very old. It was almost as bad as the time she'd unwisely described something as 'lit'. Owen had laughed about that for an entire weekend.

'Yes, Mum,' he replied, humouring her.

'How'd you know Robbie has that?'

Owen shrugged, which was an answer of sorts. In the years after Jodie's separation from Darren, she'd spent plenty of time at Fiona's house. That meant Owen had spent time playing video games with Robbie. It hadn't quite been a father-son relationship but was something more like an uncle-nephew. Robbie was the sort who'd give Owen too much chocolate or crisps – and then say he thought it would be fine. One time, Jodie and Fiona had gone out and Robbie said he'd keep an eye on Owen. He'd ended up showing him an eighteen-rated slasher movie, when Owen was barely eleven. That was the only time he babysat – and Jodie had spent less and less time at her friend's house when she knew Robbie would be there. It seemed clear Owen and Robbie were still in contact in some way.

Back in the hallway, Owen made another move for the stairs.

'We still need to talk,' Jodie said.

'Fine.'

Jodie let him pass and he stomped his way upstairs with the usual rhino-like elegance. She'd barely sat back in the living room when the rumble of his game started to drill through the ceiling.

Fiona glanced up with a half-smirk on her face.

'How is he?' she asked.

It was too big a question for Jodie to answer in the moment. She didn't particularly want to think about what was going on with her son – although she wouldn't be able to put it off for much longer.

Jodie said Owen was fine and quickly switched the conversation back to what was going on with Fiona. The mix of reminiscing and commiserating soon led to Fiona's suggestion of opening a bottle of wine.

There was a four-quid bottle of Tesco rosé in the fridge, which Jodie opened as she cooked some chicken for the three of them. Owen took his tea to his room, leaving the two women downstairs.

They had long since moved on from talk of Robbie, instead chatting about the town in general. Anything that meant they could each avoid talk of their respective issues.

The wine helped.

They watched TV together. They laughed and switched off. Jodie had said she'd talk to Owen that evening – but she left him in his room, playing his games. Another day gone without having the serious conversation they needed to have. It was easier to snack and drink and pretend everything was fine. She couldn't shake the fear that, no matter when she did it or what she said, she'd never get through to him. Or that she'd make it worse.

It had gone quiet in Owen's room when Jodie went upstairs to make up the spare bed for Fiona. The third bedroom had only been used by Fiona in the years since Jodie had moved in. It still had the grimy plain wallpaper from when she'd moved in and, as well as the IKEA bed, there were various boxes of things she'd never unpacked. They'd been in the spare room for so long that Jodie couldn't remember what was in most of them. She had a vague idea of redecorating and moving into it herself, then redoing the room in which she slept presently.

Like so many things, it had been delayed and part forgotten.

After leaving Fiona in the room, Jodie crossed the hall and nudged open the door to Owen's room. The TV and lights were off, leaving only a vague glow seeping around the curtains from the street light outside. Owen was in his bed, facing away from the door, one arm hanging limply from the covers. She'd blinked and he'd gone from baby to toddler to teenager.

It was the wine, she knew that, but she suddenly had to gulp away the tears that felt close. It was hard to think of him as enough of an adult for them to have the grown-up conversation that was needed.

And it *was* needed.

For more reasons than one.

THIRTY

Jodie was dozing when the banging echoed and blundered into her dreams. The clock next to her bedside read a little after two thirty in the morning as there was suddenly quiet. She was sitting up in her bed, not quite remembering how she got into the position, wondering if she'd dreamed the noise. She tended to be all or nothing when it came to sleep. Either easily awoken by the merest sound half a mile away – or so out of it, she'd sleep through a meteor strike.

She was still trying to figure out what had happened when the thumping started a second time. It was coming from downstairs and she tingled with déjà vu at the familiarity of when she'd been asleep on the sofa and the police had been at the door.

It was chilly outside the covers and Jodie stumbled onto the landing while fighting a yawn. The banging had stopped again as the door at the other end of the hall opened. Fiona emerged, eyelids heavy, her hair fuzzy and static.

'Sorry,' she said.

'What for?'

'Robbie.'

Jodie led the way down the stairs as the banging started again. It came in short bursts and at different volumes, probably a mixture of fists and feet. Everything had again gone quiet when Jodie opened the door, while leaving the chain attached.

Fiona's husband stood a pace away, arm raised as if about to start thumping on the door for a fourth time. As the door caught against the chain, he swayed on the spot, blinking quickly as he tried to take in what was happening.

'Where is she?' he managed. His voice was a slurred half cough.

Jodie looked over her shoulder to realise Fiona was no longer a step behind. Instead, she was sitting near the bottom of the stairs, out of sight from the slim gap between the front door and the frame.

'She'll talk to you when she's ready,' Jodie said.

'Tell her I wanna talk to her now.'

'Go home, Robbie. You can barely stand.'

He opened his mouth to say something but ended up slipping off the path onto the strip of lawn. The drop was a couple of centimetres at most – but he wobbled like a novice on a unicycle. For a moment, it looked as if he was about to topple over but he managed to right himself, even though he ended up standing at an angle.

Robbie was a little further away from the door but his toxic beer breath was still like an invading army.

'Fee!' he shouted.

'If you don't leave, I'll call the police.'

'Pfft.' Robbie's own puff of air was suddenly hilarious to him as he started giggling. He swayed from side to side and then stopped rigidly as he tried to focus on Jodie. His mouth hung open, eyes almost closed. 'I wanna have my say. I—'

Robbie cut himself off as he stumbled again, this time slipping onto the path and somehow managing to do half a cartwheel as he attempted to regain his balance. There was a bone-crunching snap as he ended up on his back, neck drooped over the edge of the path.

It was largely against her better judgement that Jodie released the chain to open the door fully. She stepped outside barefooted as Robbie groaned to himself. His eyes had rolled back into his head and his tongue flopped out of his mouth.

'Are you all right?'

Jodie stood a couple of steps away, unsure if she could help him up even if she wanted.

'Just, er...'

Robbie was on the ground, doing an impression of an upside-down turtle, apparently unable to figure out which way was up.

Jodie was almost ready to crouch and see if she could help when someone breezed past her. It took her a second to realise it was Owen, who was barefooted in a T-shirt and boxers. He crouched next to Robbie and then gripped his hand before helping him into a sitting position.

'You all right?' Owen asked.

Robbie's head bobbed back and forth, his eyes zigzagging as he tried to focus on his saviour.

'Good. You?' It was a ludicrous response, given his predicament – though Jodie was a bystander as her son helped Robbie back to his feet and brushed the grit from his front.

'D'you need a hand getting home?' Owen asked.

'Naw, mate. I'm good.' Robbie suddenly sounded coherent, though there remained a hint of a slur. 'Did I show you my gaming chair? You should come over.'

'Yeah, I'll—'

Owen stopped himself, perhaps realising the extent of the atmosphere. He stepped away from Robbie and around Jodie before wiping his feet on the mat inside and disappearing into the darkness of the house.

Robbie was no longer swaying. If it wasn't for the dirt on his palms and graze on his temple, he'd seem himself. 'Tell Fiona I wanna see her,' he said.

'I think banging on the door at half two in the morning gave her a clue.'

Robbie didn't get the sarcasm. He stared blearily towards Jodie, then turned and started to walk away, with only a hint of unsteadiness. As soon as he was off the path, Jodie stepped inside and locked the door. She crouched and brushed the dust from the soles of her feet before turning to see Fiona still sitting on the stairs.

'Sorry,' Fiona said quietly.

'It's not your fault.'

'I should've come out to help...'

Owen was standing a few stairs above Fiona, leaning on the banister.

'What was that all about?' Jodie asked him.

'Sounded like you needed some help.'

'I meant the talk about gaming chairs?'

A shrug. 'Dunno.'

Jodie eyed her son for a couple of seconds, sensing that she'd missed something. She didn't feel quite able to challenge him on it, mainly because she wasn't sure what she would've done without him. It wasn't so much *what* Robbie had said, more the familiarity with which he said it. As if he and Owen were used to hanging around with one another.

'Thanks for trying to help,' she said.

Owen didn't want the praise. He mumbled something to himself, then turned quickly and blundered his way upstairs with the usual grace.

Fiona remained sitting, head slumped towards her knees. 'Sorry,' she repeated. 'It's not your fault.'

'I should've known he'd come here.'

'Still not your fault.'

Fiona stooped a little lower, burying a hand in her hair and scratching her scalp. 'It's not fair to put you in the middle.' She looked up. 'What if *he* wants some of the house?'

It was a simple, almost obvious, statement – and yet Jodie suddenly felt as if a puzzle had been completed. When she and Darren had separated, they owned very little. There'd been no need for a formal document stating who got what because there was no house or car. Fiona and Robbie lived in the house where Fiona had grown up. She'd inherited it after her parents died and, aside from short periods, had lived there her whole life. She'd remained with him far past the point she wanted because she was worried he'd want half that house. This was home-owning in the twenty-first century. A series of hand-me-downs and divorce settlements decided who lived where because nobody at the bottom of the pyramid scheme could afford to buy. That's why Jodie herself suddenly owned the house in which she'd grown up, even though she didn't think she'd be able to live there.

Jodie remained at the bottom of the stairs for a moment before she nodded Fiona towards the kitchen. Once they were inside, she closed the door and stood for a few seconds, listening for any noise upstairs. A short silence passed before she turned back to her friend.

'I need to tell you something,' she said. 'Something big.'

'About Robbie?'

A shake of the head.

Jodie waited another few seconds, convincing herself Owen was back in bed and couldn't be listening from the top of the stairs. She crossed the kitchen and filled the kettle, then set it boiling.

She spoke quietly, barely more than a whisper.

'I found something when I was clearing Dad's house,' she said.

'What?'

Jodie tried to think of the words and, when they wouldn't

come, she opened the cupboard that contained tinned vegetables and baking ingredients. She removed cans of peas, carrots and potatoes, and then pulled forward the plastic bag from the back.

'No danger of Owen going looking in there,' she said, mainly to herself.

Jodie had come close to burning the shirt when Owen had got home from school and asked about the burning smell. Perhaps she would have done if he hadn't walked in. She'd had to act so quickly, she'd stuffed the shirt into the cupboard by the breakfast cereal before later hiding it in a place her son was definitely not going to stumble across it.

She unfolded the top and turned it around so Fiona could see the green clover logo.

Fiona squinted for a second and then puffed out her lips. 'What's that?' she asked.

Jodie didn't need to reply because, as soon as the words were out, Fiona's eyes widened and her mouth hung open. She was sitting at the kitchen table and stared up towards the shirt, frozen, before finally blinking.

'You found that at your dad's?'

'In the attic.'

'Is it...?' She stopped, not able to say the name, before trying again. 'Is that what I think it is?'

'I think so. How many other shirts like this can there be?'

Fiona nodded slowly. 'I remember Ben wearing it.' A pause. 'How'd it get into your dad's attic?'

Jodie folded the shirt back into the bag and put it on the counter. The kettle had started to boil and she crossed to pour water into a pair of mugs before dunking a teabag in each. She waited for a second, listening for any sounds from above.

'That's what I've been asking myself for five days.' She glanced across to the clock on the cooker. 'Six days.'

Neither of them spoke for a while, although Fiona opened

and closed her mouth a few times, as if she couldn't quite decide what to say.

Jodie moved the mugs to the draining board and fished out the teabags before swirling some milk into each. She passed one across to Fiona, whose blank expression hadn't changed.

'Who've you told?' she asked.

'Just Mum. I said it was still at Dad's place – and then, last night, someone tried to burn down the house.'

The pause was much longer this time. So many questions but no obvious place to start. No safe place to start. If two and two made four, then there were some very uncomfortable truths to face.

'You think your mum tried to set fire to the house?'

Jodie waited for a moment, not quite able to say 'yes'. 'I don't know,' she said instead. 'Mum might have told someone – and they could have done it.' Jodie glanced towards the shirt in the bag on the other side of the kitchen. 'If she knows what happened to Ben...' It was more a thought than a question.

'Who knows you have the shirt here?' Fiona asked.

'Just you.'

Fiona sipped her tea but Jodie didn't feel able to do anything other than hold the warm mug. Fiona was her longest friend, her *best* friend, and yet she still wasn't sure who she could trust.

After putting down her mug, Fiona turned to look at the bag on the counter. She spoke over her shoulder, her back to Jodie.

'If *your* dad had something to do with Ben, do you think mine knew...?'

It was only then that Jodie realised her friend might be right. It hadn't occurred to her before but, in the same way she and Fiona were lifelong friends, the same was true of their fathers. They were another pair who'd grown up in the town, gone to the same school, been into the same things, and ended up seeing each other more or less every day of their existence.

That was until Fiona's dad had died a few years back and Jodie's father had given the eulogy. One of them was always likely to do that for the other.

Jodie was leaning on the sink as Fiona continued sitting. Jodie didn't know what to say and it seemed the same was true for Fiona. The truth might be unknowable and, perhaps, that was for the best.

'I heard Paul McIntosh is out,' Fiona said. 'That he might be back in town.'

'He is,' Jodie replied. 'I've seen him.'

She didn't mention the near altercation between McIntosh and Ben's father but, as she was picturing that, she realised Fiona was now looking directly to her.

'But McIntosh killed Ben,' Fiona said. 'So how could your dad have the top he was wearing that day?'

'I don't know.' A pause and then, 'I don't know what to do.'

Jodie's voice cracked with something close to a sob she hadn't expected. Without a word, Fiona stood and stepped across the kitchen, where she put an arm around Jodie's shoulders and pulled her close. 'It's not your fault,' she whispered.

They stayed like that for a few seconds, with Jodie thankful for the warmth in more ways than one. She was happy not being in a relationship, except, sometimes, she craved the touch of someone else – even if it was in friendship.

When Fiona stepped away, she leaned on the back of the chair, leaving them at the same height.

'Did you find anything else in the attic?' she asked.

Jodie stared at her friend for a moment, almost answering 'no', before realising the truth. 'I didn't look,' she said. 'I found the shirt and didn't know what to do. There are more boxes in there.'

Fiona smiled slimly. 'Let's go back when it's light,' she said. 'I'll come this time and we'll see if there's anything else up there.'

THIRTY-ONE

Fiona returned to bed – but Jodie pottered around downstairs, cleaning and drinking tea as she waited for the sun to come up.

When Owen came down for breakfast, they didn't mention the middle-of-the-night moment with Robbie – and neither did Jodie raise the other things she had to talk to him about. After she'd thanked him for his help the night before, they were at something close to a truce and she didn't want another argument quite so soon. She also didn't want to put him in a bad mood ahead of his day at school. He still had to concentrate on his classes and the weekend might be a better time to raise things.

Owen ate his toast and fiddled on his phone as Jodie scrubbed the draining board with a ferocity she hadn't employed since trying to get her deposit back on the flat in which they'd previously lived.

It was a gleaming silver and her arm was sore as she stopped and looked up to realise Owen was watching her from the table.

'What's going on?' he asked.

'What do you mean?'

'You never clean.'

'Which is why it's overdue.'

He focused on her for a couple of seconds longer before the draw of his phone became too much.

'We still need that talk,' Jodie said. 'I've not forgotten.'

Owen's only response was to start tapping at the phone screen with one hand, while feeding the last of the toast into his mouth with the other. If nothing else, smartphones were turning young people into quite the multitaskers. He swallowed much of the final slice in one go and then said something that might have been 'bye' through his half-full mouth as he grabbed his bag from the ground.

The front door had barely closed when there were footsteps on the stairs and then Fiona emerged, yawning and stretching. She cricked her neck and rolled her shoulders. 'I always forget how hard the mattress is,' she said.

'Did you get back to sleep?'

'In a second. You?'

Jodie shook her head, though didn't answer properly. Despite the lack of rest, she could feel herself buzzing. 'Shall we go?' she asked.

Even though it had been her suggestion, Fiona suddenly seemed reluctant. She yawned again and rested on the back of a chair.

'Do you think it's a good idea? What if we... I dunno... find something?'

'Isn't that the point?'

It was the morning after the night before for Fiona. She didn't reply but Jodie could see it in her.

'I can go by myself...?' Jodie said.

Fiona had been staring through the window, off towards the nothingness of the alley at the back. 'No,' she replied. 'I'll come. Let's hope there's nothing there.'

. . .

As Jodie lifted the hatch, she remembered the feeling of entering the attic the first time. That childlike wonder of doing something that felt forbidden. It had been five days and somehow seemed as if it had been both the day before and weeks earlier.

The same sense of dust and dirt met her as she slipped the hatch off the side and groped for the plug. The first time she'd slotted it into the socket, the exploding orange light had almost made her fall backwards out of the attic – but the repeat visits had her ready.

The beams squeaked, the shadows stretched. Everything was as Jodie had left it.

'What's it like up there?'

Fiona was holding onto the ladder and it was only as Jodie peered down towards her that a memory bubbled to the front of her thoughts. She'd once asked her dad if her bedroom could be painted purple and he'd said yes on the condition she held the ladder while he painted. It felt so close, so real, especially as she was in the house where it had happened.

All these years on and she realised holding the ladder for her dad had never been about holding the ladder. She was too light to have truly kept it in place – and the task was more about giving her time with her dad.

'You OK?'

Jodie flicked back to the attic as she realised Fiona was talking to her.

'Just, er... dusty,' Jodie replied. She shuffled across the boards that covered the insulation, giving space for Fiona to head up the ladder and poke her head through the gap.

Fiona turned in a semicircle, taking in the space before pulling herself up and sitting on another section of board. 'Dad would never let me in the attic at home,' she said.

'Same with me.'

'I still don't think I've ever been in it. When we cleared it out after he died, Robbie went up there.' A pause. 'Men love their attics, don't they?'

Jodie replied with a soft smile and then reached for the box with 'KEEP' written on the side. She removed the lid and looked inside at the neat stack of children's books that had been underneath Ben's shirt. They'd been Jodie's when she was young – and Mike's before her. The sort of chewed, thumbed, grubby hand-me-downs that she'd have given Owen if she had known her dad had kept them. They were unrelated to the shirt that had been on top – and Jodie wondered whether her dad's handwritten 'KEEP' referred to the books, the shirt, or both.

'Anything?' Fiona asked.

'Just books. This is where I found Ben's... y'know.'

Fiona nodded and then stretched towards a box that had an old Golden Wonder logo on the side. Jodie watched for a moment as her friend pulled off the lid and started to dig inside. She soon held up a flowery pink and cream monstrosity.

'Your parents had an awful taste in curtains,' she said.

'They used to be in the living room,' Jodie replied. 'When I was four or five, perhaps. I can't remember properly.'

'Everyone had bad everything back then,' Fiona remarked. 'My mum and dad used to have a green bathroom.'

They stopped for a moment and Jodie pictured the way their old bathroom used to look, with its grimy grey-cream colour scheme – and a tatty carpet near the sink. It had been normal at the time.

Back in the attic, the beams and boards creaked with every movement, almost every breath. Fiona reached for another box, so Jodie did the same. Hers was a Crawford's Biscuits box that was coated with a thin layer of dust that came away on her palm. The contents felt heavy as Jodie slid the box towards her.

There was more dust inside, a thicker coating, even though the lid had been closed. Jodie blew the powder into the darkest corners of the attic and then, untouched and unseen for years, was a series of folded newspapers. The one on top had her dad on the cover, back when he'd had hair and been mayor. He was wearing the ceremonial gown and chain that he'd barely been able to lift as he got older. His face took up half the page, his grin wide and familiar.

Jodie put it down because she couldn't bear to look at him.

Underneath the first paper was a second that had a headline far more recognisable than the first. She'd seen it at Keith's house.

GIRL PULLED FROM FIRE BY NEIGHBOUR

She removed the crusty paper from the box and opened it out. She'd been in hospital immediately after being pulled from the shed and didn't know her dad had kept the story relating to it.

There was a photo of a fire engine on the front and, as she scanned it, Jodie suddenly knew she was being watched. She glanced up to see Fiona staring towards her and the paper. She didn't know how she knew but there was a synergy between them. They were thinking the same thing.

'It felt normal at the time,' Jodie said, defending herself against an accusation that hadn't been said out loud. That had never been said out loud.

'It felt very sudden,' Fiona said quietly. She wasn't quite able to meet Jodie's eyes any longer and was staring towards the darkest part of the attic. 'I couldn't say anything,' she added. 'You were obsessed with him. You used to draw him on your books at school. You'd ask if I knew what he was thinking, even though it was impossible. You'd talk about getting married. We were only kids.'

Obsessed.

Fiona had actually said it.

Obsessed.

The hairs on Jodie's arms raised and she knew it was true. Ben had been the centre of the universe right up until the time he disappeared. Lots of teenage girls are obsessed with their boyfriends, but she'd looked up to him as more than simply her boyfriend. Her saviour. Her everything.

'I didn't want to fall out with you,' Fiona added. 'That's why I never said anything. There were a few of us.'

'Girls at school?'

'Yeah...'

Jodie knew the girls of whom Fiona was talking – and she didn't blame them. She still saw most of them around town, or at the garden centre. They'd been the typical sort of group who'd grown apart after leaving school. When they realised they had nothing in common. They'd nod their hellos and like each other's Facebook statuses – but that was as deep as it got. It was only Jodie and Fiona who'd remained close. That's the way it had always been with the two of them. They'd shared their first cigarette and then Jodie had given it up the same day, even though Fiona had kept up the habit. They'd swapped clothes and CDs, they'd bought their first mobile phones at the same time, solely to text one another when they were apart. So many joint firsts.

'I was a bit jealous,' Fiona said. 'You had a boyfriend and I didn't. That was part of it – although there was more than that. There were days when the only thing you talked about was Ben. If he had a gig, or something like that, you'd spend the whole week leading up to it going on about it as if it was your thing.'

It felt alien and yet familiar. A time Jodie barely remembered and yet something which inhabited every part of her. Her time with Ben felt as if it had happened to someone else.

'Sorry...' Fiona said. She let it hang and Jodie didn't know how to reply. It had been a moment of understanding between them. Something that should have been said a long while before.

It felt as if they could move on, though there didn't seem much point in hunting through old newspapers. When Fiona reached for a new box, Jodie did the same.

The new one was less dusty than the previous and had 'misc' written on the side in her dad's handwriting. Inside was a mangled spaghetti of leads and power cords, a tape measure, spirit level, plug socket extensions, a light bulb and a couple of rulers. There was more underneath but Jodie went to reseal the box, figuring it really was junk, until she noticed the black eye staring back at her. She pushed aside a light switch bracket to uncover the pointy features of a garden gnome. His once green hat was speckled with chips and scrapes and a crooked hole was in place of one of his eyes.

Jodie took it out of the box and looked at it properly. There were cracks along the legs and a stump where something like a fishing rod would have once been.

It seemed familiar, though Jodie couldn't place why. She never remembered gnomes at the back or front of the house and, despite her father being a collector and low-level hoarder, gnomes had never been his thing.

Jodie put down the ornament on the board at her side and continued looking through the box, where there was more of a mishmash of items. There were half a dozen forks and knives, an old mug with a picture of a dog on the side, an empty year planner from the nineties, a small, blunt hacksaw, a bottle opener – and more mounds of tat that was fit only for the bin.

It was as she was putting everything back into the box that Jodie realised Fiona was now holding the gnome. Her friend turned it over in her hands, poking a finger into the empty eye socket and then scratching at a dried fleck of dirt on the nose.

'Take it if you want it,' Jodie said.

Fiona glanced up, eyes wrinkled in confusion. 'Huh?'

'The gnome. If you want it, you can have it. This stuff's going to the tip otherwise. I don't know where Dad got it, or why he kept it.'

Fiona looked back to the gnome and started scraping away more of the dried dirt. 'It's already mine,' she said quietly.

'What do you mean?'

'This is Gnomey. He used to live in our back garden and I'd talk to him when I was little.' She looked up, made sure Jodie was watching her. She was more animated as she continued. 'I noticed Gnomey wasn't there one day and asked Dad about it. He said he'd broken, so he'd thrown him out. I thought I'd fix him, glue him back together, that sort of thing – but, when I looked in the bin, he wasn't there.'

'Did you say anything to your dad?'

'No. I suppose I forgot about it. I was older then, fourteen or fifteen. I figured he broke a few weeks before but I'd not noticed. It's not like I was still sitting in the garden having conversations at that age...' She tailed off and turned the gnome over in her hands once more, then looked up again. 'What's he doing here?'

THIRTY-TWO

It was a largely silent journey across town as Jodie drove, with Fiona in the passenger seat. They passed the primary school, where children were tearing around the playground, their screams and shouts echoing towards the town centre. The town itself was quiet, with only a handful of shoppers shuffling between the Tesco Express and the charity shops. Past that was the outskirts of a couple of housing estates and then it was the narrower web of streets that took them past Jodie's house on towards where Fiona lived.

It was a two- or three-minute walk from Jodie's house – and yet the houses had been built at different times. Jodie's was a boxy housing association place, in among rows of identical places. Fiona's had been built in the post-war boom and had front and back gardens that tripled the size of the property.

'Robbie's car's gone,' Fiona said, as Jodie started to slow. She had been cradling the gnome on her lap, as if clutching a baby. As Jodie parked on the side of the road, Fiona unclipped her seat belt.

'Where's he gone?' Jodie asked.

'He was saying something about day labouring with one of

his mates – but I assumed he would be too pissed after last night.'

She opened the door and let herself out, as Jodie trailed around and along the path to the front of Fiona's house. It was another place in which she felt drawn into the past. When she was a girl, she'd play on the floor of Fiona's bedroom as their dads shared a drink and chat below. As they got older, they'd lie top to tail on her bed and gossip about the people from school.

And Ben, of course. Jodie would talk about Ben.

Fiona fished into her bag but, instead of removing her keys, she pulled out a cigarette and the wand lighter that should have been sitting next to Jodie's cooker.

'Sorry,' she said. 'I was only borrowing it.'

She lit the cigarette and handed Jodie back the lighter.

'I've got some inside,' Fiona said. 'But I didn't know when I'd be coming back.'

Jodie waited as Fiona leaned against her own front door, puffing on the cigarette. It was something she'd have never got away with if her dad had still owned the house. He was fervently against smoking – and had told a teenage Fiona on more than one occasion that it was a dirty, bad habit that she shouldn't begin. He hadn't known that she'd already started smoking by then.

Time passed, though Fiona seemed in no rush. The gnome sat on the ground at her feet and it was impossible for Jodie to miss her friend's frequent glances towards it.

It was a strange thing for her dad to have kept – even if it had belonged to him. The fact it was his best friend's made it even odder.

When Fiona was finally done, she pressed the end of the cigarette into a makeshift ashtray of the mug that sat next to the drainpipe by the door. That done, she unlocked the door and let them both in.

Jodie had to stop herself from mentioning how messy everything was. Fiona had never been a clean freak or minimalist – but the clutter was on the way towards reaching the standard of Keith the journalist's. There were clothes on the floor of the hallway, plus mucky dishes piled high in the sink and across the countertop in the kitchen.

Fiona was leading the way through the house but she stopped near the back door and sighed. 'I told Robbie I wasn't going to pick up after him any longer,' she said. 'I figured he might do some washing up, or clean some clothes – but he started leaving everything where it was. We've been playing a game of chicken for weeks about who'll break first.' She stared aimlessly towards the mess in the sink. 'He's not going to do it, is he?'

'He'll move out before he washes any of that lot.'

Fiona puffed a breath of resignation and agreement before she turned and plucked a key from a hook near the door. She unlocked it and then led Jodie into the yard at the back, where there was more mess. A wheelie bin had a trio of black bags sitting at the foot, while a rusting barbecue set was on its side, with a pile of charcoal speckled across the ground.

Fiona ignored that and continued towards the back. A pile of rounded, large pebbles had been spaced across a caked bank of soil. Rockeries had always seemed a pointless mystery to Jodie. At the garden centre, customers would often need help lugging bags of stones to their cars and she'd never figured the appeal. There weren't many extra clues as she looked down on the one at the back of Fiona's garden. The pebbles were coated with a mossy greeny-brown slime and it looked more like a rubbish beach than something anyone sane would want to look at.

'Gnomey used to live here,' Jodie said, pointing towards a spot somewhere in the middle of the rockery. 'Dad used to grow strawberries out here when I was young. He used to say that Gnomey was guarding them until they were ready to eat.'

It felt like the exact type of thing Jodie's dad might have told her when she was young. Perhaps the sort of thing all dads told their children?

'Why did he get rid of the strawberries?'

Fiona thought on it for a moment. 'Something about it being too much work each year... I don't remember. One day I got home from school and there were rocks here.'

'Was that around the time your gnome went missing?'

Fiona crouched and pressed the ornament into a patch of soil that rested against the fence. His smashed, angular face stared up accusingly as she stood again.

She didn't answer because she didn't need to. They both knew. It felt inevitable.

They spent a few seconds staring at the gnome before Fiona crouched again and started trying to dig her fingers underneath one of the larger stones. When she failed to manage that, she crossed to the other corner of the yard and disappeared into an A-frame that would have once been a shed. Years of rain, wind and neglect had left it barely standing. There was a gap where the door would have once been – and a bag of soil was spilling through a cracked window.

A moment later, Fiona re-emerged with a heavy-looking shovel. She headed wordlessly back to Jodie's side and thrust the spade into the ground with a grunt. She rattled it around and then stomped on the blade, sending it underneath the rock she'd been trying to dislodge. More wiggling, more grumbling – and then Fiona scooped the stone out and onto the grubby flagstones.

She stopped and took a breath, wheezing gently from what was likely a mix of effort and the smoking habit.

'Dad would have a fit if he could see that shed,' Fiona said. 'He used to paint it with that creosote stuff twice a year but I guess it all got a bit out of hand.'

Jodie turned to look at the crumbling shed again. Fiona's

dad had been a self-employed landscaper and builder. He'd won contracts for some of the council projects, including the community centre that was soon to be named after Jodie's dad.

That was another thing that felt normal at the time but, years on, had a whiff of cronyism and jobs-for-the-boys about it.

He'd died in an accident on one of his worksites a few years before Jodie's father had passed. It was easy to imagine he'd disapprove of the state Fiona was leaving his shed and tools.

Fiona thrust the spade back into the ground for a second time and wiggled out another stone. She gasped as it pinged free and she flicked it to the side before trying for a third.

Jodie offered to help and, from there, they passed the shovel back and forth to do a stone at a time. It had been a long time since Jodie had done anything like this level of manual work and, within minutes, her shoulders and elbows burned.

When Fiona took a smoke break, Jodie continued digging by herself until it was time to swap back. Jodie checked the houses behind, looking for movement – except adults were at work, kids at school. A creeping sense of dread had grown as they'd been digging, as if she already knew what would be below. Now, half the stones had been cleared and there was... nothing.

Jodie was starting to feel as if this was all a colossal waste of time. Perhaps a good workout but nothing more. It wasn't what they feared.

Fiona was digging deeper now. She shovelled mounds of dirt to the side, piling it against the fence, and so Jodie did the same when it was her turn.

The sun came out as they worked, leaving Jodie with long sweat patches along her back. Fiona was no different, using her sleeve to wipe her forehead at regular intervals.

'Better than the gym,' she said. 'Dad would be so proud.'

'Not if he knew you were digging up his rocks.'

It came out harsher than Jodie meant and the smile that had been on Fiona's face slipped a fraction. 'No...'

Jodie turned to look at the hole they'd made in the dirt. It was more mad dad digging at the beach than serious excavation – and the job was becoming harder as the earth became more like clay. The grim sense of foreboding that had been growing had cleared further. There was nothing in the ground except dirt and the odd stone. Her dad hadn't held onto the gnome as some sort of morbid keepsake.

'You're right about being better than the gym,' Jodie said. 'We've dug up all this and we're going to have to put it all back soon.'

Fiona looked from the hole to Jodie and back again. She rammed the shovel into the ground and pushed it hard into the soil before twisting and flipping more onto the pile.

'There can't be anything down there,' Jodie said. 'Shall we go in? Or put all the soil back?'

Fiona didn't reply. She was seemingly on a mission as she shovelled out three more mounds and hoofed them onto the larger pile. She didn't offer the spade to Jodie this time, instead continuing on and on... until...

'What's that?'

The hole was perhaps a metre deep at its deepest point and Fiona had stopped digging. She dropped the spade on the ground and crouched, craning forward for a closer look. Jodie joined her as Fiona pointed towards something white among the brown of the dirt.

Jodie knew what it was, even before Fiona lowered herself into the hole and stretched towards it. It suddenly felt cold.

'It's a bone,' Jodie said.

THIRTY-THREE

Fiona withdrew her arm and instead leaned in to get a closer look. Jodie hoped she was going to turn and say it was only a rock. That it was all a mistake.

When Fiona did turn, she was grey. She reached for the spade and then carefully dug around the bone until it was more or less uncovered.

That done, Fiona pulled herself out of the hole, bone in hand. She held it up to the light, like a shopworker checking the strip on a banknote. Apart from the crust of dirt on the surface, it was almost like a cartoon bone, with knobbly bits at either end and a longer, narrower section in the middle. It could easily have belonged to someone's arm or leg.

Jodie thought her friend was going to pass it across but, instead, Fiona dropped the bone back into the hole and then picked up the spade once more. She had already scooped two mounds of dirt back into the hole when Jodie found her voice.

'What are you doing?' she asked.

Fiona was using the spade to push the soil back into the hole. It was a lot faster going back in than it had been coming out.

'What does it look like?' she replied.

The bone was already out of sight, underneath the dirt that Fiona was furiously piling on top.

'Stop,' Jodie said.

'Why?'

'Because...' Jodie realised she didn't have a second part of the sentence. She couldn't quite manage 'because it's wrong'.

'We don't have to tell anyone,' Fiona said. 'We can forget we ever found anything.'

'So why did we do this?'

Fiona stopped and jammed the spade into the disappearing mound. 'Because I wanted to know.' Her teeth were clamped together with frustration and anger. 'It's not just *your* dad, is it? It's both of ours.'

Jodie had no immediate answer to that.

'It might not be Ben,' she managed eventually, trying to convince herself as much as anyone.

It was Fiona's turn not to reply. She continued to push soil from the big pile back into the hole. Each sweep of the spade came with force, with anger. Jodie knew that fury. She'd felt it bubbling for days. A frustration at all the questions she had for a father who would never be able to answer them.

Now Fiona had similar questions. A similar sullied memory.

The hole was close to half-filled when Fiona stopped and jammed the spade into the ground. 'Why would they do it?' she asked.

It didn't feel as if it was a question specifically for Jodie – even if she was the only one there.

'I don't know,' Jodie replied. 'Maybe they didn't...? The bone might not be human. Or, if it is, maybe it isn't Ben's. Or...'

She tailed off, not convincing herself, let alone Fiona. They both knew what their discovery likely meant. The secret shared by their fathers now belonged to them.

Jodie felt an odd sense of calm. As if, ever since finding that green shirt, she'd known it would end somewhere like this. In a strange way, it was almost a relief. All those years of wondering about Ben and... here he was.

Or so she assumed.

Fiona reached for the spade again – but it wasn't out of the ground before there was the sound of doors sliding open. Jodie turned towards the house – to where Robbie was standing next to the patio doors with a curious look on his face.

'Whose body are you burying in there?' he asked.

THIRTY-FOUR

Jodie stared, wondering how he knew about a body. How could *anyone* know. It wasn't until Fiona replied that she realised he was trying to make a joke.

'Don't you remember?' Fiona said. 'This is where you said you were going to bury me. I've just been showing Jodie how easy it is to dig up in case I go missing.'

Husband and wife stared at one another: Fiona with defiance, Robbie with confusion.

'I said what...?'

'When you were pissed the other night,' Fiona added. 'You said you'd hold a pillow over my face and then bury me under the rocks in the garden. I was making sure someone knew, just in case.'

They had never really been friends but Jodie had known Robbie a long time. She'd never seen him as rattled as he was when he reached towards the frame of the patio doors, missed, and nearly toppled over. He righted himself and brushed down his front. His eyes were wide.

'I never said that,' he managed eventually.

'You don't know what you said. You were too drunk.'

He swallowed. 'If I *did* say that, I mean, look, it's just...' He ran a hand through his hair. 'It was just the booze. I didn't mean that.' He looked to Jodie, pleading silently from a distance. 'I'm obviously not going to do that...'

It took her a moment but Jodie suddenly realised Fiona was acting. She turned to look at the hole and then back to Robbie.

'I said there's no way anyone would be able to dig under the rocks,' Jodie said, 'so Fee showed me.' She pointed an accusing finger at him. 'You should be careful what you say. I wanted to go to the police.'

Robbie's features creased into a frown. 'I was only messing.'

Fiona wasn't about to let it go. 'You've not even said sorry.'

'I didn't know I'd done it!'

'That's still not an apology.'

Robbie was squirming, looking at the floor. 'Obviously, I'm sorry.'

'You don't sound it.'

He threw up his hands. 'What do you want me to say?'

'You owe an apology to Jodie too – for waking everyone up at two in the morning.'

That got a loud *pfft*. The apology tour hadn't lasted long. 'What more do you want?' Robbie replied. 'You've already told me to move out. Now you want apologies for this, that, and the other.' He risked a glance towards Jodie, wanting her to be somewhere else. When he focused back on his wife, his tone had softened. 'I was hoping we could talk...'

Fiona moved away from the hole in the ground and put down the spade. 'Go on then.'

'I meant...' Another glance towards Jodie.

'You can say whatever it is in front of her.'

Jodie found herself staring off towards the collapsing shed, trying to remember if she'd ever seen it in a better state. Trying to think of anything other than the marital grief happening in front of her.

Robbie had been quiet for a moment but then seemingly decided changing the subject was the best way to go.

'You'll never guess what I heard,' he said.

'I don't care,' Fiona replied.

'Remember that Ben kid at school? That guy who killed him is back.'

He'd apparently forgotten Ben had been Jodie's boyfriend. Either that or he didn't care.

Fiona had an eyebrow raised, as if silently trying to remind her husband of the connection to the other person in the garden.

After a moment's stand-off, it was Jodie who replied.

'I know,' she said. 'I had to stop Ben's dad going after him with a knife.'

There was a silence as Jodie realised both of them were looking at her with their mouths open.

'You didn't tell me that,' Fiona said.

Jodie didn't get a chance to reply because Robbie cut in. 'Why'd you stop him? Sounds like the right idea to me.'

'You think going after someone with a knife is the "right idea"?' Jodie replied.

A shrug. 'He killed the bloke's lad. What do you expect him to do?'

Jodie should have let it go – except all she could think of was the bone that was buried barely a stretch from her. *Bones*, probably. There would be others under there. If it truly *was* Ben's, then Paul McIntosh had spent two decades in prison for something he didn't do.

'He did his time,' Jodie said quietly. 'What's the point of prison if you kill the guy when he comes out?'

That got another shrug, even more dismissive than the first. 'Too many do-gooders,' Robbie said. 'That's the problem nowadays. If it was up to me, I'd hang 'em.'

Jodie could feel Fiona staring sideways at her as it sank in that McIntosh might have given up twenty years for no reason.

The three of them stood silently for a moment, Robbie's smug expression making it clear he relished getting the last word. It was apparently that which gave him the confidence to return to his initial point.

'Anyway,' he said, turning to Fiona. 'Are you coming back?'

'I told you yesterday – and last month after our holiday – that we're finished. This has all been going on too long.'

Robbie remained defiant. 'What has?'

'You getting drunk and then pretending nothing's happened. All the arguments. You can't say you're enjoying this.'

Robbie held up his hands, as if to indicate he didn't know what she was talking about. 'We've always been like this.'

'That's the point!'

Jodie was back staring at the shed, wanting to be somewhere else.

'This is what we do,' Robbie tried. 'We fall out, we make up.'

'Not this time.'

Jodie risked a glance to Robbie, who was staring curiously at Fiona, apparently unable to believe she might be serious. She didn't really blame him, considering he was correct in the sense he and Fiona had been through an endless cycle of falling out and making up. From his point of view, why would this particular time be any different?

'You've got a month to find somewhere else,' she added. 'Not even that now.'

Robbie might not have sensed it but Jodie heard the hint of a quiver to Fiona's voice. A false confidence that if she stuck to this point, Robbie might simply move out and not stake a claim to the house.

He was staring towards his wife, perhaps waiting for a

reconciliation that wasn't coming. When it didn't – and his staring failed to achieve anything – he finally threw his hands into the air. 'Fine!'

He spun and stomped back inside, leaving the patio doors open as he stormed through the house. There was a series of small bangs, then a louder one of the front door. After that, silence.

Fiona sighed with what might have been relief but, as Jodie looked from the hole to her friend to the house, she was nursing a growing sense that everything was going to end very badly.

THIRTY-FIVE

The cool, air-conditioned breeze of big Tesco was a calming relief as Jodie ambled around with a trolley in front of her. She hadn't realised until she was halfway along the fruit and veg aisle – but the mundanity of it all was something she craved. Despite everything, she still needed to feed herself and Owen, and the car had to be filled up. Life didn't stop simply because a person was surrounded by chaos.

And Jodie's life *was* chaos.

Except the supermarket was peaceful and a delicious slice of normal.

Jodie walked aimlessly around the store, vaguely checking the shopping list app on her phone, as well as eyeing the two-for-one stickers on the shelves.

There was a girl pestering her mum for unicorn cupcakes in the bakery section, plus a pair of boys making faces as their mother picked a bag of mixed vegetables from one of the freezers.

It was comforting to be surrounded by people going about their regular lives. Normal was good – but life outside the store was anything but.

Jodie eyed the café section longingly, wondering if she could get away with spending a few hours with a cup of tea or two. Perhaps have someone cook a meal for her, for once?

Then she spotted a girl she used to know from school, which reminded her of school itself, then Fiona, then Ben, then the bone, then her dad.

It was never far away. Impossible to forget, impossible to think about.

Those bones *had* to be Ben's.

But if they were, it meant...

Jodie started a second lap of the store, rechecking the list for all the things she'd missed first time. She came in every ten days or so – and yet she could never remember where things were. Either someone was swapping everything around from one week to the next or she was getting old.

She was soon back in the bakery area, plucking a pair of Warburton's loaves from the shelf. As Owen had become a teenager, he seemed happy enough to live off a diet that was close to one hundred per cent toast. It would keep him going for a while. She grabbed him a multipack of Monster Munch, which would disappear into his room at some point over the coming week. She told herself it was normal for a teenager to survive off toast and crisps. She couldn't exactly force vegetables down his throat – but she bought them anyway. She'd still cook them and try to persuade him that broccoli and carrots weren't the route to all evil.

As she was lost in yet more thoughts of how she was a terrible mother, Jodie rounded the end of an aisle and turned into the one dedicated to various canned goods. She was eyeing the four-for-three offer on baked beans, wondering if they needed that many cans, when she realised she was being watched. She turned towards the end of the aisle, where a woman had stopped with her trolley blocking the way. She was angling her phone towards Jodie and pretending to be looking at the screen, even though the direction made it obvious she was filming.

Jodie knew a lot of faces around town – but not the woman with the phone. She was a little younger than her, somewhere in her late-twenties, with a kid sitting in the seat section of the trolley, swinging his legs back and forth.

Was she filming because news was out about Ben? Jodie had left Fiona at the house – but had she then gone online and told everyone what they suspected?

Those thoughts came and went in a second and, as soon as the woman realised Jodie had clocked her, she angled her phone to the ground. She was still pretending she'd been looking at the phone screen but the final glance along the aisle gave her away. Except the momentary gape didn't seem to be in Jodie's direction. Instead, it was behind her...

Jodie looked over her shoulder and realised the woman hadn't been filming her at all. Instead, she'd been focused on the man who was standing in front of the soup, with a can of Heinz Tomato in his hand.

Jodie almost leaped back, more through the shock of recognition than anything else. As she'd been mulling over the beans, Paul McIntosh had been standing almost touching distance away. They hadn't noticed one another but Jodie must have made some sort of sound because, a moment after she turned, he did as well.

They looked at one another, barely arm's length away. For some reason, it popped into Jodie's head that McIntosh was the same height as her. All the years they'd shared a joint past and she hadn't realised.

He'd hacked away at his beard since she'd last seen him. Instead of the wild mass of white, there was an uneven sandpapery bristle. He'd used a shaver on his eyebrows, getting rid of the sprouting long umbrellas and replacing them with an odd, shortened stubble. His clothes still hung from him: too big and too long.

As they stared at each other, Jodie felt a tingle, knowing they were being watched from the other end of the aisle. Someone was probably filming them again but she couldn't bring herself to stop watching McIntosh.

If that bone underneath the rockery at Fiona's house belonged to Ben, then it surely meant McIntosh was innocent. Countless scenarios flooded through her as they continued to eye each other in silence. She should tell him what she knew – except he could never get those twenty years back, so what good would it do? She should tell him she believed he was innocent – because she did. Except that would do no good either. She should tell him she was going to call the police and let them know what she'd found. Except, perhaps things weren't as they seemed? Her father wasn't around to defend himself, after all. Could she destroy his legacy and memory for that?

And then none of that came out because before Jodie could say a word, there was movement from the side. They both turned to see a fifty-something woman with short hair stomping purposefully towards them, finger primed to wag. She ignored Jodie as she faced down McIntosh and thrust her finger towards his face.

'How *dare* you!' She spoke through clenched teeth and with unconcealed fury.

McIntosh stumbled over something that was lost as she raged over the top of him.

'There are *kids* here,' she added. 'Don't think I won't call the police. I'm sure they'll be right down here to deal with your sort. Are you even allowed here?'

'I, er—'

McIntosh had stepped away – but that only encouraged the woman to move towards him, finger still close to his face. 'Don't you come that with me. I don't know *why* you came back.

Nobody wants you here. *Nobody.* They should have let you hang – but if they didn't want to do it, the least you can do is do it yourself.'

He was cowering from her, hiding behind a trolley as she loomed closer. It was as he tried to turn that he bumped the trolley with his hip. It squeaked forward and collided gently with the woman. There was barely enough force to knock over a one-legged child on rollerblades – but Jodie could see what was going to happen a moment before it did.

The woman hurled herself backwards like an arthritic gymnast, landing on her arse and throwing her legs high like a puppy wanting its belly rubbed. She screamed, first incoherently – and then, as she pushed herself up, actual words. 'That's assault!' She turned to where an embarrassed-looking teenager was scuffing his feet as part of a slow zombie walk towards them. 'Call the police,' she shouted at him.

The boy made no attempt to do any such thing – but that didn't stop the woman.

'You're a witness,' she shouted, now pointing at Jodie. 'You saw the whole thing, how he shoved me to the ground.' The woman was standing again, rubbing her side and gasping to herself. 'Ow! I bet I've broken something.' She started pointing her finger at McIntosh again. 'You're going to wish you never came back here. Running around hitting women and all that. You're going right back to prison, where you belong.'

McIntosh was a statue, can of soup still in his hand, as he stared at the woman. She continued raging, pointing to someone else at the other end of the aisle and saying they were also a witness. The boy, who Jodie assumed was her son, had stopped a few paces away and had his back turned, wanting to be anywhere that wasn't near his mother.

'I saw what happened,' Jodie said.

The woman stopped and turned to her. 'Good! We can—'

'I saw you harassing someone for no reason and then you threw yourself to the ground.'

'I did not!'

The woman turned incredulously, first towards her son – who was ignoring her – and then to the person at the other end of the aisle, who had disappeared. When she focused back on Jodie, her lips were screwed into a snarl.

Jodie pointed to the ceiling and the woman looked up, towards a domed security camera.

'It'll all be on there,' Jodie said. 'If you think he pushed you, I'm sure we can get someone from security to check the footage.' She plucked her phone from her bag. 'How about I call the police and we can all look together...?'

The woman's eyes narrowed in furious annoyance. She stepped towards her son, who was still pretending not to know her. She had the face of a woman who'd call the police because someone was parked in front of her house.

'I always *knew* you were in on it,' she snarled.

Jodie stared at her. She'd assumed the woman had no idea who she was.

'In on what?' she replied.

'Oh, I know you,' the woman replied. 'The lad *he* killed was your boyfriend, wasn't he?' She nodded from Jodie to McIntosh, then back again. 'In on it together, are you? I always told people you knew more than you said.'

She was sneering with confidence, even as she backed further away, stepping around her son and using him as a shield.

Jodie stared, wondering if she knew her. Perhaps the mother of someone with whom she'd been at school? Or a friend of her mum's? Or a neighbour? Or...?

Jodie had no idea who she was – but the woman had her own phone out now and was filming in portrait mode, naturally. She was still backing away, saying something Jodie couldn't make out as her son trailed. A few seconds later and they were gone.

When Jodie turned to McIntosh, the soup was still in his hand and he was shaking. He hadn't moved since the woman had come at him.

'Are you all right?' Jodie asked.

He remained where he was, staring blankly along the aisle towards where the woman had gone. 'I'm not… I didn't… I—'

Jodie placed a hand on his arm. 'I believe you,' she said.

THIRTY-SIX

Jodie helped McIntosh find the grocery items he'd written on a scrap of paper. There was bread, butter, milk, Rice Krispies, soup, beans, teabags and instant coffee. Nothing exciting, or expensive. He barely spoke as she shepherded him around the store, ignoring the handful of sideways stares from other shoppers.

When they were done, he seemed confused by the self-checkouts, so Jodie scanned and then put him in a taxi outside. After that, she went back inside to complete her own shop. By the time she reached her own car, Jodie felt dazed. Those moments of boring peace she'd felt while ambling up and down the supermarket aisles felt a long way away.

She checked her phone, wondering if someone had taken pictures of her helping McIntosh and put them on Facebook. Gossip had always travelled fast around town – and things like Facebook had only made it worse. Jodie scrolled around the town's page and then her own – but there was nothing recent, except some woman wondering if she should call the police because she'd seen a 'lout' sitting on a wall close to her house.

Jodie put down her phone and pressed backwards into the head rest, then closed her eyes.

She understood why Fiona had immediately reburied the bone after finding it. There was a part of her that was glad. She and Fiona could pretend it had never happened and try to remember their fathers as the kind men who'd brought them up.

McIntosh complicated that.

He'd lost decades of his life for something Jodie felt sure he hadn't done. If she and Fiona were to pretend they'd found nothing, it would also mean no investigation into the bones. It would mean condemning McIntosh to never having the chance to clear his name. He would never have peace, even with such ordinary things as going to the supermarket.

Jodie opened her eyes and watched the stars of light swarm. She wanted to sleep. She wanted to be somewhere that wasn't the town in which she'd grown up.

Except there was Owen. It wasn't only her home, it was his as well. He was moving into a period where GCSEs would be on the horizon and whatever she decided to do was going to affect him and his schooling. Revealing what she'd discovered about Ben would bring all that attention back to her again.

And him.

It would be worse than ever before precisely because of things like Facebook. Jodie's father's legacy would be destroyed – but he was Owen's grandfather too.

It would be impossible to go to the police with Ben's shirt and the bones in Fiona's yard, without having the chaos and gossip bounce back onto Owen as well.

As she drove home, Jodie wrestled with what to do. There didn't seem to be a good option.

She was so lost in her thoughts that she didn't notice the man on her front lawn until she'd already parked on the drive. He was around Jodie's age, in jeans and a jacket. Jodie looked sideways through the driver's window towards him and suddenly realised he wasn't *only* standing on her lawn, he was shouting angrily at someone else who was at the front of her house.

At Owen.

Jodie tried to get out of her car so quickly that the seat belt locked in place and she had to fight to untangle herself. A few seconds passed until she finally managed to stumble onto the driveway – and the slightly overgrown patch of lawn beyond.

Owen was in his school uniform, bag hanging low on his arm, as the stranger towered over him menacingly. Owen was fumbling with his keys, trying to get the extra few steps towards the front door. As soon as he freed them from a pocket of his bag, the man lunged and snatched the keys before turning and throwing them towards the road. It happened so quickly that Jodie barely had time to realise what had happened.

The man had apparently not noticed that Jodie had arrived because his focus was entirely on Owen, who was cowering in a way Jodie had never seen. He was hunched slightly, as if his neck had shrunk into his body. When he looked to Jodie, to his mum, his eyes were pleadingly wide with a terror she didn't know. Owen continued to shrink as the man advanced another pace towards him.

'Not such a big man now, are you?' the man growled.

Owen stumbled over a sentence that never finished forming. He ended up coughing and then keeling over further.

The man took another step forward and pushed Owen hard in the chest. Owen stumbled, tripping on his own feet but managing to stay upright. Jodie had been momentarily statue-like from the shock of what was happening but the push released her.

'Come on, fight back,' the man was saying. 'You're the big man, aren't you – so pick on me.' He stretched and pushed Owen again, though with less force second time around. Owen stumbled again and his bag dropped to the floor as Jodie darted between them. The man blinked in surprise at her appearance – but it was only a moment until he puffed up his chest again.

'Who are you?' Jodie shouted.

'You're his mum, are you? Like mother, like son, is it?'

He took a small step back, allowing a gap between them as Jodie half turned to check Owen was all right. Her son had backed to the edge of the lawn, barely a step from the front door and safety beyond.

'Your boy's been bullying my son,' the man said. There was still anger in his voice but a hint of a something else too. It took another sentence for Jodie to realise the man was close to tears. 'Flushed his head down the loo,' the man said. 'Threw his bag in the canal.' He was up on his tiptoes, angling past Jodie and pointing towards Owen. 'Not so brave when you're up against someone bigger than you.'

Jodie was torn between trying to defend her son while simultaneously feeling sick at what he was being accused of.

'Look,' she said, trying to think of what to say next. 'I'm sure we can figure this out.'

Her attempt at appeasement only angered the man, whose voice cracked halfway through his reply. 'What, like your son figured it out when he sent my Elis home bleeding? Him and his mates. Four of 'em on one before they threw his bag in the canal.' The man focused on Jodie. 'Is that the kid you're raising?'

It was a horrifically charged question. One that left Jodie feeling as if *she'd* been knocked backwards, even though he hadn't touched her.

The worst thing was, there was no answer to give other than 'yes'.

'I'm not going to defend him,' Jodie said. 'It's just this isn't the way to do it.'

'What's a better way then? I tried going through the school and they haven't done much. As if four people beating up one is fine because the four say they didn't do it and the one says they did.'

He was back on his tiptoes, eyeing Owen once more, though with greater menace. Jodie could see something in his face – and it wasn't tears any longer. He was furious.

She stepped to the side, shielding his route towards Owen, and holding her arms wide. 'I went into the school—' she started.

'And what have you done about it? I still see him with his mates. He's still at school. He's got away with it.' The man flexed his muscles. 'Bullies only know one language.'

He stepped sharply to the side and Jodie moved towards him, trying to block his path. The time for talking was done, though, and he shouldered through her like boiling water through ice cream. He didn't shoulder her hard but Jodie was off-balance and tripped over her own feet, falling onto her arse as the man barrelled past – and loomed over her cowering son.

THIRTY-SEVEN

Jodie felt something bristle past her other side and then, in a blink, there was a fleshy thud as someone slammed into the man's side. The pair of bodies crashed to the ground and there was a series of grunts and moans as two men rolled in the dirt, swinging wild and inaccurate punches at one another.

It took Jodie a moment to realise the second man was Fiona's husband, Robbie. The last time she'd seen him was as he huffed his way out of Fiona's house when she told him they were still separating. They lived a few minutes from one another, so there was every chance he was on his way home for the evening.

Robbie and the other man continued rolling and snorting, though they were so tightly clamped in each other's grasp that they were doing more damage to the grass than each other. They snarled vague threats, though it was more *drunken men in a pub car park* than anything serious. Jodie's nights out in town when she was barely old enough would almost always end with her and her friends walking past a similar scene in the early hours of the morning.

It took a few seconds but the men eventually disentangled themselves from one another. They hopped up, fists clenched, biceps tight, chests heaving, a couple of paces apart.

Robbie was standing between the other man and Owen. 'Like picking on women and kids, do ya?'

The man pointed past Robbie towards Owen, who was no longer cowering with fright. He was bouncing on his heels, eager for more. He hadn't spoken but she saw an exhilaration and excitement in her son she'd never seen before. She knew then it was all true. He *was* a bully. He *had* thrown another boy's bag in the canal. He *had* flushed his head down the loo. It had probably been going on for months.

'He's been picking on my boy,' the man said breathily. 'You his dad?'

Robbie didn't get a chance to reply because Jodie did it instead. She stepped across the lawn, putting herself in front of the bullied boy's father.

'Did you say your son's called Elis?' she asked.

The abrupt intervention left the father rocking on his heels. He was so surprised, he answered immediately. 'Yes.'

She turned and peered around Robbie, towards where Owen was still standing on the doorstep. She used the voice that only came out when there was no alternative. The tone that every parent knew. The one of not just *being* angry – but *showing* it. 'This ends now,' she said. 'If you even *look* at Elis the wrong way, I'll change the Wi-Fi password and cancel your phone contract. If I hear any report, from anyone, about you bullying other kids, the same happens. I've had enough.'

Owen was looking at the floor now, the bravado gone.

'I didn't hear you reply,' Jodie added.

'Fine!'

'I'm not messing around. You can look at me and give a proper response.'

Owen looked up, eyes blazing with embarrassed anger. '*Fine!*'

It would have to do for now.

Jodie twisted back to Elis' father. 'Can I do anything else?' she asked. 'You can have my number and—'

'Forget it.'

The man sized up Robbie one final time and, for a moment, Jodie felt sure they would start fighting again. Robbie pushed himself onto his tiptoes, primed for what might come, but then the other man stepped away. He moved slowly at first but then turned and strode away at pace before disappearing around next-door's hedge.

Jodie breathed.

Robbie sank back to his regular height. There was a scuff of dirt on one of his cheeks and a reddening graze on his forehead. 'You OK?' he asked.

Jodie couldn't quite bring herself to thank him, so replied with a soft 'yeah'. She answered at the same time as Owen – and only then realised Robbie wasn't talking to her.

'Don't talk to him,' she snapped. She'd been speaking to Owen – but it was Robbie who smirked and blew a raspberry with his lips.

He winked towards Owen. 'The Wi-Fi always works at my place,' he said.

A smile crept across Owen's face, though he immediately tried to hide it by looking away.

Jodie could feel her own anger bubbling. Her eye was beginning to twitch as she focused back on Robbie. 'How's the search for a new place going?'

His features darkened. 'You should be thanking me.'

They stared at one another for a couple of seconds before Robbie turned. He muttered a 'see you around' to Owen – and then stomped back to the street and headed in the direction of his house. Of *Fiona's* house.

Jodie breathed again. She wasn't exactly a gardening enthusiast but could see the flattened patches of grass from where the men had been rolling and fighting. One more thing to sort out at some point. She looked up to see Owen hurrying past her. For a moment, she thought he was heading after Robbie – but then she realised he was looking for the key Elis' father had thrown into the road.

She still didn't know the man's name.

Before she could help look, Owen crouched and picked up his keys from the pavement. He crossed back to the house and unlocked the front door before letting himself in. He was already on the bottom stair as Jodie called after him.

'Where do you think you're going?' she said.

'Upstairs.'

She started to reply but he was already clumping to his room. Jodie wasn't in the mood to leave it there, not after putting things off for so many days. She followed him up and opened the door to his room a moment after he'd slammed it.

'What do you want?' he said.

Owen had dumped his schoolbag on his bed but spun to look at her, eyes narrow.

Jodie moved to his television and crouched. She pulled the wires from the back of his Xbox and then coiled them on top of the console before stepping away with it all in her hands.

'What are you doing?' he said, as shocked as she'd ever seen him. 'You can't take that.'

'I can – and I am.'

'You said if I go near Elis and I won't.'

'I said I'd change the Wi-Fi password and cancel your phone contract if you went near him again.'

There was an air of panic to Owen's voice as Jodie stepped back towards the door. 'So why are you taking that?'

Jodie put down the Xbox on an empty shelf of his bookcase and held up the phone she'd been holding in the other hand.

She opened the photos app and loaded the one of Owen breaking in through the back window of her father's house. She turned it around, so he could see.

'Because of what you've already done to Elis – and because of this.'

THIRTY-EIGHT

Owen boggled at the image on his mum's phone. The security footage from over the fence at the back of Jodie's dad's house offered a clear image of Owen's face. It offered a few of his arse too, as he disappeared through the window.

Jodie lowered her phone. 'You're lucky I don't take this to the police,' she said.

Owen remained speechless – but Jodie was suddenly putting the pieces together.

'You took Dad's medals, didn't you?' she said. 'I told you I'd promised them to Mike and you figured they must be worth something. You decided you'd get them before he could. That was the night I took those sleeping tablets. I asked you the next morning if you'd heard anything in the night and you said "no". Except the noises I heard were you sneaking out and back.'

His eyebrow twitched in silent acknowledgement.

'Where are they?' she asked.

'What?'

'The medals. I want them back or I really *will* go to the police.'

Owen sized her up for a second or two, perhaps wondering

if she was bluffing. Jodie knew it was because she so rarely followed through with her threats and punishments. She had to share a single space with her son and didn't want to be at war with him. She wanted them to get on. She wanted their home to be happy. It was because of that she went easy on him. Because of that they'd ended up where they were.

But she wasn't bluffing – and Owen must have seen it because he turned and knelt. He pushed the covers up onto his bed and stretched underneath. Moments later, he pulled out a plastic supermarket bag and thrust it towards Jodie. She took it and the weight sagged in her hand as he let it go. She opened out the handles and looked inside to see a mangled pile of metal and ribbon.

Even though she'd seen the photos of him breaking in, Jodie could still barely believe her son had actually done it. It wasn't just playing up, it was criminal.

Her *son* was a *criminal*.

Jodie tied the handles of the bag and put it on the shelf next to Owen's Xbox.

'Why did you do it?' she asked. 'I said you could have whatever you wanted of Dad's. We could have gone there together.'

That got a trademark shrug, though she already knew the answer. Mike wanted the medals, so Owen figured they were worth something. Perhaps the biggest surprise was that he hadn't already sold them.

Jodie picked up the Xbox and the bag and balanced them with her phone. She moved into the doorway. 'I can't even begin to tell you how disappointed I am,' she said. 'Not just about the medals. The bullying as well. I don't know what would have happened outside if Robbie hadn't turned up.'

That got an uninterested huff and, suddenly, Jodie was dialled to eleven.

'Don't you make that noise at me,' she snapped. 'And stop shrugging. You know right from wrong.'

He swore under his breath but loud enough for her to hear, as she was meant to. 'What do you want from me?' he huffed.

'I didn't raise you to be a thief or a bully.'

He scowled and glowered, clenching his teeth, wanting to say something back, although the glance towards the Xbox gave the biggest clue as to why he chose not to.

'When can I have it back?' he asked.

'When I've decided you're sorry enough – and you've got a lot to be sorry for. You're lucky I'm not taking your phone away.'

Owen swallowed and glanced towards his window. 'I *am* sorry.'

'Are you? You didn't look it when Robbie and that other man were fighting. You looked like you were enjoying it. Not only that, I *specifically* asked you if there was anything I needed to know before going to your school – and you said there wasn't, even though you knew you were in trouble for bullying. And then, on top of all that, I only know you broke into Dad's house because there was security footage. You wouldn't have told me otherwise. What have you got to say for yourself?'

'Nothing... I didn't mean any of it.'

'You *accidentally* flushed someone's head down a toilet? Accidentally threw Elis' bag in the canal? And you *accidentally* broke into a house?'

Owen flopped into a sitting position on his bed. He hugged his arms around himself and continued staring towards the window. Jodie so wanted to be furious with him – and yet, in the moment, he seemed so small and vulnerable.

'There's this new game out next month but I don't have the money,' he said quietly. 'I thought...' He tailed off, not adding that he thought he'd steal from Jodie's dad. It was more or less as she'd guessed.

'You're paying for that window,' she said. 'It's coming out of the birthday money I'd have given you next month.'

His mouth hung open as he turned back to her. 'You can't—'

'I can. I had to spend that to fix the damage you did.'

Money she couldn't afford. Even more on her credit card. It was no excuse but Owen didn't know that.

Jodie could see the blend of anger and annoyance flitting across her son's features. She told herself there was at least some regret there too. He had to know he'd brought it all on himself.

His eyes again flicked to the Xbox on the shelf. 'All my friends play on there,' he said.

'You'll have to find another way to talk to them. You could try actual *talking*. Either that or find better friends, who aren't bullies.'

He rolled his eyes. If he wasn't in such trouble, Jodie knew he'd have said she was so old for suggesting such a thing.

'What can I do to get it back?' he asked.

'Like I said, you can act as if you're *actually* sorry.'

'I am!'

Jodie pointed to five cups and glasses dotted around the room. There were at least two plates as well. 'You can show it by cleaning your room,' she added. 'You can do the washing- and drying-up every morning and evening. You can get home from school on time – and show me that your homework is actually done. It'd be nice if you vacuumed the living room, the hall, stairs and landing.'

Owen had slumped lower as the jobs racked up.

'It's your granddad's naming ceremony tomorrow and half the town is going to be there. You can turn up, dress properly, *act* properly – and that'd be a good start.' She tapped the Xbox. 'Do all that and we'll see how things look after the weekend.'

He sighed. 'I can't have it back 'til Monday?'

'That's if you're lucky – *really* lucky – and I'm not making any promises. It all depends on your behaviour over the next few days.'

Owen scratched his head, eyed his Xbox as if it was the

long-lost love of his life, which it probably was, and then pushed himself up.

'Where's the hoover?' he asked.

'Where it always is.'

He almost rolled his eyes, though narrowly caught himself. 'Where's that?'

'The cupboard in the hallway downstairs.'

'Fine.'

Jodie picked up the pile of stuff and nudged the door open with her elbow. She was a step into the hallway when Owen called a gentle 'Mum...'

She turned, expecting him to start haggling for a way to get his Xbox back. Instead, he was squirming, looking at the floor.

'What?' she asked.

'The other night, when I was in Granddad's house...'

Jodie felt the anger rising again. When he'd *broken into* his granddad's house. 'What about it?' she replied.

'There was someone at the front door,' he said. 'They were trying to get in.'

Jodie froze. 'What do you mean?'

'There was this scratching, like they were trying to use a key that wasn't working. I accidentally bumped into a chair and made a load of noise. They went away after that.'

Jodie waited for more, though her son was silent. 'Who was it?' she asked.

He shook his head. 'I don't know.'

THIRTY-NINE

Jodie hid Owen's Xbox under her bed – and then put the cables into separate sections of the old bags that were buried at the bottom of her wardrobe. He'd be *really* pushing his luck if he went looking for his things but, even if he did, he'd be unlikely to find it all. Not only that, if Jodie caught him, the time he spent without the Xbox would only be extended. She'd give it away to a charity shop before she let him have it back early.

He did the jobs she'd asked that evening, which was the most housework she'd ever known him do. Jodie even checked the skirting boards in the hall and he'd vacuumed across the top of those.

She didn't tell him, preferring to let him stew, but it was a job well done. Not that housework could undo the pain her son had caused another child.

After that, he went up to his room, leaving the house the quietest it had been in a long while. She wondered if he was actually doing his homework.

Fiona arrived a little later in the evening. She'd been at an exercise class in town and then shared a drink with the trainer.

She showered and then pottered around the kitchen before making small talk about how clean everything was.

She acted as if they hadn't found the bone in her garden. As if they hadn't been led there by the gnome in Jodie's father's attic. As if everything was normal.

When she went up to the spare room, it left Jodie by herself in the living room. The house was still and quiet, though haunted by Jodie's destructive thoughts. She should go to the police but she couldn't. She should clear Paul McIntosh's name – except to do so would forever tarnish her own family's – and possibly Fiona's as well.

All that – and she still didn't know what had happened. Had her brother tried to set fire to the shed with her in it? What was her father's role in covering up Mike's fascination with fire – and Ben's disappearance? Did her mum know the whole time?

She drifted in and out of sleep as the television blinked its way through the late-night chat shows into the early hours of rolling news. Jodie had told Owen to dress smartly for the naming ceremony but, when she'd said that, she hadn't been certain she was going to go herself. How could she stand in front of the town and listen to people saying how great her father was when she was riddled with doubts about the truth?

By the time Jodie made it into her bed, it was barely worth it. She grabbed a few hours of spoiled sleep but morning light peeped around the edges of her curtains far too early.

There was noise coming from downstairs – and she arrived back in the kitchen to find Owen leaning on the counter, apparently waiting for the kettle to boil.

'Can I make you something?' he asked.

For a moment, she couldn't figure out what he was doing. He never had hot drinks and she wouldn't need many fingers to count the number of times he had been up before her. Her muddied mind took a couple of seconds to remember she had his Xbox.

Jodie plopped herself at the kitchen table and told Owen he could put some toast in for her. At least she knew he could cook that. He hurried to the bread bin and grabbed some slices, then dropped them into the toaster before fiddling in the cupboard for a teabag.

When that was done, he turned and leaned on the counter once more. 'What time is Granddad's ceremony?' he asked.

'One o'clock at the community centre.'

He nodded along and asked what she wanted him to wear – which was the first time he'd ever done such a thing. It was as if he'd been replaced overnight.

Punishment or not, she didn't think she could take too much of her son clumping around the kitchen, even if he was trying to be helpful. She wanted a good relationship with him, though she also liked having space to herself, where she could eat and wake up in peace.

Jodie sat by herself, eating the toast and convincing herself it wasn't the right day to tell the police what she knew. *Tomorrow*, she figured... although that little voice told her that it would always be tomorrow. She was in a dead end of having *some* idea about what happened to Ben, while having *no* idea of how to work out any more. That same little voice told her she didn't want to know any more.

She drifted through the morning, finding a muted dress that wasn't *daughter in mourning*, while avoiding anything too *night out in town*. Owen was wearing his school blazer and had dug out a dark tie for himself. The fact he'd opted to wear one, without being forced for school, was another first.

The community centre was buzzing by the time they arrived. A stage had been set up close to the front and there was a curtain covering the doors. A crowd of well-dressed, largely older, locals had gathered in small groups and were chatting among themselves. It was like the bit after a wedding when everyone's standing around, not knowing what's happening. There were even a couple of photographers floating around, likely documenting everything for the council's website and their hundred or so Twitter followers.

Past them, an opportunistic ice cream van had parked in one of the 'No Parking' spaces at the side of the centre and was doing a roaring trade from the children who were tearing around the playground beyond. A handful of parents were on the benches at the side, half watching their kids, half checking their phones.

Milling close to the stage was the usual crowd of councillors and officials. The sort of people who Jodie knew through osmosis, even though almost all their names eluded her. Owen peeled away from her not long after they arrived – though she didn't blame him. She was surprised he'd hung around at all.

Jodie's brother Mike was standing with Samantha close to the road. There in presence but wanting no part of the actual proceedings. She couldn't blame him either. Samantha was studiously avoiding eye contact and it felt like weeks before that she'd stormed around, demanding half the house. Jodie had to count on her fingers to realise it was only six days.

Jodie and Mike exchanged a brief wave but that was the total of their interaction. Jodie couldn't look at him without remembering that their father had covered up the story about him starting a fire by the council offices.

A few paces away, Jordan was on his phone – and was quickly joined by Owen. The two teenagers turned their backs to the adults and mumbled among themselves. Jodie figured Owen was probably telling him about his lack of Xbox – and that he had to at least appear to be on his best behaviour.

Jodie did a lot of nodding as she made her way to the front. The benefit of having some involvement in proceedings was that she didn't have to stop for a conversation with anyone. Her boss, Ian, said something about the weather – and then Darren, with a very pregnant Chandra, told her it was a fantastic turnout.

The same conversations, with the same people, for infinity.

Jodie's mother was hidden under a large hat and unnecessary sunglasses, as if she was set for a day at the races. She was with a few other women, drinking tea out of paper cups that were being served by a girl with an urn on top of a fold-up table.

It was all a bit summer fete. A bit coffee-morning-at-the-church-hall – which her father would have loved, of course. That was his scene and, even more than his funeral, this was a fitting send-off.

Rows of seats had been placed on the path at the front of the community centre. They were the sort of straight-backed, spine-mangling chairs that only existed in places like schools and function rooms. They were neither comfortable, nor stylish – and the only benefit was that they could fold down and fit in a small space.

Names of the various councillors had been printed on cards and placed on each, though there was one tactfully marked 'daughter' that Jodie assumed was hers.

Things kicked into gear when the town's current mayor arrived in the full regalia of blue gown, cape and heavy chains. It was the same gear Jodie's dad had worn so many times, like a carnival pirate without the eye patch.

There was a lot of handshaking and glad-handing; smiles and tilted-head *how-are-you-doings?*

Jodie hadn't paid a lot of attention to the emails she'd received about the order of the day – but it was the mayor who rang a giant bell to get everyone's attention. He gave a short speech about how Jodie's father had 'inspired the town and a generation'. Jodie doubted that, considering nobody under the age of sixteen or so likely knew who he was.

In another time, probably even a week before, Jodie would

have enjoyed the way the town was celebrating her father. After everything that had happened, she couldn't help but think how much of a fraud it all was. There were so many celebrities from when she was a kid who were now banished from public life for various indiscretions that had come to light – and now her father could be the same.

There was a silence as Jodie realised everyone was looking to her. The mayor was beckoning towards the stage and one of the councillors leaned in to whisper, 'Do you need a hand?'

Jodie stood, feeling the weight of the town upon her. She went up the handful of steps, becoming the focus of attention, as someone passed her a pair of scissors. She was confused for a moment, holding them up and almost asking what to do before realising the mayor was pointing to a red ribbon which had been tied between the pillars at the front of the centre.

She'd seen her father snipping ribbons to open things when she'd been a kid. It was another thing that was easy to accept as normal when a child but appeared odder with age.

Jodie went with it and cut the ribbon as someone off to the side pulled on a string that opened the curtains behind the stage. Past that, a glimmering plaque had been installed above the door – and, though she could make out her dad's name, the rest of the engraving was too small to see from distance.

People clapped and then the town's band burst into the national anthem for some reason.

Jodie stood alone on the stage, twisting the scissors in her hand and not knowing where to look. There was a microphone barely three steps away and she dreamed of grabbing it and telling everyone how fake it all was. That her father wasn't who they thought he was. That he wasn't who *she* thought he was.

Instead, she continued twiddling the scissors until the anthem was done and the bloke who'd given her the scissors offered to take them back.

Photos were taken, more people talked about the weather

and the turnout – and then the doors were flung open and someone announced there was a buffet inside. They might as well have said there was free gold for everyone – because the stampede wouldn't have been any worse.

Jodie waited as people from the town streamed past her, following the promise of free food. Darren came across and kissed her on both cheeks, saying she 'did great' before adding that he had to get Chandra home. Given how pregnant she was, Jodie was sympathetic – and it was only as they headed for the car park that Jodie realised she hadn't told him about Owen breaking into her dad's house. As far she knew, father and son hadn't actually spoken during the ceremony, despite only being a short distance from one another. It felt like another broken relationship, in among a family that didn't know anything else.

Inside, people were milling around with paper plates piled high with slightly soggy cheese and tomato, or egg, sandwiches. There were sausage rolls, Mr Kipling Battenbergs and some open boxes of Family Circle biscuits. The sort of thing her dad lived for. *It's a lovely spread*, he would have said. One of his catchphrases whenever he had to attend events. Someone could've served up a massive bowl of cabbage they'd grown themselves, and he would've called it a lovely spread.

Jodie watched the crowd separate off into smaller groups, wondering how long she might have to hang around without looking rude for leaving. She was scanning the throng for Owen when she realised her mother had appeared at her side.

'I wasn't sure you'd be here,' her mum said.

'I could say the same.'

Jodie's mother didn't acknowledge that she'd spoken. 'You got yourself in quite the state the other day,' she said. 'I was worried you'd run off and do something silly.'

She was partially right about that. Jodie had told her about finding Ben's top in the attic – and her mother's response had been cold indifference.

'Like what?' Jodie whispered.

Her mother's reply was a hissed warning. As if Jodie was a child, being told off for not eating all her tea. 'Don't cause a scene,' she said. 'Not on your father's day.'

'Dad's dead, Mum. He doesn't have days of his own any more.'

It came out harsher than Jodie meant... or perhaps she wanted it to be that cruel. She wasn't sure any longer. The man she thought had raised her was apparently someone else.

Jodie's mother rocked onto the balls of her feet, nodding and smiling at someone in a suit who passed them with a glass of something fizzy in his hand. Jodie and her mother were a pace apart but it might as well have been an ocean.

Jodie waited until the person had passed and then she continued, her voice measured and quiet. 'I told you about Ben's shirt being in Dad's house and then, that night, someone tried to set the house on fire.'

Her mother took the news of the attempted arson with the calmness of someone who already knew.

'Mike told me,' she said, heading off Jodie's thought process. 'He said he had to find out via Samantha seeing it on Facebook.'

'I *only* told you what I found,' Jodie said quietly, ignoring the implied criticism.

She expected indignance – but all she got was a continued calm.

'If you've got something to say, then say it,' her mother replied.

Jodie almost did – except accusing her mum of trying to burn down the house in which she'd raised her children seemed too big a stretch.

'Did you tell anyone else?' Jodie asked instead.

Her mother answered by not answering. 'I said *not* to cause a scene,' she replied. 'We can talk another time.'

Jodie was about to ask what they'd talk about on another

day, when there was a creak from the speaker system. She turned towards the stage, where a man was standing in the centre, microphone in his hand.

There was a collective gasp as everyone realised at the same time who it was.

Paul McIntosh was about to address the town.

FORTY

Paul McIntosh's clothes still hung loosely from him, like a child in his dad's Sunday best. His hand trembled as he flicked at the cord connected to the microphone, making the speaker system whine again.

'I, um... wanted to say something,' he said with a stammer. 'I just, er... don't want any trouble.'

He bobbed from one foot to the other with the nervousness of a teenager about to ask out a girl for the first time. The only other sound in the room was a gentle hush of people asking who it was – and then being astonished when told.

McIntosh was about to say something more when a man's voice shouted across the quiet. 'What about Ben?'

An excited murmur flitted through the room and then another groan went up from the speaker system.

'I never killed anyone,' McIntosh said. 'It was all a mistake.'

Jodie had never heard a quiet like it. The silence of an abandoned mine.

'I never—'

McIntosh's lips continued moving but there was no sound. For a moment, Jodie couldn't figure out what had happened, then she saw one of the suited councillors at the base of the stage, with a power cord in his hand. He'd pulled the plug – and was motioning frantically for McIntosh to get off stage. A pair of councillors started ascending the stairs, as McIntosh held up his hands to indicate he hadn't meant any harm. The men continued towards him, so he hurried in the other direction, dropping down from the stage and disappearing through the closest fire exit with a clang. It happened so quickly that the dumbstruck crowd stared to one another, as if to make sure they'd all seen the same thing.

Jodie looked to her mother, whose calm appearance had been replaced by something closer to interested bemusement.

'Why would he do that?' Jodie asked, largely talking to herself. She didn't expect a reply – but she got one.

'I heard someone put his windows through last night,' her mum replied.

'Is he OK? Did he call the police?'

'How would I know?'

Jodie thought on it for a moment. McIntosh hadn't said very much: mainly that he hadn't killed anyone and that he didn't want trouble. It had felt stumbling and barely coherent – but, in context, it was a nervous, scared man asking people to leave him alone in the most public way possible.

What other option did he have?

'What if he's innocent?' Jodie said. She spoke in a whisper, worried about anyone overhearing.

'What if he is?' her mother replied. 'It's not like anything can be done now.'

Jodie examined her mother, who was studiously ignoring the stare. On the surface, it was a factual statement – but the coldness with which it had been spoken said so much more than the words. There had been times in the past when Jodie struggled to see how they were related but it had never been more apparent.

She didn't get the chance to reply because Mike appeared, Samantha in tow. He had a similar look of confused amusement that so many of those around the hall were sharing.

'What about that?' he said, nodding towards the stage. 'After what he did. He's got some nerve. I still can't believe he came back.'

'You're one to talk about nerve,' Jodie replied.

Mike's brow creased. 'What d'you mean?'

'It wasn't a lightning strike that set the shed on fire when I was kid,' Jodie said. 'It was you.'

FORTY-ONE

Jodie hadn't planned to accuse her brother, even though it had been in the back of her mind ever since she'd spoken to Keith the journalist.

Mike stared at her, brother and sister, another huge divide.

'What do you mean?' he said.

'I know about you starting that fire near the council offices,' Jodie replied. 'Dad kept it quiet to protect you. I know you had a thing about starting fires.' A beat. 'Maybe you do now...?'

Mike was still for a moment, then he glanced sideways to his wife. He and Samantha were holding hands and Jodie saw his arm muscle tense as he squeezed her fingers.

'It's not like that,' he said.

'Isn't it? Are you saying you didn't start a fire at the council building?'

Another squeeze of Samantha's hand. 'Yes... well... I wasn't trying to burn it down. It was a mistake.'

'But Dad covered it up because he knew people would think you set fire to the shed with me in it.'

Mike glanced to their mother and then focused back on Jodie. 'I didn't do that.'

She wondered if she believed him. Whether it mattered. Their family was broken and, in many ways, it was irrelevant what he did. The fact she thought him capable was enough.

'Did you try to set fire to Dad's house the other night?'

Jodie didn't know from where her boldness was coming.

Mike opened his mouth to reply but Samantha got in first. 'Course he didn't,' she said. 'That's Jord's inheritance. Why would he burn it down?' She let go of her husband's hand and batted it dismissively towards Jodie, like a someone shooing a fly. 'You've lost it.'

Jodie turned to face her sister-in-law – and, this time, her confidence wasn't forced. 'It's *not* Jordan's inheritance,' she said firmly. 'It's *mine*.'

She spoke so ferociously that Sam took a quarter-step back. It lasted barely a second until she straightened herself. 'We'll see about that.'

'No, we won't. You're getting exactly what you deserve.' Jodie waited a moment, relishing the power of a pause and then, 'You're getting nothing.'

Samantha's eyes narrowed dangerously. 'How do we know you didn't try to start the fire?'

'Why would I set fire to something I own?'

'I wouldn't put anything past you.'

Mike thrust an arm across his wife's front, anticipating there might be more than angry words. 'I think we're all overreacting,' he said. 'It's an emotional day, what with Dad and all.' He lowered his arm and motioned towards Jodie. 'It's not like she poured lighter fluid through the letterbox herself, is it?' After that, he turned to his sister. 'For what it's worth, I didn't set fire to the shed. Yes, I was caught at the council offices – and Dad said he'd try to keep it out of the news. It was just... I dunno, stupidity.' He broke into a gentle smile. 'Didn't you do anything stupid as a teenager?'

Jodie looked through her brother, towards the other side of

the hall, where Jordan and Owen were standing next to Robbie. The cousins were laughing at something the older man had said. Teenagers doing stupid things was a touchy subject.

As her mother, brother and sister-in-law all looked at her, Jodie suddenly felt very small and embarrassed. She'd said things and made accusations that couldn't be taken back.

'I've got to go,' she said, stepping quickly around Samantha.

Her mother started to say something but Jodie ignored her as she weaved around a couple of women in muted dresses. She strode through the crowd, across to where Owen and Jordan were still laughing. A nod from Robbie towards Jodie was all it took for the two boys to turn and spot her coming. The smiles instantly left their faces as they looked to the floor.

'We're going,' Jodie said.

Owen wavered for a moment – but the silent threat of not getting back his Xbox meant there was no complaint.

'See ya soon,' he said.

It was only when they were halfway back to the car that Jodie realised she didn't know if he was talking to Jordan or Robbie.

FORTY-TWO

Jodie drifted through the rest of the day. She ignored a text from Mike, saying they should talk soon, and instead flopped on the sofa, wishing she could go back and never enter her father's attic.

Fiona had gone to a spinning class instead of the naming ceremony – and they danced around one another through the afternoon, neither bringing up the one thing they should be talking about.

Afternoon became evening and quiz shows became talent shows. Fiona was on the other side of the living room, reading something on her phone as Jodie stared aimlessly at the television. It was like her mind was being read as Fiona finally spoke.

'I'm sure it's not what it looked like,' she said. There was a forced decisiveness about her, as if she was trying to convince herself as much as she was Jodie.

'We found Ben's shirt in Dad's attic – and a bone in your garden. The gnome from your garden was in my dad's attic. What else does it look like?'

Fiona gazed unfocused towards the TV. 'It might not be Ben's bone.'

Jodie picked up her phone from the arm of the chair. 'Shall I call the police and ask them to find out?'

She was struggling to contain an anger at a man who'd never have to face it.

Fiona didn't reply at first. She sucked on her bottom lip and continued not watching the television. 'Our dads would have had a reason,' she said quietly. 'You must know that.'

'What sort of reason?'

'I don't know but they were good dads. Look at everything yours did for the town. They just named the community centre after him. It's not like they do that for anyone.'

A week before and it would have been true. They'd each had good fathers and yet it didn't feel like that any longer. Jodie didn't know if she'd ever go to the police but she also didn't know how she could cope with not knowing what happened. With not knowing who her father actually was. She wanted Fiona to be right. She wanted there to be an explanation that made sense but couldn't think of one.

'What about McIntosh?' Jodie said. She thought of him standing there on stage, trembling. Of the shouting woman in the supermarket. Of how someone had thrown something through his window.

'What about him?'

'He lost all those years for something I don't think he did.'

'We can't give them back to him.'

'...But we can let everyone know he's innocent.'

'I'm not saying it's right,' Fiona said, 'but what's done is done.'

It was perhaps the biggest dilemma with which Jodie had been wrestling. She could never return the years that had been taken from McIntosh – so was it worth it to destroy other lives? Her father's legacy didn't only impact her, there was Owen as well.

Fiona wasn't done. 'Even if you tell the police what you

know, there will still be people who think McIntosh did it. It's not like he's got a wife or kids. It's just him – and, if he didn't kill Ben, then he already knows the truth. If you tell people, who are you helping?'

Jodie tried to think of a reply better than something about it being the right thing to do. Perhaps Fiona was correct – and right and wrong wasn't as black and white as she wanted it to be. She pressed back into the chair and closed her eyes.

'I'm not saying I agree with it all,' Fiona continued, 'but I don't know how anything gets better if you hand in Ben's shirt. Or if the police dig up my garden.'

Jodie kept her eyes closed for a few moments, then opened them to stare at the dimpled ceiling. The thing Fiona was missing was that Jodie didn't think she could keep going with things as they were. She knew too much but she didn't know enough.

She excused herself and headed for the stairs and then the bathroom. She had been happy for Fiona to stay at hers as a respite from Robbie – but now she felt trapped by her friend's knowledge. It felt as if *they* were in on something together, even though Jodie didn't know what.

Jodie went into the bathroom and perched on the toilet seat for a while, running through the same dilemmas that had been stuck in her mind for days. She ran the taps and washed her hands and face, then went back onto the hall. She was on the top step about to head downstairs when she noticed a gentle hum coming from Owen's room. Without his Xbox, the usual sound of simulated warfare had been replaced by a general silence. Jodie hovered, trying to figure out what he might be watching or doing. It was probably something on his phone, except something didn't sound quite right.

She knocked on his door and said his name. She half expected the noise to go silent, except it continued at the same level as before.

'Owen...?'

No reply.

Jodie nudged the door open, first by a crack and then the whole way. A part of her thought he might have hunted down his Xbox and taken it anyway. The truth was worse.

The TV was on, the volume low, and there was no sign of her son.

FORTY-THREE

Jodie checked her room and the spare one in which Fiona was staying. She then went downstairs and looked there before making sure Owen wasn't in the yard.

He was gone.

She headed back to the living room, where Fiona was swiping at her phone.

'Have you seen Owen?' Jodie asked.

Fiona glanced up. 'Not since we ate. I assumed he was in his room.'

'Me too. He's not home.'

Fiona put down her phone on the side. 'I didn't hear him leave.'

Jodie waited in the doorway, trying to remember whether she'd heard any sounds from the stairs or the door. The truth was she couldn't remember much of anything after the naming ceremony. She'd been lost in her own daydreams.

'He's never snuck out before,' Jodie said, before realising that he'd done precisely that a few nights ago when she'd taken a sleeping pill – and he'd gone to her dad's house. 'He must've gone out his window,' she added. 'You can get onto the porch from there and jump down...'

Fiona didn't reply – there wasn't much to say – so Jodie grabbed her own phone from the side and called Darren. Her ex-husband didn't answer on the first attempt, so she hung up and tried a second time. He'd barely said 'hello' when Jodie asked if he'd seen Owen.

There was a coughed pause and then, 'Not since earlier.' He took a breath and then, 'Why?'

Jodie waited a moment, wondering if it was worth saying that their son had snuck out of the house and that she didn't know where he was. It sounded bad because it *was* bad. Or maybe it was a teenage thing. Hadn't every kid snuck out of home or school at some point?

'No big deal,' she replied, trying to sound breezy. 'He's just a bit late. He's probably with Jordan. I'll try there – but let me know if you see him.'

Darren sounded distracted. There were voices in the background and some sort of banging. When he replied, it was as if he was talking away from the receiver. 'I will,' he said – and then, before Jodie could hang up, he was gone.

Jodie could sense Fiona watching, so she withdrew into the kitchen, wanting to be by herself. She called her brother, something she couldn't remember doing at any point in the recent past. They communicated by text and vague nods or waves if they saw one another. Actually speaking on the phone felt too personal, especially after the day they'd had.

He answered on the second ring with a confused-sounding 'Jode?'

'Is Jordan there?' Jodie asked.

'He's upstairs. Why?'

'Because Owen's snuck out and I was wondering if he's with Jordan.'

There was a gentle 'oh' followed by a swift 'I'll check. Hang on.'

Jodie winced as her brother put down his phone too hard on something. The clunk echoed through her ear as she waited, back turned to the living room. The vague sound of a television hummed in the background of the call.

Soon, there was another clunk as Mike picked his phone back up. Jodie knew from the hesitancy in his voice that something was wrong.

'Jordan's gone as well,' he said. 'He left his telly on, with some sort of YouTube video of someone playing games. It sounded like he was in there playing, like he always is.' He waited a moment, sighing and lowering his voice. Jodie assumed he was yet to tell Samantha. 'Do you think they're together?' he asked.

'I would've thought so.'

'I'm coming over.'

'You don't have—' Jodie didn't finish the sentence because her brother had gone. He'd sounded urgent and worried in a way he rarely was, though, if anything, the fact *both* boys were missing gave Jodie a small amount of reassurance. At least Owen hadn't disappeared by himself.

Jodie turned and realised Fiona was hovering in the door. She offered an apologetic shrug and then, 'We should check my house. They might be with Robbie.'

Jodie had been thinking the same.

Fiona went upstairs to grab her house keys and then the two of them hurried along the street.

'Does Owen often come to yours?' Jodie asked.

'Not really – but I've seen Robbie talking to a few of the lads here and there. I think they play Xbox online together.'

Jodie had no idea who Owen played against when he was on his Xbox. She'd assumed it was his friends from school –

although, if it was Robbie as well, it would explain Owen and Robbie's familiarity around each other.

Fiona unlocked the door of her house and led the way inside. She went through to the empty living room, where the Xbox sat unused underneath the television; and then into the kitchen. Jodie looked through the window, towards the space at the back, where Fiona had uncovered, and then recovered, the bone. The rocks were back in place and it was as if the moment had never happened.

There was nobody in the kitchen, nor the garden. Fiona darted up the stairs and there were footsteps from above. When she reappeared in the hall, she shrugged at Jodie.

'Nobody's home...'

Jodie checked her phone and then tried calling Owen. It should have been her first option but, for some reason, it hadn't occurred to her.

There was no answer. She hadn't received any messages from him either, so she hammered out an angry:

WHERE ARE YOU?

She almost sent it – except she wondered if letting him know that *she* knew he was gone would make things worse. If he'd snuck out, he'd obviously planned to return at some point in the not-too-distant future. Tipping him off that he would be in almighty trouble for doing so might only encourage him to stay out longer.

And he would be in almighty trouble when she found him.

Jodie deleted the message without sending it.

She and Fiona got back to Jodie's house just as Mike's green van was pulling in. He buzzed down the passenger-side window and craned across.

'Any sign?' he asked.

'Nothing,' Jodie replied.

'Jord's not answering his phone.'

'Neither's Owen.'

Mike stretched and opened the door for her. 'We'll drive around town,' he said. 'They're probably with their other mates. They can't've got far.'

Jodie told Fiona she'd catch up with her later and then climbed into Mike's van. It was only as he pulled away, and the rumbles of the engine vibrated through her, that she realised she'd never been in a vehicle with only her brother before. They'd spent hours in the backs of cars together, when they were kids and their dad was driving them to the seaside. They'd even have days out at the 'big' supermarket away from town during the summer holidays, if it was raining. They'd play I-Spy, or count coloured cars... and then, one day, they were too old for it all.

It had been a long time since she'd felt connected to him in such a way – even if it had been barely hours before that she'd accused him of setting fire to the shed when she was inside.

Mike was driving in the direction of the town centre, one hand on the wheel, one on the gearstick.

'Has Owen snuck out before?' he asked.

Jodie pictured the security camera shot of him going in through the window of their father's house.

'I don't think so,' she replied.

'I don't think Jord has either. If he has, we've never noticed.' He paused to give way to someone on a roundabout and then added, 'Did you ever sneak out as a kid?'

'Never. You?'

'Once. Mum and Dad were arguing and I decided I was going to run away. I got to the bus stop and it started raining, so I changed my mind and went home. Nobody noticed I'd left.'

Jodie smiled to herself. They felt like more innocent times. It had been so much simpler when they were children and other people made all the decisions.

Mike slowed as they reached the outskirts of the shopping area. There was a group of teenage boys spread across the pavement, each trying to trip one another up. Jodie vaguely recognised the biggest of the group – but none of them were Owen or Jordan.

Mike sped up, continuing along the high street and out the other side. He doubled around to do a loop of the supermarket car park, though there was no sign of the boys on the patch of land past the car wash, where lads played football sometimes.

After that, he drove the other way along the high street, before heading into the housing estates. They slowed past various playgrounds, arches and alleys. The sorts of places where Mike might have hung around with his friends when they were young. There was no sign of Owen or Jordan.

It seemed almost inevitable they would end up back at the house in which they'd grown up. Jodie told Mike to stop and he parked outside while she let herself in. She called Owen's name and then checked the back window and door, both of which were still in place. She looked upstairs, just in case, but there was nobody there.

Back in the van, she answered Mike's unasked question. 'Owen took those medals you wanted,' she said. 'He broke through the back one night this week. I was furious.'

Mike eased off the clutch and pulled away, his attention on the road. 'What? Why'd he want them?'

'I'd said that they were going to be yours – and he thought that meant they were worth something. He was going to sell them but I got them back first. They're in a bag at home. You can take them later.'

Mike remained quiet as he stopped at the end of the street and let someone in a people carrier reverse onto the road. He drummed the steering wheel.

'I wasn't going to sell them,' he said quietly.

'I never said you were.'

'They were...' He stopped himself, gulped, and then added, 'They always remind me of Dad. We'd polish them together when I was a kid. Just me and him.'

There was no need for Jodie to reply. She had those same moments with her father when it was only them and she felt like the most important person in the world. A break from constantly sharing him with the whole town.

The woman had finished reversing and gave a thank you wave as she pulled away. Mike followed behind as they continued towards the edge of the estate.

'I don't know what to do with Owen,' Jodie admitted. 'He's in trouble for bullying at school and now he's sneaking out. I took away his Xbox.'

That got a kindly snort. 'I bet that went down well.' A pause. 'What about his dad?'

'I tried to get Darren to have a word but Chandra's due any day and he's more focused on that.'

'Do you want me to talk to him?'

The thought hadn't occurred to Jodie. At least somebody else was helping and it wasn't all her. 'Maybe,' she said. 'Let's find him first.'

Mike continued driving. They passed a few groups of young people but there was no sign of either Owen or Jordan. Mike tried phoning Jordan again but there was no answer, and he fielded a separate call from Samantha, where he explained that he was yet to find their son.

The next time they ended up outside their father's house, Mike slowed again. The scorch marks around the front door were still burned into the corners of the brickwork. Jodie found herself wondering if they would come out with a scrub, or if it would need repainting.

Mike had already driven past when it felt as if he'd read her mind. 'I can come round and clear that off on Monday, if you want,' he said.

'Will you have time?'

'I'll make it work.' He slowed for a corner and changed gear down and then back up. 'Did you ever find out what happened...?'

He was fishing but it felt like something had changed with the journey and the shared goal of finding their sons. It was the closest Jodie had felt to her brother in years.

Which is perhaps why she suddenly remembered what he'd *actually* said back at the community centre. She'd been focused on herself at the time, angry at her mum and the ceremony and, more than anything, her father for not being there. She'd taken it out on Mike by accusing him of setting fire to the shed with her inside.

She'd been *so* angry she hadn't listened to what he was saying.

Except, now she was.

'How did you know?' she asked.

Mike shifted in his seat, though remained focused on the front. 'Know what?'

'Back at the community centre, you said it had been an emotional day for everyone.'

'It had.'

'Samantha reckoned I might have tried to set fire to the house myself – but you said something like, "It's not like she poured lighter fluid through the letterbox".'

Mike glanced sideways and suddenly sounded unsure of himself. 'I'm assuming you didn't...?'

'Of course I didn't.' Jodie paused and reran the moment from the community centre in her mind. 'But how did you know someone poured lighter fluid through the letterbox?'

FORTY-FOUR

Jodie heard it in the hesitancy of her brother's voice the moment he replied. 'I suppose I was guessing,' he said. 'It was a turn of phrase, that sort of thing...'

He tailed off but she knew.

'The fire marshal told me it was lighter fluid,' she said. It was a lie but he didn't know that. 'So how did *you* know?'

'I didn't. I was guessing.'

'It's such a specific thing to guess. You could've said petrol, or anything.'

Mike continued driving but his fingers were twitching on the steering wheel.

'Stop the van,' Jodie said. She heard her own voice quiver.

It might have been a flinch of the foot but Mike sped up. 'It's not like that,' he said.

'So what is it like?'

A car was trying to merge from an intersection but Mike powered through, almost ramming the vehicle in front before easing off.

'You have a history with fire,' Jodie continued. 'There was

that one by the council offices that Dad covered up. Now Dad's house. What is it? Some sort of disorder?'

'No.'

'So what then?'

Mike broke abruptly and turned into a side street. Jodie jolted forward in the seat, breastbone slamming into the seat belt, which left her gasping. Mike accelerated towards an old factory, where the wire fence had long since collapsed, leaving a large patch of rubble and cement. He swerved around the shattered chain-link and stopped in the shade of the old factory, hidden from the road and the houses beyond.

'Did you set fire to the shed?'

Jodie could feel her heart racing, and not only from the shock of the seat belt. It felt as if her entire life hinged on his reply.

'No,' he said.

Jodie didn't believe him. She unclipped her belt and reached for the door handle. The moment her fingers touched the plastic, the central locking slammed into place. She tried the handle anyway – but the door was sealed shut, with the pair of them inside.

She turned to her brother. 'Let me out,' she said.

Mike shook his head slowly. 'I can't do that,' he replied.

Jodie tried the handle again, clicking it forward and back, all to no result.

'Please don't break my door,' Mike said quietly.

'Let me out.'

'No.'

Jodie looked at the sternness in her brother's stare. There was steel that she'd never seen before, which sent a shiver along her back. She moved quickly, stretching across and hammering the centre of the steering wheel. The horn blasted three long toots until he pushed her away.

'You want to hear this,' Mike said.

'Let me out.'

Jodie lunged for the horn again but her brother grabbed her wrists and held her at bay.

'Just *listen*,' he said breathlessly.

Jodie was flailing, trying to get her feet out from under the glovebox. After a couple of seconds, Mike let go of her wrists and pushed her away. He pressed something on his side of the divide and the locks clicked up.

'It was me,' he said.

Jodie was holding the door handle. She levered it partway forward, though not enough to open the door.

'You set fire to the shed...?'

He shook his head. Gulped. Sighed. Glanced up, then down. Sighed again. 'I killed Ben.'

FORTY-FIVE

There was a long, long pause until Jodie realised she was still clasping the door handle. She let it go and pressed back into the seat, no longer wanting to escape.

'What do you mean?' she said.

'Dad got rid of the body,' Mike added. 'I don't know where or how. Just that he did.'

Mike was staring straight ahead as Jodie turned to look at him. A part of her wondered if it was some weird joke – but his features were still.

'I don't understand.'

He took a breath and ran his tongue across the bottom of his teeth. 'It was sort of an accident,' he said.

It didn't sound real. 'You killed him *by accident?*'

Mike didn't reply for a while. He pushed into his seat and rested his neck against the back.

'I did it for you,' he said.

The words were clear but it was like he'd spoken another language.

'What are you on about?' Jodie managed.

'You were at the cinema with Ben,' Mike said. He was

speaking slowly, choosing his words. 'I'd gone next door to drop off a set of guitar picks. I didn't know Ben was out and I didn't know you were with him. His mum told me and I asked if I could leave the picks with her. She said something about forgetting where she'd put them, so said I could leave them in his room. I went upstairs and their house is the mirror of ours.'

He started to ask whether Jodie had ever been inside but stopped himself because of course she had. She'd spent hours in Ben's room at various times when they were seeing each other.

'I'd never been in his room before,' Mike said. 'He had the same room as me but on the opposite side of the house. I put the picks on his bed and I was going to leave, except...'

He tailed off and bit his lip.

'What?' Jodie asked.

'Did you ever look out his window?'

It was an odd question. Jodie thought on it for a second. 'I guess.' The hairs on her arms had risen. 'I don't remember.'

'*I* remember,' Mike replied. 'Ben said he'd seen the shed fire from his window and that he'd rushed down to save you.'

'Right...'

'Except you can't see the shed from his window. I remember looking towards the yard and thinking it was a dull view compared to the one from my window. I'd started to leave but then I don't know why I thought of it. I went back to the window and realised the angle was wrong to see the shed. You wouldn't have even seen a glow from a fire because it's facing the wrong way.'

As soon as he said it, Jodie realised he was right. Ben's bedroom window overlooked a corner plot of the neighbour's garden on the other side. The only way he could have seen the shed from there was if he could somehow twist his head to face the opposite direction and see through another wall. He'd said he'd seen the fire from his window and nobody had bothered to check, because why would they? They were too busy calling him a hero.

Jodie had a sense of what was coming before it did.

'I left Ben's house and almost went home to tell Dad,' Mike said. 'It suddenly seemed so obvious – but it didn't feel like I could tell anyone. I ended up walking for ages – and then, you were there. Both of you. Holding hands. I guess you were heading home from the cinema. I watched for a while and thought about asking him in front of you – but then you separated. You were heading towards home and he turned and walked back along Bramble Alley. We almost bumped into each other because I wasn't that far behind.'

He paused and switched off the engine that Jodie hadn't realised was still running. There was a flicker of movement from outside and Jodie turned to where a crow had landed on a mound of rubble and started pecking at the top.

'I told him I knew about the shed,' Mike continued. 'He laughed and said he didn't know what I was on about. I said I'd been in his room and knew he couldn't have seen the fire.'

Mike gulped.

'I suppose I'd been trying to tell myself that it was a mistake. That maybe he'd been in a different room, something like that. But I saw it in his face. I remember him looking both ways along the alley. I wondered later if he'd been looking to see if you were still there – but I think it was to see if anyone was there. He didn't want to be overheard.'

'What did he say?' Jodie wasn't sure she wanted to know.

'That he didn't know you were inside the shed. He'd read something about Jimi Hendrix setting fire to a guitar and thought it'd be cool – except he didn't want to set fire to his own guitar. I don't know how he came up with it but he thought he'd set fire to our shed instead. It was so stormy that night, so loud, and I guess no one noticed him going over our back gate.'

Jodie wondered if a small part of her had always suspected.

'I don't know how he got it going with the rain that night but he watched it burning. Enjoyed it. He said he didn't know you were inside,' Mike continued. 'That's what he *said.* But I suppose I wondered if he knew all along. He said he'd started to walk away after a while so he didn't get caught but he heard a noise from inside. That's when he ran back and pulled you out. By then, me and Dad had noticed what was going on and we were outside. I think Dad said Ben was a hero and, after that, he was stuck. He could hardly admit he'd started the fire. He went along with it.'

Jodie had been unconscious at the time but she could picture the scene. In the confusion of the storm, the fire and the shock of a daughter being rescued, it was no wonder her dad had got the wrong end of the stick. He always looked for the good in people – and he'd found it in Ben.

'Are you saying he knew I was in the shed when he set it on fire?'

A shrug. 'Maybe. Even if he didn't, he wasn't that bothered. He got to be a hero.'

Jodie thought on that for a moment. There was no way of ever knowing – and it wasn't as if either version was good for her.

'You said Ben's death was an accident...'

Mike didn't reply and, for a while, Jodie wondered if he ever would.

Outside, the crow on the rubble had been joined by a second and the pair of them poked and jabbed at some sort of food wrapper until one of them lost interest and hopped away.

'It's hard to describe,' Mike said. 'He was sort of... *gloating* about it. It wasn't something he said, it was his face. It was... *him.* Like it was this big, clever trick he'd pulled off. He put you in danger, saved you, and everyone thought he was a hero. Not only that, people thought you were this perfect couple...' He took another breath and then added, 'You thought the sun shone out of his arse and I remember having this vision of you being older and married with kids. His parents even encouraged it. You'd still be together if he was still here, but it was all a lie. I was thinking that and he smiled and I just...'

Jodie didn't want to hear the rest – except she needed to. 'You what?'

'You remember my apprenticeship?'

It was a question out of nothing. 'What's that got to do with anything?'

'I'd not long started and I used to wear my tool belt everywhere. I think my boss had said something about getting used to wearing it and I'd taken it a bit too literally.'

Jodie nodded as she remembered. It had felt normal at the time – but he had worn his belt through evenings and weekends, when he wasn't working.

'I'd not realised it the whole time I was out – but my wrench was on that belt – and then it was in my hand. He had that look on his face; that cocky, clever look, and I hit him. I didn't even think about it. It was automatic and then, next thing, he's down. It was only one blow and he was in that ditch with all the brambles. It was like I blinked and it all happened.' He let out a long breath.

'How did no one see?'

'I suppose it was because it was so overgrown. You used to have to dodge around the thorns and he'd rolled down the bank, to where it was at its thickest.'

'What did you do then?'

'I went and told Dad.'

The chills were back on Jodie's arm and she suddenly didn't want to hear the rest, even though she couldn't resist asking. 'What did Dad say?'

Mike leaned forward and rested his head on the steering wheel momentarily before pressing back again. Outside, both crows had disappeared.

'He said he'd deal with it. He asked where Ben was – and that was the last time we ever spoke about it. I never asked what he did and he never said. Then everything happened. The police spoke to you and arrested that McIntosh guy. I figured he'd get off because he hadn't done anything...'

There was no need to finish that thought because they both knew how that had gone.

Brother and sister sat in silence for a while. Jodie felt a strange sense of completion, even through a mask of revulsion. She wondered if she'd always known something wasn't right. It was hard to know how to feel about Mike and what he'd done, apparently for her.

'Did Mum know?' she asked.

Mike was chewing the inside of his mouth. 'I think so. She told me about the shirt you found in the attic and I don't know why she'd have done that if she didn't.'

Jodie needed a second or two. It was all true.

'It *was* you who tried to set fire to the house.'

The reaction was sudden and explosive as Mike banged the steering wheel. 'Because you changed the locks! What were you thinking? My key had worked for thirty-odd years and then you changed it.'

'Because I didn't want Samantha going in there.'

Mike's anger disappeared as quickly as it had arrived. He huffed long and low as he sank down in the seat. 'I didn't know how else to get rid of that shirt. I didn't know Dad had kept it. When Mum said it was at the house, I went over to get it. I couldn't get in and sort of... panicked.'

'What if the fire had caught next door? Jim and Elaine would've been sleeping.'

'I know. I wasn't thinking. It was so stupid. I wish I hadn't done it. I've been expecting the police to come round any day. I thought there might be fingerprints, or something like that.'

Jodie let him stew on that for a minute or so. She couldn't

get past their neighbours being trapped inside a burning house, where the fire had spread from Mike's stupidity. It wasn't simply reckless, it was criminal. In the minutes before he'd pulled into the shadow of the factory, Jodie had felt closer to her brother than she had in years. Now, she barely knew him.

'The shirt wasn't at Dad's house that night,' she said.

Mike didn't flinch. 'Where is it?'

Jodie refused to answer. She now knew why she'd been left the entirety of the house. Her father had never forgiven his son for what he'd been forced to do to protect him. It wasn't *only* subduing a story about a fire, it was a murder. Her dad was a kind man, a councillor, a mayor. Getting rid of a body was so far outside his expertise that he'd done the only thing he could think of – ask his best friend for help. That's how Ben had ended up under the rocks at the bottom of Fiona's garden. Her father, the landscaper, had done the ultimate favour. There was little doubt now that's where the rest of Ben's remains would be found.

'Why'd Dad keep the shirt?' Jodie asked. It was more a question for herself than her brother. 'He washed it, folded it, put it away...'

'I've been wondering that ever since Mum told me,' Mike replied. 'I think it's because he kept everything important. All those clippings on the walls. The photos and certificates. He wasn't a hoarder but he could never quite get rid of anything that was big in his life. Maybe he'd have got rid if he knew he had something terminal – except he didn't know he was going to die. It just happened and then...'

Jodie thought on it for a few seconds, figuring her brother was probably right. It explained the gnome as well. Every major thing in her father's life had been documented and kept – and what happened to Ben was another of those things. Perhaps it made sense as a moment of protective madness, where nothing made sense.

'What about the council offices?' Jodie asked.

'How do you know about that?'

'Does it matter?'

Mike was in a mood where it felt as if he'd answer anything Jodie threw at him. 'Another mistake,' he said. 'After I found out about Ben and the shed – and then with what happened later... there was no one to talk to. I thought it was only Dad who knew and he never looked at me the same. I suppose I started to obsess about Ben and what he'd done. Why he did it. Then I started setting small fires. Matches and twigs at first, in the middle of nowhere. And then, I guess, I wanted to try something bigger...'

Jodie couldn't understand how her brother had got to that point – but then she'd never killed anyone and had to live with it. Perhaps it was another thing that made sense to the person most heavily involved?

'What about McIntosh?' she said.

Mike pushed himself up and, for the first time in a while, turned to face her. 'What about him?'

'If you did it, and Dad covered it up, how did he get done for it?'

They looked at one another for a moment, strangers and family as one.

'I thought about that a lot,' Mike said. 'I assumed he'd be found innocent because there was no body. Then, when he wasn't, I read all the papers to try to figure it out. I don't actually know – but I do have a theory.'

'What?'

'Did you ever see Ben trying car door handles?'

Mike didn't need to explain more because Jodie instantly knew what had happened. There had been a couple of times when they'd been walking somewhere together that she'd noticed Ben trying to open a series of car handles as they passed. He'd always laughed it off as something to do. She'd never understood – but was too infatuated to press any further. He'd done it on the last day she'd seen him.

Mike must have seen the acknowledgement. 'There was this time when we were on our way from school and there was this long row of parked cars. As we walked past, he tried every handle, seeing if any were unlocked. We were almost at the end when one opened. He poked his head inside and then got back out and closed the door. I asked what he was doing and he shrugged. Said it was something to do. I never saw him do it again – but it felt like something he'd done before. I figured he was looking to see if there was anything worth nicking. Later, I wondered if he'd done it with McIntosh's van. Sat inside it for a bit, even. It was just really bad luck that traces of him ended up in the same van that you saw at the church.' He took a breath and then added, 'If it wasn't that, then I don't know.'

It was another thing that felt true to Jodie. A stupid series of coincidences that had ended up with an innocent man in prison for the best years of his life.

'What are you going to do now?'

Jodie took a moment to realise her brother was asking her the question. Everything was in the open and it was up to her what came next. The door was unlocked and she eyed the handle, thinking about letting herself out and making a run for it. Those seconds of danger in which she'd been locked inside felt a long way off. The man next to her was a killer... but also her brother.

'Let's find our sons,' she said.

FORTY-SIX

Mike pulled away from the factory and bumped across a kerb before swerving onto the empty road. He got to the corner and then took the turn that would take them towards the high street.

He drove in a silence that Jodie didn't feel like breaking. What was there to say? She had no idea what to do. The important men in her life – her father, her brother, her first boyfriend – had all been people she thought they weren't. Of them all, it was only her father with whom she had a degree of understanding. If Owen came to her saying he'd done something terrible, her instinct would be to protect him in the way her dad had saved Mike. Maybe she could even see that with how she handled the bullying and why she'd put off talking to Owen for so long. Her father did something terrible because the alternative was also terrible.

Jodie was lost in her thoughts when Mike pulled to the side of the road. A couple of teenage boys were sitting on a wall and Mike buzzed down his window before craning out. When he spoke, he was carpenter Mike; man-down-the-pub Mike. 'D'you know Jordan Parker?' he asked.

One of the boys looked at his feet, while the other suddenly seemed interested in his phone. It was answer enough.

'Where'd you see him?' Mike asked.

'School,' replied the first boy.

'Where'd you see him *today*?'

The one who'd been looking at his feet squirmed and started scratching his head. The other pretended nothing was happening. Mike delved into his pockets and pulled out a ten-pound note that he offered out the window.

'First one who speaks...'

From nowhere, the lad with the phone leaped from the wall and grabbed the money in one quick movement. He pointed back the way they'd come. 'There were a few of them,' he said.

It wasn't much to go on, except, from nowhere, Jodie knew exactly where her son was headed.

'McIntosh's house,' she whispered.

FORTY-SEVEN

Mike did a U-turn and barrelled back towards the other side of town. Jodie remained quiet as he turned left through a red light and sped up as they went through the twenty zone.

It wasn't Owen that Jodie was worried about, not specifically, it was the company she suspected he was keeping. Not that he was innocent in everything. When she found him, at the very least, they were going to have a serious conversation about his friends – and about any time he was spending with Robbie, even if it was online.

Her brother must have felt something too, because he was doing almost fifty as they barrelled out of the twenty into a thirty. His phone was ringing, with Samantha's name on the screen, but Mike ignored it as he surged through a give-way sign without doing anything of the sort.

Jodie clasped the edge of her seat as her stomach gurgled with worry. There was no good reason for Owen to be at McIntosh's house.

It felt as if she'd been holding her breath the whole time until, minutes later, Mike screeched to a halt outside McIntosh's house. It was looking more dilapidated since Jodie had last visited. Bin bags were piled four deep close to the front door and all of the downstairs windows had large, splintered holes in the glass.

The gate was unlocked and Jodie led Mike onto the path as they edged towards the house. Jodie could hear voices, though it was difficult to know if they were coming from the house or...

Someone had shouted. She was sure of it. She only realised she'd stopped moving when her brother bumped into her back, before stepping away. 'What?' he said.

'Did you hear that?'

Jodie held up a hand, pointing towards the sky as if that would help her hear more clearly. There was silence, except she was sure she'd heard something.

'What?' Mike repeated.

There was a rustle of breeze, a distant hum of a car and... nothing.

Jodie took a few more steps until she could see where the front door was hanging open. One of the hinges had been broken and it was resting at an angle.

'Do you see—'

Mike never finished the sentence because, as he pointed towards the door, something boomed loud from somewhere within the house.

FORTY-EIGHT

Jodie swivelled on the spot, her body surging towards the house as her brain dragged her away. It sounded as if a cannon had gone off. It had been so loud, she'd *felt* it. She almost tripped over herself and, by the time she'd sorted out her legs, a blur emerged from the open door.

Jordan bounded across the threshold, breathless and wild, as he motioned towards the house behind. He was moving so quickly and desperately that he had bumped into his dad before he realised where he was.

Mike caught him and held him up as his son's feet scuffed at the ground. 'What happened?'

Before Jordan could answer, Robbie burst from the house. His eyes were as wide and frantic as Jordan's and his legs were moving too quickly for his body as he almost overbalanced forward. He bounced off the corner of the house, oblivious to the presence of Mike and Jodie as he weaved through them and dashed for the gate.

'What happened?' Mike had Jordan by his shoulders and was shaking him.

Before the reply could come, a third person flew from the

house. Jodie recognised him as one of Owen's friends, though she couldn't remember his name. He was wearing a cream top with a splattered effect across the front and it was only as he hurtled towards them that Jodie realised the red wasn't a pattern.

Jordan had dinner plates for eyes. He glanced sideways towards the boy with blood on his front and had to be physically turned so that he was again facing his father.

'Where's Owen?' Mike said. The panic and urgency in his voice made Jodie shiver – although it seemed to spur Jordan back to the present. He coughed and waved towards the house, which was enough for Jodie.

She dashed to the front door and inside, feeling Mike a step behind. It was dark and glass crunched underneath as she found herself next to a sink where the tap was running.

'Owen...?'

Jodie's voice echoed into a dark hall that ran off the kitchen. A faint orange glimmered from the far end and there was a shadowy hint of movement across the light. Jodie entered the hallway, Mike still a step behind.

'Owen...?'

No answer, although a creaking, scratching seeped through the darkness, like two knives rubbing together.

There was a shadow on the bottom step. Legs outstretched into the circle of light on the bare floorboard. A foot was scraping back and forth and there was another sound too. Something below the scraping: deep and otherworldly. Something Jodie could *feel* more than she could hear. It took her a second to realise it was sobbing. The sort of chest-heaving, guttural, deep-down cries that made it feel as if a person's stomach was swallowing them from the inside.

When Jodie reached McIntosh, his head was between his knees as his body rocked back and forth. The ripped wallpaper on the walls was speckled with a muddy, reddy, brown.

Mike noticed it first. Jodie had stopped in the spotlight and he stepped around her, crouching in the shadows within touching distance of McIntosh, where he reached towards something long and metallic. He withdrew his hand without touching it, though Jodie had seen it too.

A shotgun lay on the floorboards, with a spent cartridge at its side. There was more red on the ground, more still at McIntosh's side, and even more on the stairs above.

Jodie only had the merest glimpse, a fleeting half-second, but it was enough.

Mike stepped across her, blocking the view and holding her tight into her shoulder. 'Don't look,' he whispered, except Jodie already had.

Because, above McIntosh, splayed across the stairs at the top, head limp through the banisters, was the unmoving body of a teenage boy.

FORTY-NINE

WEEKS LATER

Another wake.

It was worse this time. Much worse. The worst of all.

Teenagers in ill-fitting suit jackets and crooked, dark ties gathered in small groups. There was a lot of nervous smiles, not because it was funny or joyous, but because nobody that age knew how to deal with what had happened. In the corners, away from the adults, the younger ones were trying to trip up one another. That, or loading plates with too much food. Boys being boys, Jodie's dad would have said.

Almost nobody dared to speak to Jodie. She felt people's eyes flick across her before they hastily moved onto someone safer to speak to. She didn't blame them. What was there to say? She'd heard it all when her dad had died and that was nothing compared to this.

There was one exception, well two. Ben's parents found Jodie as she was trying to hide behind one of the pillars in the community centre hall. The Martin Parker Community Centre. She couldn't look them in the eye as Elaine pulled her in for a hug she didn't want.

They truly were two people who knew how she felt.

'We're so sorry, love,' Jim said.

Jodie kept her head down and nodded a vague acknowledgement. She might have even mumbled something but it was difficult to know what was thought and what was said. It all blurred into one.

She blinked and she was outside, away from the crowd and apologies she didn't want. There were younger children on the playground at the back. A pair of boys were unbothered by their smart trousers and waistcoats as they climbed the slide. Jodie had no idea who they were – but she hadn't been paying much attention to everyone at the funeral and now the wake. Perhaps they were children of a friend she knew?

'You OK?'

Jodie turned from the playground, to where Fiona had materialised at her side. She was holding an unlit cigarette in one hand and a lighter in the other. Jodie motioned for the cigarette, which Fiona let her take – and then lit for her.

They stood together, both smoking as if they were teenagers once more. It had never been Jodie's thing, except maybe it had. In the moment, it was what she wanted.

'I'm sorry,' Fiona said. She waited and, when no reply came, she added, 'If I knew Robbie was going to take the boys there, I'd have done something. I didn't know he had such a hold on them. I thought...'

She left it there. It wasn't the first time she'd apologised, even though it wasn't her fault. Jodie knew it wasn't down to her, but it was easier to think it was.

They stood and smoked, watching the boys move from the slide to the climbing frame. There were grubby scuffs on the front of both their waistcoats and muck on their hands.

'Where are you sleeping tonight?' Fiona asked. When she didn't get a reply, she added, 'There's always a room at mine.'

Jodie shook her head. Her own house was full of ghosts and so was her dad's. Then there was Fiona's, with what they both knew to be under the rockery. Not to mention the place where Robbie had lived. The man who led her son to McIntosh's house.

Fiona finished her cigarette first. She pressed it into a metal box on the side of the building and then stood with her arms folded, waiting until Jodie did the same. Jodie instantly wanted another, although didn't want to ask.

She watched as the boys hopped down from the climbing frame and began wrestling among the bark chips. They were laughing as they rolled in the dirt, until a woman that Jodie hadn't noticed sprinted from a pair of benches. She was calling the boys' names but they ignored her until she dragged them up by the arms. Even as they were being shouted at, the grins never left their faces.

Roll back a decade or so and it could have been Owen and Jordan. Jodie had never been hard enough with Owen. Perhaps that was the problem?

'Hey...'

The boys had disappeared from the playground and Jodie was sitting with Fiona on one of the benches at the side of the centre. Darren was standing over them, looking as smart as she'd seen him in a pinstripe dark suit. They'd come a long way from teenage idiots who thought they were in love.

They'd barely talked since *it* had happened. Actually, Jodie had barely talked to anyone. There had been odd sentences here and there. A few words when needed. Or maybe they were thoughts and not out loud? Jodie still couldn't remember.

'I've got to get back to Chandra and the baby,' he said.

'How are they both?' Fiona asked.

Darren was blinking quickly. 'Good,' he said. 'Seven pound seven when she was born. Both sleeping a lot but, y'know...'

He swivelled awkwardly on the spot, not wanting to be

there but also not wanting to walk away. Jodie knew how he felt. Guilt hung between them. His at rarely being there, hers at not being a good enough mother. They'd never say it out loud to one another but they knew.

'You should get back,' Jodie thought, although she realised she'd actually said it when Darren coughed an appreciation.

'Right,' he said. 'We should um, y'know, stay in contact and, um...'

His voice was cracking and he turned and hurried away before he lost it completely.

Jodie remained sitting on the bench as Fiona said something about a chill coming in. She blinked and there was a coat around her shoulders that wasn't hers. Fiona had one too, although Jodie had no idea from where they'd appeared. It was darker than it had been moments before and the street lights around the car park were starting to murmur their way to life.

'I know it's not the time,' Fiona said quietly. 'But I've not seen you much and I need to say something.'

Jodie sat and stared towards the red lights at the back of the cars who were pulling out of the car park.

'I've been wondering about our dads,' Fiona said. 'I don't know if you...?'

'I haven't told anyone,' Jodie said. 'It's only us who knows.'

A part of Jodie envied Mike's obliviousness to what had actually happened after he'd told their father what he'd done. He didn't know about the bones and the rockery. There seemed little point in telling him.

'Oh!' Fiona said, as she failed to hide the relief in her voice. 'That's good. I mean... I know I shouldn't have asked. I wasn't, I didn't...'

Jodie had heard the knocking on her door in the past week or so. She figured it was Fiona and that this question would come.

Even though Fiona was sitting at Jodie's side, she would

always be the woman whose husband led Jodie's son into that house. There was nothing she could have done about it, before or after, and yet Jodie didn't think she'd ever be able to look at her properly again.

According to the things Jodie had read on Facebook – the things she hadn't responded to, despite people endlessly tagging her – Robbie and his makeshift gang of teenagers were attempting to scare away Paul McIntosh. Except McIntosh had a shotgun hidden under the floorboards that the police had never found when he'd been arrested for Ben's death two decades before.

After his windows had been smashed the day before, McIntosh had dug out the gun. When Robbie, Owen, Jordan and the other boy had ignored his plea to be left alone and broken into his house, a terrified McIntosh had shot from the hip in an attempt to scare them away.

Owen had died instantly, they said. There had been no pain and someone at the hospital had said he probably didn't know it had happened. The man had meant it to be a comfort, and perhaps it was, but Jodie was stuck picturing that head flopped between the banisters before Mike pulled her away. Robbie and the boys had spent all that time playing virtual shooting games and then...

'Have you visited him?' Jodie asked.

Her question was met with an immediate 'no'.

Robbie had been arrested not long after McIntosh. For McIntosh, it was for something he actually *had* done this time around. Thinking of McIntosh broke Jodie's heart all over again. His whole life in ruins, twice – because of her. She didn't blame him for what happened to Owen, although everyone seemed to think she should.

For Robbie, he'd been found in the pub, off his head on cider, almost certainly knowing what was coming.

That left the whole town wondering why Jodie was a bad enough mother to let her bully of a son sneak out to terrify an old man. The same man they'd wanted gone, of course, but everyone had forgotten that. Jodie had read the Facebook posts. She'd searched her name on Twitter. She'd seen the news stories and, worse, the comment sections. She couldn't stop.

In the distance, their outlines illuminated by the street lights, Jodie watched Mike, Samantha and Jordan disappear into the shadows of the car park. Mike and his wife were holding hands, while Jordan trailed a pace behind, his head bowed. He would have known that it could have been him if he was a step forward or back from Owen.

Jodie didn't know exactly what had happened in the house, who had gone in first, who had led the line. She didn't want to know – although she was sure it would come out if there was ever a trial. Those people would be back on Facebook and wherever else to make sure she knew.

She and Mike hadn't spoken since he'd pulled her away from the house as the sirens descended. He'd called and texted but she hadn't replied. He'd been at the funeral, of course, and the wake – but Jodie had skipped around him to the point that he'd obviously got the message.

His secrets of twenty years before seemed so inconsequential given what had happened. Jodie would go hours without thinking of any of that because all she had on her mind was Owen. Then she'd remember that they were where they were because everyone had betrayed her. Because her whole life had been a lie on a lie.

Fiona's chilled fingers rested on Jodie's arm, who wanted to shrug her off, but didn't. 'Is there anything I can do?'

'I want to be on my own,' Jodie replied.

Fiona shuffled on the bench, though didn't stand. 'Are you sure? It's just—'

'I'm sure.'

Fiona stood this time, hovering at the edge of the bench. It felt as if she was going to say something important but then she settled for 'call me if you need me' – and then she was gone to the darkness of the car park. Mike was gone too.

Everyone was.

Jodie finally stood. Her back creaked and her backside was numb from all the sitting. She was wearing someone else's coat, padded and warm, with no idea whose it was. She set off towards the pavement, feeling herself shiver. She was under the lights and then she wasn't. She crossed a road and then another... and then she was home, in her room, sitting on her bed, without knowing how she'd got there. The coat was at her side and she was wearing the black dress and black tights she'd picked out that morning. Or maybe it was the day before?

Jodie reached under the bed and slid forward the shoebox before taking off the lid. Inside was the green T-shirt that had started it all. She held it up, as she had every day for as long as she could remember. Each crinkle and crack in the clover print was the same as it had been when she'd last looked.

She wondered, as she always did, whether things would have been different if she'd never gone into her dad's attic. She would have been focused more on Owen, instead of on what happened to Ben. She'd have been a better, more observant, mother. He'd have never sneaked out. He'd be in his room at that very moment, with the chatter of his war game soundtracking her weekend.

Jodie folded the shirt back into the box and held it on her lap. She had the same question every time she looked at it and yet the answer never came. Should she give it to the police and tell them what she knew? It would destroy the legacy of both her and Fiona's dad. It could, or would, send Mike to prison to join McIntosh.

A big part of her family, the biggest, was already destroyed – so should she finish off the rest?

Jodie cradled the box and asked herself that question again, knowing she'd do it again the next day, then the next. Then she crouched and put the box on the floor before nudging it under the bed.

KERRY WILKINSON PUBLISHING TEAM

Editorial
Ellen Gleeson

Line edits and copyeditor
Jade Craddock

Proofreader
Catherine Lenderi

Production
Alexandra Holmes
Natalie Edwards

Design
Lisa Horton

Marketing
Alex Crow
Melanie Price
Occy Carr
Ciara Rosney

Publicity
Noelle Holten
Kim Nash
Sarah Hardy
Jess Readett

Distribution
Chris Lucraft
Marina Valles

Audio
Alba Proko
Nina Winters
Arran Dutton & Dave Perry – Audio Factory
Emma Newman

Rights and contracts
Peta Nightingale
Richard King
Saidah Graham

Lightning Source UK Ltd.
Milton Keynes UK
UKHW040251090622
404155UK00004B/59